LAST SECRET
CHAMBER

PHIL
PHILIPS

A cataloguing-in-publication entry is available from the catalogue of National Library of Australia at www.nla.gov.au.

Requests to publish work from this book should be sent to:
admin@philphilips.com

Philips, Phil, 1978-

ISBN-13: 978-0-6482724-0-3
ISBN-10: 0-6482724-0-0

Typeset in 11pt Sabon

For more information visit
www.philphilips.com

Dedicated to my wife Marie

Death Mask of the boy king Tutankhamun.

Fact:

Ancient Egypt's most iconic treasure – the golden face mask of the boy pharaoh Tutankhamun – was in fact a second-hand family hand-me-down.

Very careful examination of the hieroglyphic text found inside the mask shows that Tut's name was actually inscribed over an earlier individual's name.

His mother Nefertiti.

Chapter 1

Cairo, Egypt
April 17th, 2018

Benjamin P. Fontaine woke up to a spinning room. Still drowsy, he regained his focus and glanced around his apartment, unable to believe his eyes. The tiles looked like a Jackson Pollock painting. His personal notes and drawings, his life's research and work, were scattered across the floor as if they were unimportant. Furniture had been toppled.

He felt a sharp, burning pain on the left-hand side of his jaw. He tried to move his hand to touch it, but found he couldn't. His wrists and ankles were restrained by a double-braid nylon rope that was tied up against a cane chair he had purchased not long ago. The black rope was well knotted, allowing him to move his palms apart slightly, but tight enough to cut off his circulation if he tried to budge.

He spotted someone in the kitchen. His eyes widened with trepidation until he realized the figure he was seeing was his business partner, a French-born Muslim named Youssef. However his relief was short-lived when he saw that Youssef was standing behind the marble island benchtop with a smug, evil-eyed expression on his face.

'What's going on, Youssef?' Benjamin asked coldly. 'Why am I tied up to this chair?' His temper rose a little more with each second of silence that followed. 'And why does my apartment look like it's been ransacked by thieves?'

'I need you to tell me the code to your safe,' said Youssef with an air of nonchalance.

Benjamin snapped his head around to face the north wall. His safe – which was supposed to be hidden behind a glass-framed beach scene – now lay face down on the hard porcelain tiles. 'Why do you want to enter my safe?' asked Benjamin, scowling. 'You've seen the granite stela and the key many times.'

Youssef casually poured himself a cup of cold water from a jug in the refrigerator, as if having his best friend tied up like this and held hostage in his own apartment was the norm. After taking a sip from his glass, he lifted the lid of a pot sitting on a gas cooktop and took in the smell from last night's leftovers.

'Spaghetti bolognese … nice,' he said casually. 'Bolognese always tastes better the second day.'

'What's going on, what do you want, Youssef?'

'I want the key you have in that safe of yours, so I can enter the Hall of Records.'

Benjamin grimaced as he tried to force his hands free, rocking the chair from side to side, but to no avail.

'Why are you doing this? We've discussed this before. We were going to reveal what we have when we discovered the final key described in the granite stela; the key that will lead us to the last secret chamber. That was the plan from the very beginning.'

'It's been two years now!' Youssef shouted, staring at his partner with menacing blue eyes. It was clear that Youssef's patience had come to an end. 'Why keep what we have a secret? You've got the first key to enter the hidden chamber within the Sphinx. I can't wait any longer. You have a winning lottery ticket, but you're too chickenshit to cash it in.'

'Youssef, you know why I've kept it quiet for so long. Once the Egyptian antiquities experts find out what we're in possession of, it's game over. They'll take control, find the treasure and bury the information, like they've always done in the past. I don't trust that Zahi Hawass and his team of misfits. That's why we need to find that all-important last key before we act.'

Youssef stalked over to the safe, drinking more of his water, and seemed to regain his composure. 'Benjamin, I've known you most of my life. Please, just tell me the code.'

'Your father would not have approved of what you're doing right now,' Benjamin replied, squeezing his hands into fists. He knew this was a sore point. Youssef had hated his father.

'Yes, my father. I know you two were close,' said Youssef bitterly. 'My old man always wanted me to be more like you. In his eyes I was always a failure, but in the end it'll be my name that lives on through the ages, not yours.'

Benjamin didn't know how to reply to this last comment and instead waited for Youssef's piercing gaze to catch his own. He remembered the last time he had seen the man before him, a man he'd considered to be his closest friend. It was just this morning that Youssef had surprised him with breakfast, bacon and eggs and a skim latte, just how he liked it … Then it came to him.

'You drugged me?' Benjamin felt blood rush to his face as his fury grew, the veins on his forehead throbbing as he leaned forward, up tight against the ropes. 'Take these off me now!' he yelled through gritted teeth.

'I don't think so,' replied Youssef, whose eyes remained fixed ahead. 'It's my turn to shine now.'

Regret washed over Benjamin. In hindsight, how he longed to go back and take a different path. If only he had found another way to fund his research, he never would have needed his rich friend to become his business partner and he wouldn't be in this current predicament. In fact, he recalled now, at one point Youssef's father had warned him against doing business with his son. He should have listened.

'Once you get what's in my safe, then what … are you going to kill me?' said Benjamin, feeling vulnerable as he bit his bottom lip.

Youssef flashed a sly grin. 'Tell me the code.'

'I can't,' said Benjamin, every word cut short by fear.

'The code!'

'No!'

His rage visibly building, Youssef threw the glass of water hard against the wall, where the glass smashed into pieces, and then called out in Arabic.

Benjamin turned to face the door.

A towering giant of a man with bulging biceps entered the room with a dry cough. He was dressed as if he were an undercover detective in blue jeans and a black polo shirt that clung to his body. His dark skin was that of someone who lived in the heat of the desert. Along with a twelve o'clock shadow, he had clipped hair and was armed with a semiautomatic weapon that could be seen protruding from his expensive shirt.

Walking behind the muscle was a shorter, older man with graying hair. He wore thick-framed glasses and carried a plump, nut-brown leather bag. He glanced around the vandalized room and spotted Benjamin tied up in the chair. His eyes quickly flicked to the ground as if he hadn't seen anything, and he followed the bigger man to the safe.

'What's going on?' Benjamin asked, his adrenaline spiking as he tried once more to set himself free. After a short, fruitless struggle, he stopped and faced the shorter man, who positioned himself in front of the wall safe.

It seemed like the stranger was focused only on the objective at hand, studiously oblivious to Benjamin being held hostage in his own apartment. He extracted a variety of high-tech tools from his leather bag, which rattled as he laid them out on the tiled floor; it became clear to Benjamin that he was a locksmith paid to do Youssef's bidding.

'Youssef, you're like my brother, don't do this,' he begged.

Youssef ignored Benjamin's plea for mercy and

turned back to the safe, gesturing for the locksmith to begin.

The drilling into the steel frame began and the smell of burnt metal filled the air.

The locksmith struggled for twenty drawn-out minutes, sweat beading on his brow, but eventually he managed to force open the safe door. Youssef advanced toward it and scrutinized the contents within, then extracted an old stone container roughly the size of a shoebox. He hefted it in his hands, careful not to drop the heavy three-thousand-year-old artefact, and carried it over to the marble kitchen benchtop.

The armed giant thanked the locksmith and handed him an open envelope filled with what appeared to be Egyptian pounds, before escorting him to the front door.

Benjamin caught sight of the treasure in Youssef's deceitful hands, which immediately brought to mind the memory of the moment when he had extracted it out of a cave in Cyprus a little over two years ago. The secret underwater cavern was located at the baths of Aphrodite. The cave was meant to be a shrine for Alexander the Great, but instead laid a trail to his final resting place and a swap that had happened over two thousand years ago. The venerated tomb of St Mark in Venice contained not the evangelist, but the body of the most famous warlord in history, his mummified remains buried beneath the altar of St Mark's Basilica.

As an archeologist, it had been the biggest find of Benjamin's life, and it had yet to be shared with the world. It was a discovery only known by one other person, a man he thought he could trust. But now, it was in the hands of a man possessed by hatred and greed.

Benjamin could do nothing but stare at Youssef, who reached inside the box to remove the first object, which he knew to be a key. He held the solid iron, a tri-spiral design extruding outward from its base which was embedded in a triangular single piece of rock-hard limestone.

The limestone core bore many unique holes and grooves and was surrounded by intricately carved Egyptian hieroglyphs.

1st key

The tri-spiral shape symbolized the creation of the universe, and could be found throughout the world in the relics of many ancient civilizations. Benjamin had deduced that it had been created from a single meteorite rock that had fallen to the Earth thousands of years ago.

A masterpiece in itself.

Youssef carefully left the solid four-inch key on the marble benchtop and took out the next object – a rectangular-shaped rose granite stela – and ran his fingers across the indented hieroglyphics.

'You have what you want, now let me go!' said Benjamin vehemently.

As soon as he spoke the words, there was a heavy thump.

With lightning speed, Benjamin turned to face the doorway, only to see the locksmith lying face first on the floor. A kitchen knife protruded from the back of his neck as blood cascaded out from the wound onto the Italian tiles.

Benjamin's hands shook and his mouth went instantly dry. A whimper escaped him as he stared at the dead body by the door, knowing this was going to be his own fate.

'What have you done?' said Benjamin, trying to calm down enough to think.

Youssef spoke to the bigger man in Arabic and was handed a silenced pistol, as if this had been preordained. Benjamin's eyes followed the weapon as Youssef approached him and kneeled down so that their eyes met close up.

'What are you going to do with that?' asked Benjamin, nodding toward the firearm, while the murdering giant was collecting the priceless artefacts behind them.

'I'm sorry, my friend, this is the end for you,' said Youssef, aiming the nine-millimeter Heckler & Koch at Benjamin's chest.

'Wait ... I was the one who found these artefacts,' he said desperately. 'I'm the brains in our operation. If you kill me you'll never find the key to the last secret chamber.'

Youssef smirked, dangling the weight of the gun in his right hand. 'There's no need to search for it anymore, my friend,' he said. 'I know exactly where it is.'

Benjamin followed the dark barrel.

'Your father would be rolling over in his grave,' he spat.

'My father would not approve. Yes, you're right. I know you two were tight, but he was wrong about one thing.'

'What's that?'

'I was never the dumb one.'

Youssef shook his head and with a cold detachment he aimed the silenced gun at Benjamin's chest once more. Benjamin arched his back and pressed his lips together, preparing for the bullet to enter.

Youssef's hands trembled and he shut his eyes. For a second, it seemed like he might not be able to go ahead with it. They had history together. They were long-time friends. Just as Benjamin began to feel hope that he might survive, Youssef regained his menacing composure and squeezed the trigger.

Chapter 2

It had become their morning ritual: breakfast with a view on the balcony of his penthouse suite.

Joey winked at his girlfriend, Marie, all the while enjoying the Californian ocean breeze, which smelled lightly of salt while ruffling his sun-bleached hair. As the last living member of the Peruggia family, Joey had inherited everything at the tender age of twenty-six. The sports cars, the boats, and his father's most prized possession: the Beach Club. This he had renamed Joey's Beach Club in order to escape the shadow cast by his father; a man so many people had feared. Even though he was not living a life of crime a year and nine months after his father's death, Joey could never escape the family name. The Vitruvian Man tattoo on his wrist was a permanent reminder of who he was and where he came from. He had tried to perform an act of altruism to help repair his family's tainted reputation, returning the real *Mona Lisa* his great-grandfather had stolen, but that hadn't ended as he had planned.

Joey sipped his freshly brewed coffee, as Ellie, a young employee at the club whose main duty was to greet customers and make bookings, interrupted them.

'I'm so sorry to intrude on your breakfast, sir, but there's someone here who wants to see you. He says it's urgent.'

Joey gave Ellie a sidelong glance.

'He also told me to tell you it's a matter of life and death,' said Ellie, holding her palms upward in a confused gesture. 'What would you like me to do?'

'Send him up,' said Joey, placing his cup of coffee on the glass table in front of him and revealing the tattoo on his wrist. 'Just make sure he's not packing; you can never be too careful.'

Ellie gave a nod and hurried away.

'I wonder what that's all about?' said Marie as she sipped her own coffee. The Californian sun that hit her tanned legs showed off her pedicured toenails. Marie, a sworn-in American citizen with a culturally diverse background of British, Swiss and French, was ten years older than Joey, though her baby face belied her age.

Moments later, a clean-cut male in his late teens, dressed to impress in a navy single-breasted suit with pointy brown leather boots, knocked on the already open bifold doors. His smile stretched from ear to ear.

'Oh my God, it's Boyce!' shouted Marie, almost dropping her coffee cup in her excitement as she bounced out of her chair.

Joey practically jumped out of his seat as well. 'Boyce! … What! … I can't believe you're here!'

Marie was the first to wrap her arms around her old friend. 'Look at you. You've grown up so much!'

Joey moved in and gave him a bear hug, while Marie pulled up a chair so he could sit down beside her. 'What brings you to America?' asked Joey, and without waiting for a reply, peppered the youth with rapid-fire questions. 'It's been over a year and a half since we last saw each other in Paris. How's life? How's your new job with the DGSE?'

'It's actually the reason I'm here,' said Boyce, opening up the last button on his suit jacket to sit down.

'I can't believe it's you, Boyce,' said Joey again, looking at the young Frenchman with proud eyes, as if he was the long-lost younger brother he hadn't seen in years.

'Don't let the suit fool you, guys,' said Boyce, adjusting his tie. 'I'm still the same homeless teenage kid that once lived in his dad's old fishing boat.'

'You sure scrub up well,' said Marie, giving him a friendly wink. 'And your English is flawless!'

Boyce smiled modestly.

'Ellie, the girl who ushered you up, told us you needed to see us as a matter of life and death. Is everything okay within the French Intelligence Agency?' asked Joey worriedly.

'Hang on, before I get to that,' said Boyce, glancing curiously around. 'Is this the penthouse where you found the real *Mona Lisa*?'

'It sure is,' Marie said with a smile. 'Before we ended up running for our lives.'

Boyce nodded his head in agreement. 'I'm still trying to forget it.'

'Come on. I'll show you where we discovered it,' replied Joey, standing up to lead the way inside the enormous penthouse suite that had once belonged to his notorious gangster father. Alexander Peruggia was the man who had been entrusted with the masterpiece passed down from his infamous grandfather, Vincenzo Peruggia, the person who had stolen the painting from the Louvre in 1911.

The three of them strolled past a billiard table and stopped to face a twenty-foot-wide dark-mahogany bookcase filled with books. The intricately molded carvings were all handmade, and a moveable slide ladder sat to the far left-hand side. Joey slid the purpose-built ladder along its tracks to far right-hand side of the bookcase and climbed up the three steps to face an old brown Bible. He tilted it forward until it clicked into place, and part of the bookcase opened slightly outward.

'It feels like it was only yesterday,' said Marie to Joey, reminiscing about the first time they had found this secret room. She helped pull back part of the heavy bookcase and Joey led them inside. The automatic sensor light fluttered on from above as Boyce took in his surroundings, then Marie pressed the brown button underneath Joey's father's desk and the boy's jaw dropped.

A hidden wall slid open and an item moved forward. It sat on a retractable ledge that looked like it floated in midair. An empty thin glass chamber presented itself, and a single LED light strategically placed on the ceiling above it switched on.

'So that's the temperature-controlled environment where you found her,' said Boyce, stepping closer to touch the glass.

Marie looked over to Joey and shook her head sadly. 'I still can't believe you destroyed the original *Mona Lisa* in the fire.'

Joey could sense the rebuff in his girlfriend's tone. Marie was regarded as one of the best, most respected connoisseurs in the art world, having worked all over the globe, including at the Louvre. Her passion for the arts was unquestionable and he knew that the event in Paris would always be a touchy subject in their relationship. She restored paintings, never destroyed them.

Joey stepped over to Marie while Boyce studied the glass chamber. He placed his hand on her shoulder consolingly. 'I've told you before, babe. It was the only way to keep them from killing me.'

Marie dropped her gaze to the ground.

'As long as I knew the clue to Alexander the Great's tomb they wouldn't dare—'

Joey broke off. He darted his eyes to Boyce in mid-thought. 'Hang on, we never found out the truth about Alexander the Great's resting place. Do you know now if it was true?'

Boyce flashed a cheeky grin.

'That's right,' Marie said, her face now bright with interest. '*The exchange that secured his final resting place.*' She quoted the phrase they had uncovered in an underwater cave at the baths of Aphrodite in Cyprus.

'Was it true?' asked Joey.

'Was what true?' replied Boyce, playing dumb.

'Are the bones of Alexander the Great inside the Basilica?' asked Marie, her voice rising with excitement. 'Have the people of Venice been praying to the general all this time instead of their St Mark?'

Boyce stood there with a poker face. 'If I tell you I'd have to kill you,' he said in jest.

'Come on,' begged Joey.

Boyce shrugged helplessly. 'I take my job with the DGSE seriously, sorry. Some things just need to be kept a secret.'

'So it is true,' murmured Marie.

'Speaking of my job,' said Boyce, clearly relieved to be able to change the subject, 'do you remember my boss, the general, Julien Bonnet?'

Marie and Joey agreed with a nod.

'He is sending me on my first solo mission due to the connection I have with this new case.'

'What connection?' asked Joey, wanting to find out the real reason Boyce had come all this way. 'What's the case?'

The teen's expression became somber, as if the fun and games had ended and it was time to talk business. 'Joey, do you remember the dog tag you found inside Aphrodite's cave? The tag that bore the name Benjamin P. Fontaine?'

'Actually, it's funny you bring that up,' said Joey, not breaking eye contact with Boyce. 'I received an email from a Benjamin about a month ago claiming he was my long-lost uncle and wanting to meet up in Egypt.'

'We were planning to go on vacation there next month,' said Marie. 'Catch up and hand him back his dog tag.'

'What did he say in the email?' asked Boyce.

'He wanted to make contact with his last living family connection. At first I was skeptical, but then he sent me photos that sealed the deal. Photos of my grandmother and a couple of himself. The man is the spitting image of my father. There's no denying that the resemblance is uncanny.'

'Was anything else mentioned?' said Boyce, his demeanor even grimmer.

'He invited Marie to come too, which I thought was strange because he knew her by name, but that's about it.'

Marie darted out for a second and brought back two printed photographs. She handed them to Boyce to examine. One was of Joey's father and the other of Benjamin P. Fontaine.

Boyce scanned both pictures, but it seemed like he didn't need to.

'What's going on?' asked Joey cautiously, reading Boyce's negative body language.

'Joey, Benjamin P. Fontaine was a relative of yours. It's been confirmed. He was your father's half-brother.'

'What do you mean *was?*' Marie responded hastily.

'I'm sorry to be the bearer of bad news, but Benjamin was recently murdered in his Egyptian apartment while trying to stop a robbery attempt. Both he and the thief were killed and the contents inside his apartment's safe were stolen.'

'Oh no ... I can't believe it. I was really looking forward to meeting him.' Joey took a moment to process this news. 'So ... why are they sending you?' he asked eventually, his mind sifting through the possibilities. 'What's the French intelligence got to do with this?'

'The DGSE was notified by Benjamin's business partner, a man called Youssef Omar. It seems your estranged uncle was hiding artefacts in his personal safe that he had extracted from the same cave we entered in Cyprus.'

'What artefacts?' said Marie, her eyes wide with wonder. 'We found nothing but a gold throne.'

'The plot thickens,' said Joey, shaking his head.

Boyce took a breath. 'I'm here to ask you both if you would like to join me in Egypt while I investigate this tragedy. I thought with him being your lost uncle, you might want to tag along.'

'I'm in,' Joey quickly responded.

'So am I,' said Marie.

'As long as this trip doesn't end up like our previous holiday in Paris,' said Joey. 'I don't want to get shot at, or drive a car off a cliff, or swim across a freezing-cold lake. If there's any sign of danger I'm out of there.'

'Don't worry,' said Boyce, a smile blossoming on his face. 'You'll be under my personal supervision. You're in safe hands. Trust me.'

Chapter 3

Joey snuck to the bookcase in his penthouse suite and spotted a dull auburn hardback book with a thick spine. The writing on its hard-covered surface was illegible with age. He extracted it from the shelf and sighed as many pleasant memories of his father flooded his mind. The book had belonged to him and Joey felt a sentimental attachment to it.

'Hurry up, babe, your driver is here waiting to take us to the airport,' Marie shouted from the bottom of the stairway along the corridor.

Boyce was with her, making sly jokes about Joey taking longer to get ready than his female counterpart.

Joey's attention drifted back to the book in his hands. He opened it with care to see a gaping hole cut out where the pages should have been. Inside, the interior was lined in red velcro with custom-made pockets to hold his father's precious watch collection. There was a shiny vintage Rolex, a forty-four-millimeter titanium Submariner, as well as an eighteen-carat-gold Invicta and his father's favorite, a rare Vacheron Constantin Tour de I'Ile worth $1.5 million. They were exquisite to say the least and they now all belonged to him, but they weren't what he was searching for. A smile crept over his face when he extracted from one of the pockets a four-claw one-carat princess-cut diamond ring. Its flawless beauty was breathtaking as it shimmered in his fingers. He brought it up close to his face for one last glance.

Marie was the woman he wanted to spend the rest of his life with. From the moment he had laid eyes on her, he had known she was the one. Even though she was a sophisticated woman who had seen far more of the world than he had, she was a child at heart. He also felt that the difference in their ages meant that Marie was comfortable letting her guard down and being her true self around him.

Joey had been holding on to this diamond for months now, trying to decide how he would pop the all-important question. He had come close a couple of times, but he wanted the moment to be special. Marie was an incredible person and she deserved a fitting proposal, one that she would remember forever.

Egypt was to be that memorable place. Her eyes were always wide with excitement when she spoke of it. Their trip had been brought forward due to this tragedy, but he wasn't going to let it ruin the plan.

He played out the proposal in his mind.

If the time of day was right and the Sahara sunset was dazzling on its dunes, as it did in the movies, he would build up enough courage to get down on one knee, among the camel shit, flies and limestone rock, and pop the question. Their new-found engagement would start in front of the only one of the Seven

Wonders of the Ancient World to have survived to the present day: the Great Pyramid of Giza.

Joey took a nervous breath and calmed himself, shoved the ring into his pants pocket, and left his penthouse suite. Only time would tell if this adventure to the Middle East would be one that he and Marie would remember and cherish forever.

Chapter 4

Exiting the terminal at Cairo International Airport, Joey assumed the blistering heat of the Egyptian desert was going to hit him in the face, but the weather was a pleasant 78 degrees Fahrenheit. However, the air was thick and gray and held a haze that seemed unlikely to dissipate.

Joey pinched his nose. There was something unsettling about the smell; like driving behind an old car that was coughing out thick exhaust.

He followed Boyce and Marie to a man standing beside a navy BMW parked in what seemed to be a loading dock. The car's light-blue number plate mixed English and Arabic letters and numerals. Boyce shook the stranger's hand as if they knew each other, and then stepped into the driver's seat.

'Let's go, get in,' Boyce announced, entering an address on the sat nav fixed within the wooden dashboard. 'We have a fifty-minute drive to Garden City. I've been told the traffic here can get crazy, so we should get started.'

Joey slid into the back seat and let his girl enjoy the ride from the front. He knew she would soak in the history that had once made this country one of the greatest ancient nations in the world.

'What's in Garden City?' Marie asked, fastening her seatbelt.

'We're going to Benjamin's apartment,' said Boyce, taking off on the right-hand side of the road. 'Youssef, his business partner, is meeting us there.'

Joey gazed out his grimy window. He had imagined Egypt to be a vast desert filled with yellow sand as far as the eye could see, but Cairo was the complete opposite. The city was simply urban, with ubiquitous skyscrapers smudged by the smog-filled sky. They drove through a maze of tall buildings, and it seemed like every street was a marketplace covered with bright cloth stalls. Some stalls sold fish, some hard bread, while others traded shimmering jewels. He watched children playing on the road, kicking a can like it was a soccer ball, and spotted glimpses of the Great Pyramid in the distance.

'The Pyramids,' said Marie over her shoulder with an excited grin, then turned back in her seat. Her luminous skin was shining in the Egyptian sun.

'When we get a chance we must go and see them up close,' said Joey casually, thinking of the object in his pants pocket.

'We have plenty of time for sightseeing,' said Boyce, driving past a cylindrical fort-like building, shadowed by many other grand structures in the Islamic architectural style.

'You have reached your destination,' spoke the sat nav in a female American accent.

Boyce pulled up beside the curb and parked the BMW. The area was a quiet upscale residential district in central Cairo that spanned the east side of the Nile. Its leafy street, landscape, architecture, and general atmosphere had a European feel to it.

They strolled over to the front entrance of an apartment complex that looked like a cutout from an architectural digest magazine. A young woman dressed in a maroon burka was coming out of the building. Boyce responded swiftly, catching the edge of the heavy security door with his right leg and opening it wide again.

'What are you doing?' Marie asked in a whisper. 'Aren't we supposed to be meeting Benjamin's partner?'

'It won't hurt to go and have a peek,' said Boyce with his boyish grin, and Joey found himself smiling in return as they stepped inside.

'You sure have changed, my friend,' Joey said as the stainless-steel doors to the lift opened, inviting them in. After a short ride up that ended with a formal *ding*, they found themselves in the plush carpeted foyer of the one and only apartment spanning the entire level.

'Seven is my lucky number,' said Marie, eyeing the shiny numeral secured on the solid oak door.

Joey grabbed hold of the knob and turned it. 'It's locked,' he reported with a grimace.

Boyce swept the hallway, and his eyes landed on Marie's ponytail. 'May I?' he said, lifting his arm above her head.

Marie stood still, clearly understanding what he was up to.

Boyce extracted a bobby pin from her honey-brown hair and spun to the door. He fiddled with the keyhole aggressively, as though he had done this a hundred times before.

'Look at this,' wisecracked Joey. 'Young Boyce thinks he's MacGyver.'

Marie giggled at Joey's comment, but stopped short when the lock gave an audible click and the door swung open.

'You *are* MacGyver!' said Joey, surprised. It had been a year and a half since they had last seen each other and in that limited amount of time Boyce seemed to have transformed into 007.

Boyce handed Marie back her bobby pin and led the way into the apartment, while Joey scanned its sumptuous surroundings. The open-plan apartment had been turned upside down. Furnishings, clothes, bedding and books overwhelmed the space in a chaotic mess. Letters, documents and personal drawings had been ripped to pieces and scattered about the room like confetti.

'Looks like the cleaner hasn't been in,' Joey said sarcastically.

Marie picked a clear path across the room and headed for the sizeable bay windows. 'Nice view,' she commented, impressed by the site before her. 'You can see the Nile and a little bit of the Egyptian Museum from here.'

Boyce examined the paper trail on the tiled floor

and picked up a bunch of drawings that were still intact, while Joey encountered a bookcase half-filled with books on Egypt. The rest of them were strewn around his feet. He came across two framed diplomas from Cambridge University. One was an advanced diploma in Theology and Religious Studies, while the other was for Ancient and Medieval History.

He took a snoop in his uncle's bedroom to find the same mess. The sound of cracking glass almost made him jump as he accidentally stepped on a picture frame. He picked it up to see Benjamin with his squadron dressed in their military attire. Resting it on the bed, he joined the group back in the main living area.

'Joey, you two are definitely related,' said Marie, hovering over the pot of pasta in the kitchen. 'He was cooking your favorite meal.'

Boyce walked over to the empty safe. At his feet a glass-framed painting lay face down. He flipped it over and his face lit up.

'What is it?' asked Joey, seeing the excitement in his eyes.

'Isn't this the site we visited in Cyprus? *Petra tou Romiou?*'

Joey approached to take a closer inspection. 'Yes, it is.'

'I wonder …' said Boyce, finding a small shard of glass on the tiled floor. The other broken pieces led to a shattered cup resting in the corner of the room.

Marie joined them, while Boyce turned the painting back to the reverse side, which was covered in an inexpensive dull gray paper. He sliced through it with ease using the broken piece of glass, and to everyone's surprise, they found a compact chocolate-colored leather journal.

'I think we just found your uncle's personal journal,' said Boyce, flipping the pages.

'I wonder if it explains about the artefacts he took out of the cave?' asked Marie. 'It would give us a better understanding of their importance and why he was murdered.'

A brief silence ensued until Boyce came across three photographs that were tucked inside.

A stone box.

An unusual item made of limestone and three spiraling iron prongs.

A tablet with hieroglyphics on it.

'These must be the artefacts,' whispered Boyce in growing excitement. He turned the page again to find a detached folded piece of paper wedged into the spine.

'Here, give me that,' said Marie, easing the sheet out of the journal. She unfolded it with care and discovered a chalk rubbing of the tablet in the photo. The intricacy and detail of the carved hieroglyphics were in plain sight, each letter and drawing easily distinguished.

'Benjamin decoded it,' said Marie, pointing to the scribble that was found underneath every shaded hieroglyphic, her eyes widening with elation.

'What does it say?' asked Joey.

At that moment, as Marie recited the first letter of the translation, Joey heard the *ding* of the elevator reaching their level. He immediately snatched the journal out of Boyce's hands and wedged it behind his back, inside his jeans, lifting his shirt over it to conceal it. 'We can't trust anyone,' he warned quickly. 'Remember when we trusted the Louvre curator and that nearly got us killed?'

'I agree,' Boyce replied. 'Hide the paper,' he instructed Marie quietly.

Marie faced the doorway and hastily concealed it in her pocket.

Waiting for the company to join them in the apartment, Joey's stomach sank, leaving him feeling almost ill. His mind wandered back to the first time he had met the Louvre curator and his treacherous security team. At first it was all smiles; after all, Joey was returning the real *Mona Lisa* to its rightful home. Everyone was going to prosper. His family name would be restored. But it hadn't gone at all as planned, and had ended up almost costing him his own life.

Staring into space, replaying in his mind everything that had gone wrong in Paris, he vowed to be more cautious this time. With a guarded anticipation, he watched as a narrow stream of light spliced through the room, and a shadow quickly followed.

Chapter 5

Two men entered the room. The shorter of the two was dressed smartly and looked like a man who enjoyed the finer things in life. Otherwise well groomed, his unruly mop of black hair was plentiful, thick and curly. It reminded Joey of Boyce's haircut the day they had met on the bank of the Seine a year and a half ago.

He strolled inside, ignoring the vandalized apartment as he flashed a warm smile. The other less polished figure positioned himself a meter behind the manicured man. He had a commanding presence. He was a giant of a man with a broad frame, clipped haircut, tattoo on his neck and a scar on his bottom lip. He stood, feet apart, and observed them intently with a serious scowl, as if he had spent his life frowning at people. Joey knew straight away that this rugged, unshaved man was the muscle, even before he spotted a shape that protruded out from his sweater, presumably a gun.

'Hello. Tell me, which one of you two is Boyce?' said the manicured man in perfect English, the hint of a British accent signaling that he most likely had been educated at a prestigious school.

'That would be me.' Boyce stepped forward with an arm raised and a fresh-faced smile.

'It's an honor to have you in Egypt, Boyce,' the man said, shaking the teen's hand. 'My name is Youssef Omar. Benjamin was my business partner and long-time friend.'

'I'm very sorry for your loss, sir,' said Boyce solemnly, while Marie and Joey watched on.

'Yes, it's a travesty.' Youssef's eyes shifted to the floor and became glazed with a glassy layer of tears. 'I've known Benjamin for a very long time, we were inseparable.'

'How did you two meet?' asked Boyce.

'We were in the French Army together,' said Youssef. 'That's how I know your boss, Julien. We all served at the same time.'

The muscle in the back coughed uncontrollably into his inner fist.

'I'm sorry, how rude of me,' said Youssef. 'The gentleman behind me is Nader, he is my geologist.'

Nader nodded his head and cleared his throat some more.

'Smoker's cough,' added Youssef in disgust.

Joey nodded absently, giving Nader a suspicious glance. He definitely didn't possess the appearance of an educated man, nor that of a scientist. He bore a resemblance to one of Joey's father's thugs whom he had grown up with, and the way he stood a meter behind his boss was exactly the stance of a bodyguard keeping a watchful eye on things.

'These are my friends, Joey and Marie,' said Boyce with an open hand gesture.

Youssef turned to Joey and Marie with that same charming smile. 'The Americans,' he said, displaying his straight white teeth for all to see.

Joey didn't respond, unsure whether or not he meant that as an insult. As a kid growing up with murderers and criminals, he rationalized quickly that it was better to say nothing than to upset the wrong person and have your head blown off.

'I know all about your trip to Cyprus,' Youssef uttered mysteriously, as though he was the puppeteer pulling all the strings.

'How much do you know?' asked Marie with barely concealed suspicion.

'Let's just say I know enough,' he replied evasively, before he turned toward Joey with a somber expression. 'I'm very sorry for your loss, Joey. Your uncle was an amazing man and, as I mentioned, a close friend of mine.'

The fact that Youssef knew that Benjamin was related to him puzzled Joey, but he stayed focused and asked him a simple question in reply. 'You said you were in the army together. How did you end up becoming business partners?'

'After our time served we moved to England and lived as frat brothers, studying at Cambridge University. We both shared a love for the ancient world and later we decided to combine our businesses as one. We started the Benjamin, Youssef, Expedition, Research & Development, known as BYERD.'

Joey felt perplexed. There were so many questions that he wanted answered, but he wasn't sure where to start. His thoughts were interrupted when Boyce asked Youssef to fill them in on what had happened in the apartment.

'As you already know, Benjamin and I were business partners. I funded a lot of his research and development. On regular occasions we would meet here to catch up, have a coffee and discuss projects.' His tone was stiffening with each word. 'About a week ago I found him on the floor with a bullet in his chest and his safe broken into.'

'Do you know if he had any enemies?' asked Boyce.

'Not that I'm aware of,' replied Youssef. 'But this is Egypt.'

'What was in the safe?' Marie interjected.

'It's the reason why you're all here,' said Youssef, walking around the apartment, clearly familiar with his surroundings. 'Over two years ago, Benjamin extracted out of the same cave you entered in Cyprus a stone box that contained a spiral object and a small rose granite stela.'

Boyce glanced over at Joey remaining po-faced.

Marie flashed an expression of excitement on her face.

Youssef continued. 'Needing money to fund his stay in Egypt and to have access to high-tech software that could decipher the oldest forms of hieroglyphics, we decided to become business partners. The catch to our partnership was that he wanted me to keep his find a secret until we translated what was inscribed on the tablet.'

'Did you decode it?' asked Joey, eyeing the Egyptian as he strolled around the room.

'We did, and what we discovered turned Benjamin's quest into an obsession.'

'What did you discover?' asked Boyce, stepping away from the Hulk standing near the front door with folded arms and a cough that wouldn't end.

'After translating the text on the stela, we uncovered that the spiral object in our possession was actually an ancient key that would open the door to, wait for it – the Hall of Records found deep within the Sphinx at Giza.'

Marie sighed with pleasure.

Joey was bemused. 'The Hall of what?' he said, unfamiliar with the reference.

Boyce jumped in quickly, ignoring his American friend's ignorance. 'So did you find out if this place exists?'

'Sadly no,' said Youssef, stopping to face the three of them before him. 'Benjamin kept this a secret. He didn't reveal it to anyone because of a second key that was also mentioned on the granite stela. This supposed secondary key was said to lead them into a deeper chamber within the complex, a cavity created by our pre-dynastic ancestors and later concealed by Queen Nefertiti for some reason.'

'Complicated,' said Joey dryly. 'Here we go again. Here come the conspiracy theories, the ancient worlds and the secret texts.'

Marie shook her head, holding in her irrepressible laughter.

'Do you know if this second key exists?' asked Boyce.

'We spent a long time trying to find it but had no luck,' said Youssef, then he stopped and looked down at the painting left on the floor with its backing slashed.

Joey stole a furtive glance at Youssef, who peered away in the opposite direction and continued to speak.

'Now all that work, all that history, is gone in the blink of an eye, not to mention all the money I poured into developing an app that could decipher hieroglyphics.' Youssef's expression grew annoyed. 'That's when I decided the police here would not be of any use to me and I needed outside help, so I called Julien.'

'Why Julien, what good is he to you in Egypt?' asked Joey.

'For one, I knew I could trust him. Plus, he has deep connections here. Tonight at 7:00 pm, he has arranged a private meeting with the heads of the Egyptian antiquities at the Cairo Museum. They've agreed to assist us with the investigation and give us a better understanding of the importance of the artefacts stolen.'

'How can they help us?' asked Marie.

'I have photos,' said Youssef. 'The thieves might want to sell the items to a collector. If they do, we'll be notified and we can track them down.'

Boyce nodded, then his gaze darted over to Joey, who yawned openly.

'My friends, you must be tired from your long trip. We have plenty of time to talk about this tonight. How about you check in to your hotel—the Grand Nile Tower, isn't it?—and let's meet up again at 7:30 pm in front of the Egyptian Museum. It's only a short drive from there.'

'That's an excellent idea,' said Marie with a long,

weary sigh. 'Gives us time to eat and freshen up.'

Boyce thanked Youssef with a firm handshake and headed for the lifts with Marie behind him. Joey was the last to exit the room. He eyeballed the muscle standing near the doorway, still coughing. He had not spoken a word the entire time. He reminded Joey in some way of Frederic, the French major who had almost killed him not so long ago. The muscle's eyes came into contact with Joey's, but Joey was the first to look away. He didn't want to provoke Nader in any way. Eyes strictly to the ground, he followed the others to the lift.

Chapter 6

The luxurious landmark Grand Nile Tower is poised directly on the magnificent Nile with a prime location in central Cairo. Joey, Marie and Boyce entered the five-star hotel, appreciating the grandness the building had to offer, including a shopping mall, an outdoor pool and a rotating restaurant. They checked in and were shown to their room.

Marie entered ahead of Joey, who watched his girl jump with glee, excited that they had been allocated a penthouse suite. She made a beeline to the oversized glass windows that framed a spectacular hundred-and-eighty-degree city skyline view and offered an uninterrupted vista across the river Nile.

'I love my job,' said Boyce with pride, his hands held up high, as if he was a referee who had just awarded a team a goal.

Joey gave him a friendly shove and meandered to an office area in the open-plan room, complete with antique desk and two matching wooden chairs. Resting on the tabletop was a notepad and pen, each with the crest of the hotel's logo stamped on them. Joey made himself comfortable and pulled out the journal he had stolen from Benjamin's apartment. 'Let's have a look,' he said, turning the pages slowly, one at a time, taking in all the information like a forensic scientist.

Boyce came in close and pulled the other chair beside Joey, while Marie joined them, hovering from above as she too scanned the handwritten text. Boyce removed the three photographs wedged inside and placed them atop the table, where the three of them examined them more closely.

'That has to be the spiral object Youssef was talking about,' said Joey, looking up at Marie's emotionless face. 'The key that'll open the door to the Hall of Records,' he continued. 'We never did discuss what the hell is actually inside that place.'

'It's a mythical ancient library rumored to be constructed at the time of Imhotep,' said Marie, channeling her extensive historical knowledge.

'I love it when you talk like that,' mocked Joey, although he was secretly very proud of Marie's deep intelligence. 'I wish I had your brain,' he added adoringly. 'Could you be any sexier?'

Marie leaned forward and gave him a peck on the lips as a thank you, which turned into a passionate display of affection.

'Can this wait until I'm not in the same room?' said Boyce, breaking the couple apart.

Marie composed herself, eyes still locked in Joey's direction, and continued to explain her thoughts. 'Many academics have suggested it's under one of the paws of the Sphinx, and now we know that could well be true. It's been alleged the Hall was used to hide information that dates back to the beginning of recorded time. Ancient scrolls, tablets and books were supposedly kept there, including much of the Library of Alexandria that wasn't destroyed.'

'So this would explain the connection with Alexander the Great and why these artefacts were found in a cave designed for him,' said Joey evenly.

'I guess,' replied Marie, deep in thought.

'This has to be the reason why Benjamin was murdered,' said Boyce. 'Maybe someone discovered what he had in his possession?'

'People have killed for far less,' pointed out Marie. 'We're talking about the Library of Alexandria. What an extraordinary find, one worth millions, billions even, that has the potential to rewrite our history as we know it.'

'Either that or his business partner was involved in some way,' said Joey openly. 'He knew about the key.'

'But, they were old friends,' said Marie. 'Do you think he is capable of murder?'

'When it comes to money and fame all bets are off, as we have learned in the past,' said Joey. 'I only mention it because I saw something strange when we were in the apartment. It could be nothing, but ...'

'What was it?' asked Marie curiously.

'I caught Youssef staring at the framed beach scene where we found the journal. It was as if he was stunned to see it slashed apart, but then he carried on as if nothing had happened.'

'I noticed that too,' said Boyce. 'Don't worry, I'm not counting him out as a suspect. For now, we just need to play along and see where this investigation leads us before coming out with all guns blazing.'

Joey turned back to the journal on the desk in front of him and flipped over the page to see sketches and cut-out pictures that were glued down to form a sort of reference book. It started with the *Petra tou Romiou*, a monumental sea stack of rocks located in Cyprus. Following that was Aphrodite's underwater cave where twelve Greek god tablets lay, and an image of the golden throne that led to Alexander the Great's resting place. Finally there was a picture of Da Vinci's most famous masterpiece, the *Mona Lisa*. A story was being told, one that the three of them had been involved in not so long ago.

Two pages remained, and the contents of the first made Joey flinch.

'Hey,' said Marie. 'Why the long face?'

Circled in pencil was a name: *Alexander Peruggia – guardian.*

Joey's father's name was written in the journal next to a black-and-white picture of the *Mona Lisa*. A jumble of emotions ran through Joey, leaving him with more questions than he had answers for. Had Benjamin known he had a half-brother? Had he known that Alexander had obtained Da Vinci's original masterpiece? And if he had, was this the reason he had written *guardian* next to his name? Joey hesitantly flipped to the last page and froze, lost for words.

A chill slowly ran up his spine.

A picture of a young man was staring back at him. In his lap sat two boys barely out of nappies. It was his father. 'So Benjamin *did* know about us,' he said, gazing off into nothingness.

'I don't understand,' said Boyce.

Snapping out of his reverie, Joey turned to Boyce. 'That's me when I was little.' Joey then touched the image of his older sibling with his index finger. It had been almost two years since his brother's death, and the emotions of not having him around struck home once again. It had never become an easy thing to cope with. Joey stood up to catch his breath and stepped up to the panoramic view.

'That's Joey's father and brother,' Marie explained to Boyce, filling in the blanks. 'It explains how Benjamin would have found the secret cave in the first place, because it too was passed down from his grandfather, Vincenzo Peruggia.'

'I wonder if my father knew he had a brother?' said Joey, watching the dot-sized boats sail away in the distant river Nile.

'Hang on, do you still have Benjamin's rubbing?' Boyce asked Marie.

Marie extracted the small piece of paper from her pocket and laid it open on the desk for Boyce to see. Her enthusiasm was contagious as she used her index finger to read out the two long paragraphs translated in English.

'The secret to humanity lies within. I, [Nefertiti cartouche] wife of [Akhenaten cartouche], God of the Sun, will guide your truth and teach you, for I am God and will rise again in the afterlife. Two keys etched out of the iron sent to us from the gods in the sky

protect the secret, hidden away to thee who is worthy to find them. Under the right paw of Anubis, the first [tri-spiral symbol] will lead you to the sacred temple of the Hall of Records. Beware, for where the second [tri-spiral symbol] will guide you, for those who have found the last secret chamber will discover the beginning of time. The [mask symbol] inscribed with a map for the afterlife will show the way.'

After reading the first paragraph, she wore a puzzled expression, the way she always did when she was perplexed by a problem. Joey knew that the more she mulled it over, the more questions her brain would generate. She focused back on the second passage and started to read aloud once more.

'... *Your right eye is the night bark [of the Sun God], your left eye is the day bark, your eyebrows are [those of] the Ennead of the Gods, your forehead is [that of] Anubis, the nape of your neck is [that of] Horus, your locks of hair are [those of] Ptah-Soker. [You are] in front of the Osiris [Tutankhamun], you guide him to the goodly ways, you smite for him the confederates of Seth so that he may overthrow your enemies before the Ennead of the Gods in the great Castle of the Prince, which is in Heliopolis... the Osiris, the king of Upper Egypt Nebkheperura, deceased, given life like Ra.'*

Marie gasped as understanding dawned. 'The last verse is a spell.'

Joey felt his guts churn at her tone.

'This entire second paragraph is engraved on the shoulders and on the back of Tutankhamun's death mask. It also appears in the masks of the Middle

Kingdom, some five hundred years before the time of Tutankhamun. It was later incorporated in the Book of the Dead, intended to protect the mask.'

'What do you think this has to do with the Hall of Records or this secret chamber?' asked Boyce, scratching his head.

'I have no idea,' said Marie as her stomach growled. 'But what I do know is that I'm starving. I couldn't eat the food on the plane.'

Marie headed for the kitchen, where there was a cordless phone.

'It's no wonder why Benjamin never found the second key,' said Boyce, looking over at Joey, who was once again deep in thought. 'It's way too cryptic.'

Marie could be heard ordering room service in the background. By the sound of the order she placed, she had ensured that she would have enough to feed a small army.

In the warm embrace of the sunlit sky reflecting off the river Nile, Joey yawned. The view was a wonder to behold, but he was struggling to keep his eyes open. 'We should all get some shut-eye before we go to this meeting tonight,' he said.

He excused himself and headed to one of the two bedrooms within the suite. The secret behind the second key would have to wait.

Chapter 7

Egyptian Museum
7:30 pm

Total darkness had descended by the time they arrived at the Museum of Egyptian Antiquities. Commonly known as the Egyptian Museum or Museum of Cairo, it was home to an extensive collection of ancient Egyptian antiquities. Boyce, who was in the driver's seat, found the landmark with ease using the inbuilt GPS, and parked the hire car a couple of blocks away. Joey, Marie, and Boyce walked to the site of the massive two-story pink-toned building which was framed by lanky palm trees and arched windows and was illuminated by spotlights, making it resemble an enormous castle.

'Cool building,' Boyce said, taking in the courtyard that led them to the entrance, complete with artefacts strewn around the garden and a fountain filled with papyrus and lotus plants.

'That pink granite Sphinx over there is of Thutmose III,' said Marie, pointing to where it was positioned on the left-hand side of the walkway.

'You're turning me on,' said Joey, putting a smile on his young friend's face.

'If that turns you on, you should see how much she ate this afternoon,' muttered Boyce. 'She cleaned out two entire plates of falafel wraps.'

Marie sighed. 'I was hungry.'

The boys laughed it off as she stomped ahead, not appreciating the teasing, and led the way to where six men were lingering around a grand white archway with columns on either side. Joey spotted Youssef and his geologist friend, dressed for the occasion in single-breasted charcoal suits, although Nader's frame was almost bursting through the fabric's seams. He stood a few feet away from everyone else and took a couple of puffs from his cigarette before they entered the smoke-free building.

It appeared that Youssef and Nader had already greeted the two distinguished gentlemen in ink-black tailored suits who were standing there waiting like old politicians about to pass a vote. There was no need to introduce the other two men in this group, who were dressed in green military attire from head to foot.

These armed guards were paid to make sure there was no foul play inside the museum tonight.

'Hello, nice to meet you all,' said Marie. She was a sight for sore eyes, dressed in an off-the-shoulder formal black gown and open-toe high heels.

Joey observed his girl interact with the men. She appeared to have them already twirled around her little finger. She was beautiful and feminine, but he knew she could man it up if she had to. This, along with her happy nature and zest for life, made Joey feel proud that one day soon he might be able to call this woman his wife. One day.

Standing behind Boyce, Joey was the last to introduce himself. Although a little underdressed for the occasion in his black jeans, red t-shirt and Nike Air Jordans on his feet, he didn't care. He was comfortable.

'Welcome to our museum,' said one of the black-suited men, a slightly overweight older man in his seventies, bald with a snowy-white beard. He stepped forth, assisted by his wooden walking cane. 'My name is Ahmed Daher, and I'm the director in charge of all Egyptian antiquities at this institution. This is a colleague of mine, Hazim Saliba, head of all restorations and the spokesman for our news coverage.'

Indeed, the man named Hazim possessed a news reporter's appearance, polished and groomed as if he was going to be in front of a camera.

'Thank you for having this meeting with us,' said Boyce. He was wearing the same navy suit he had worn when he came to see Joey and Marie in the States. 'Any help you can give us to bring Benjamin's killer to justice and to find the artefacts that were stolen from his safe would be much appreciated.'

'Of course,' said Ahmed. 'If there's anything we can offer you, we'll be glad to assist. Benjamin was a good friend and a regular scholar at our museum.'

'If you don't mind,' added Hazim, 'before we enter the gallery, a quick search, please.' He gestured over to one of the security guards who had a hand-held metal detector.

One by one they posed with their hands aloft while a thorough scan was carried out. The need for precaution was understandable, as they would be the only people inside the building tonight; God forbid a place like this fell into the wrong hands.

'Welcome to the home of the treasures of the greatest civilization in the world,' said Ahmed with a sense of pride and joy in his words. 'Cairo Museum is a portal through which the visitor is transported back to the mysterious realm of ancient Egypt.'

Joey was expecting to be amazed, but he found himself flabbergasted by the grandeur as he was directed inside. The sound of Ahmed's cane and their party's footsteps echoed in the vast space as he gazed upward to the atrium.

'This is the Great Hall,' said Ahmed, escorting them all down a flight of stairs flanked by columns and archways. 'The giant statue in the back is Amenemhet III and his family.'

Joey observed the sarcophagi and enormous statues, feeling like an ant in an ant farm. 'I feel like I'm in a horror movie set,' he said, as the moonlight shone through the windows from above.

'The difference, babe,' said Marie with a grin, 'is that the props in the movies are fake. In here, they're real.'

'Yep, lots of thousand-year-old mummies in here,' joked Boyce, playing on Joey's discomfort.

'Let's just hope they stay dead,' said Joey. 'This place gives me the creeps.'

Ahmed flashed a charming smile. 'Before we get into the meeting we have planned for tonight, would you like a private tour?'

Youssef's mouth twitched, which may have been the man's attempt at a grin, and he said, 'Can we see Tutankhamun's treasures? Every time I've come to visit its been flooded with tourists. It would be nice not to be rushed, since we have this place to ourselves.'

'Our most prized possessions,' said Ahmed with an exultant look on his face.

Marie and Boyce wore delighted grins, as if they were kids and their parents had just told them they were going to Disneyland.

'The artefacts on the ground floor are from the New Kingdom, the time period between 1550 and 1069 B.C.,' said Ahmed, leading the way with his cane, his security detail falling in at the rear. 'All these enormous statues, boats and coffins are laid out in chronological order.'

Taking the southeast stairs, the group headed up to room forty-five. A sign mounted on the wall read: *Galleries of Tutankhamun.* Outside the entrance, a substantial-sized poster illustrated the tomb and treasures as they were discovered.

'The pieces in this room are roughly in the same order as they were laid out within the tomb,' said Ahmed. 'As we enter, on either side of the doorway you'll see two life-size statues of Tutankhamun that were found in the antechamber to his tomb. They are made of wood coated in bitumen, their black skin suggesting an identification with Osiris, and the rich, black river silt symbolizing fertility and rebirth.'

Joey observed Marie taking in the information and looking as though she was enjoying herself way too much. The lights were dull, ambient and eerie, causing a cold shiver to run down his spine.

'Proceeding to room three,' said Ahmed. He probably would have shown this collection to millions of people, but it was as if he was showing it for the first time. Without doubt, this was a man who loved his job. 'Here are Tutankhamun's inner and outer coffins.'

Youssef nodded his head and quietly examined the detailed sarcophagus.

'Wasn't Tutankhamun found in three coffins?' asked Marie. 'Each one within the next?'

'That is absolutely correct,' answered Hazim,

stepping forward, his parted ash-brown hair glistening as he moved into a spotlight that shone from above. 'The largest outer box is still in the original tomb in the Valley of the Kings, along with his mummy.' He flashed her a smile and continued while Joey stood watching. This idiot was flirting with his girl, he realized irritably, playing on her fascination.

'The middle coffin here is made of wood covered with gold, semiprecious stones, glass and obsidian.' He moved to the next one as if giving Marie her own private tour, trying to impress her with his knowledge. 'This is the inner casket made of solid gold and weighing two hundred and forty-two pounds.'

Under the picture of Tut's innermost coffin was an inscription that Marie began to read out loud. *'The image of the Pharaoh is that of a god. The gods were thought to have skin of gold, bones of silver, and hair of lapis lazuli – so the king is shown here in his divine form in the afterlife.'*

A look of awe crept onto everyone's face.

'What's something like this worth?' asked Boyce, standing up front with Marie and Youssef.

'Ahm, say,' Hazim said, pausing for dramatic effect. 'Its material value would be close to a million in gold and in US dollars, but priceless in a historical sense.'

Marie raised an eyebrow.

'Why is it so dark in here?' asked Joey, standing behind Marie, Boyce and Youssef. Behind them, along with the museum security guards, Nader strolled at a leisurely pace.

'The lights can damage the artefacts, so it's essential

that they be dim,' said Ahmed. 'That's one reason why we don't allow flash photography in here.'

Joey scanned the modern glass cabinets exhibiting the Pharaoh's vast collection of royal jewelry, but his eyes caught sight of the mask he had seen on TV.

'And here it is,' said Ahmed, pointing the way. 'The most important piece in the museum: Tutankhamun's death mask.'

Even Joey, someone with no knowledge of the finer points of Egyptian antiquities, stopped to study the magnificent piece before him.

Ahmed gave Hazim a nod, as if to tell him it was okay for him to take the lead in the presentation, and rested both hands on top of his cane.

'It's made of solid gold and inlaid with semiprecious stones,' started Hazim. 'Tutankhamun is depicted wearing the striped Nemes headdress, a head-cloth typically worn by Pharaohs in ancient Egypt. The vulture's head upon the brow, symbolizing sovereignty over Upper Egypt, is also made of solid gold, apart from the beak, which is made of horn-colored glass. He wears a broad collar which ends in terminals shaped as falcon heads. The back of the mask is covered with a spell from the Book of the Dead, which the Egyptians used as a map for the afterlife. This particular spell protects the various limbs of Tutankhamun as he moves into the underworld.'

Joey, Boyce and Marie glanced at each other, recognizing the similarity between this description and the translation they'd found in Benjamin's journal.

Hazim continued. 'He also wears a false beard that

further connects him to the image of a god, as with the inner coffin. The false beard is commonly associated with Pharaohs, and even female rulers of Egypt such as Hatshepsut.'

This last comment brought a cheeky half-smile to Youssef's face.

Chapter 8

Standing in the shadows, Abdul gracefully approached the newbie guard near the entrance working the late shift. Muhammad possessed a boyish face, the skin on his chin as smooth as a twelve-year-old's, his hair clean-cut and combed over to the side and his nails trimmed. He stood roughly the same height as veteran Abdul and carried himself well for his age.

'Looks like it's going to be a long night,' whispered Abdul in his native Arabic tongue, trying to keep a low profile. 'Once Hazim gets started, you can't shut him up. He thinks he's the new Zahi Hawass.'

Muhammad gave a wry smile, but kept his youthful eyes on the party while maintaining a serious and self-contained demeanor.

'I haven't seen you here before,' probed Abdul, a rugged character and not one you would want to get in a fight with. His thinning black hair displayed his tanned Egyptian skin, and his ghostlike gray eyes looked out from a deeply creased fifty-eight-year-old face. There was a seriousness about him, and his hands were calloused and raw, as though he'd had a difficult life and worked twice as hard as anyone else for everything he had attained. His loquacious nature had earned him a reputation among the guards at the museum. He was a little annoying, but perfectly suited to training new recruits like Muhammad.

'It's my first week on the job,' Muhammad whispered.

'First week … wow,' said Abdul, remembering his first time. 'It seems like an eternity for me. I've been here for twenty-five years. Trust me, nothing exciting happens here, but I'm doing this to help pay for my son's education. I should have retired already, the wage here is dreadful, but I persist because I have to.'

Muhammad continued to listen, turning ever so slowly to glance at Abdul out of politeness.

'My son, he's the first in my entire family to go to university,' said Abdul with a note of pride in his voice. 'It's a big deal for our household.'

Muhammad gave him a grim smile, while Abdul took a moment to himself. Saying those words had almost brought tears to his eyes. He portrayed a rough character, tough and manly, but on the inside he was a gentle soul who wanted only the best for his family.

'Has there ever been a robbery here?' asked Muhammad, relaxing a little and inadvertently lightening the mood. He looked more comfortable now with his new partner.

'Never,' Abdul said with a disdainful sniff, 'not under my watch.'

'But it must happen sometimes. I heard in the news a while back that looters vandalized a museum and got away with more than a thousand artefacts.'

'That was from the Malawi National Museum.

They are a bunch of idiots over there, it didn't surprise me when it happened.'

Muhammad nodded his head approvingly.

'The raiders stole hundreds of artefacts to sell on the black market. You'd be surprised how much they go for.' Abdul wrinkled his brow, eyeing the boy inquisitively, then asked, 'You're an educated kid, aren't you? And this job is just a filler for you?'

'Yes, sir, I'm studying Archaeology at Cairo University. I'm hoping to get a job at the new Grand Egyptian Museum when it opens. They say it'll be ready mid-year. When finished it'll make this place seem insignificant.'

'Yes, there's no denying it,' said Abdul with the glum realization that everything he had worked so hard for could be taken away from him if they decided to close down the smaller Cairo Museum. The newly built eight-hundred-million-dollar museum would have it all, and its location was only a little over a mile away from the Pyramids at Giza.

Muhammad agreed excitedly with a nod.

'By the way, how are you coping with your university fees?' asked Abdul, taking into account the years of savings he'd put aside to help his own child.

Muhammad blushed. 'Actually, I come from a rather successful family. My father paid it all in full.'

Abdul flashed an unamused face. 'You're very lucky,' he said, his tone flat.

'I know I am,' Muhammad replied quietly.

Abdul turned away. He couldn't bear to look at the boy, feeling he was unworthy of his respect. He was another rich kid, a trust-fund baby, who probably didn't have to work a day in his life if he didn't want to. The type of person who walked through life without a worry in the world and with the resources to get by comfortably; nothing like his son, who needed to earn his keep.

After a moment of silence Abdul spoke again.

'I'll give you a tip, Muhammad, about how to succeed in this world, on the house.'

'What's that, sir?'

Abdul took a deep breath. 'Sometimes in life you need to do evil to get ahead. To help the ones you love.'

'I don't understand—' said Muhammad, but then broke off when he saw Abdul's eyes widen.

'Did you hear that?' warned Abdul, turning to face the doorway they had just come through.

'What is it?' asked Muhammad with trepidation.

'Hang on, did you lock the outside door before we moved to the first floor?'

'No,' said Muhammad. 'I didn't know I was supposed to do that.'

'You were, sorry, it's my fault, I forgot to tell you,' said Abdul apologetically. 'Listen … I can handle this group on my own. Quietly, leave and check it out. If there's a problem, use the radio. I've set my frequency to channel three.'

Muhammad backed out of the room at a snail's pace and without a sound. Hazim's voice could still be heard describing the details in Tutankhamun's death mask, unaware of the possibility that a threat could be lurking downstairs.

* * *

Muhammad darted to the front entrance to find that it was locked, and he breathed a sigh of relief. As he climbed back up the southeast stairs, careless with relief, he was unexpectedly attacked from behind. His perpetrator had hidden behind an alcove in the wall. Muhammad fought back, struggling to shake the vice-like grip that was wrapped around his neck. He used his elbows to swing at the man's ribs, but to no avail. He moved backwards, trying to use the concrete barrier as a battering ram, but the more he tried, the more he struggled to breathe. He fell to one knee, and a heartbeat later the second knee gave way too.

A voice broke the silence as Muhammad toppled in reverse against the stairway, facing up at the ceiling as he lay on top of the perpetrator.

'Shhh!' a raw voice said, brutal against his ear. A voice he recognized.

Muhammad grappled against his strong arms.

'Don't fight it,' said Abdul, now in complete control over his younger, inexperienced opponent.

'What are you doing?' squeaked Muhammad, trying to gasp for the oxygen that had left his lungs.

'I'm sorry, son, you picked the wrong night to be on guard.'

Abdul pushed his right palm into Muhammad's neck while using his left to push his head the other way, choking him.

Muhammad fought against the pressure that was shutting his airway.

The killing part was Abdul's least favorite task; it

was a necessary chore rather than a pleasure. This was Abdul's evil-doing; the job he had to do in order to give his only son the opportunities in life he had never had. He knew he was selling his soul to the devil. Guilt washed over him as he ended the young man's life and left his body to fall limp.

'I'm sorry,' he mouthed again, dragging the young man's spread-eagled corpse by the leg from the staircase and hiding him out of sight to deal with later. He extracted Muhammad's firearm and headed back to the dim room of the boy Pharaoh, leaping over every second step.

Having only been gone for a couple of minutes, he slid back into position, composed, and waited for Youssef to catch his eye. Everything on his end had gone as planned.

Chapter 9

Through the thick-paned glass sat Tutankhamun's death mask; one of the most well-known works of art in the world. Its shiny gold surface reflected the lights that shone up from below, giving it a majestic aura.

Hazim cleared his throat, a short reprieve from his constant babble, and then continued to explain the details of this prized possession. 'The mask depicts an actual likeness of the young boy Pharaoh, who reigned between 1332–1323 B.C. and died at the tender age of nineteen. It weighs twenty-two pounds and measures twenty-one inches in height and fifteen inches in width. The workmanship is quite exquisite and its value is priceless. Made out of gold and inlaid with semiprecious stones and colored glass, the eyes are made of obsidian and quartz.'

Joey took in the infamous three-thousand-year-old mask, discovered, he knew, in Egypt's Valley of the Kings, where stories circulated that those who dared violate the boy king's final resting place had faced a terrible curse, dying under mysterious circumstances.

He observed Boyce and Marie's elated faces as they studied the mask intently and with a childlike wonder. Guided by Ahmed and Hazim, they strolled around the glass box barrier, their eyes never leaving the artefact. Youssef, also front and center, seemed to be truly enamored by the beauty before him, though Joey assumed that as a citizen of Cairo he had seen the mask before.

All of a sudden Nader coughed profoundly into his palm. At first Joey thought it was nothing, just the smoker having his usual attack, but then he noticed something out of the ordinary.

Youssef shifted his gaze away from the mask and peered into the darkness of the room. A hint of a smile crept onto his face. Joey followed his line of sight to the back of the room, where he saw one of the guards, standing alone. *Where is the other guard?* wondered Joey, sweeping his eyes across the treasure trove of Tutankhamun's most valued collection. Maybe it was the intrigue, or perhaps it was a gut feeling that something wasn't as it appeared, but he felt unsettled.

'Sorry to interrupt you, Hazim,' said Youssef, placing his arm onto the other man's shoulder. 'If it's okay, can we discuss the reason why we're all here tonight?'

'Yes, of course,' said Ahmed, waiting to hear

the enquiries Julien had pre-organized for them to have answered.

'I have many questions to ask you,' said Youssef.

'I am happy to help,' replied Ahmed.

Subdued and without emotion, Youssef said, 'I have reason to believe the Hall of Records exists and is under the Sphinx here at the Giza plateau.'

All eyes turned to the white-bearded man who seemed to be taken by surprise.

'Is it true?' asked Marie, eyebrows raised.

Joey and Boyce waited patiently for a response.

'No, it's not,' said Ahmed, letting out a long sigh. 'What kind of question is that? I don't understand the relevance. I thought we were going to talk about the artefacts stolen from Benjamin's safe.'

'We'll get to them,' said Youssef, stepping closer to the hunched-over man holding on to his cane, dwarfing him. 'Tell me the truth.'

'No, it's inaccurate in many ways, just a myth created by archeologists wanting to make a name for themselves,' responded Ahmed, bending his neck backwards to glance into Youssef's blue eyes. 'If it were true, trust me, I would know about it. I sit at the head of the committee of antiquities and future discoveries.'

Youssef looked on dubiously, while Joey, Marie and Boyce took a back seat and let the two talk it out. It seemed like Youssef was leading up to something. His questions were a little direct, but he came across as a passionate advocate in the pursuit of the truth.

'There's no need to keep this a secret anymore, I already know,' said Youssef with his finger up against his lips, as if to say, *Kindly shut up and listen.* 'The entrance to the Hall of Records is located under the right paw of the Sphinx. The timber decking was placed there to hide an opening that was found by Zahi Hawass, who kept it a secret. He has done nothing but lie to the people.'

Hazim, whose side profile bore a resemblance to the actor Richard Gere, shook his head. It seemed by his reaction that he didn't much like his former minister of antiquities either.

'That is partly true. Yes, an underground crypt was found,' said Ahmed, turning to face his colleague, 'but nothing else, just limestone rocks that led to nowhere; a dead end.'

'That's because you didn't have the key,' said Youssef. 'The key to enter that sacred place.'

'What key?' asked Hazim, confused.

'What are you talking about?' demanded Ahmed, irritation written all over his face.

'Inside the Sphinx on one of the feature inner walls, isn't there a tri-spiral symbol etched an inch deep into the limestone?'

Joey saw the connection now, as did Marie and Boyce, and they all seemed to be holding their breath.

Ahmed gave Hazim a *how did he know this?* kind of stare.

'Did you bring the photos of the stolen artefacts to show them?' asked Joey now, addressing Youssef, who glanced back suspiciously.

Youssef eased his hand into his inner suit jacket pocket, extracted a bunch of photographs and handed them over to the experts, who wore baffled faces. 'These are the artefacts Benjamin had in his apartment safe. Do you recognize this symbol?' he said, pointing to the solid tri-spiral item.

'Yes, I see where you're going with this,' said Ahmed with conviction. 'You are correct, this shape is depicted inside the Sphinx … but what of it?'

'That's the key,' said Youssef. 'That'll lead you inside.'

Ahmed shrugged and once again looked toward Hazim.

'How did Benjamin come to get these artefacts?' asked Hazim.

'He found them inside a secret cave in Cyprus that was meant to be the resting place of Alexander the Great. He extracted a rose granite stela engraved with hieroglyphics as well as the tri-spiral object you see in those pictures. At first we didn't know what it was, but after months of decoding the symbology we discovered that this unusual shape was actually a key that would open the doors to the Hall of Records.' Youssef drew a breath and the next comment caught them by surprise. 'We also learned that the first key was only one of two keys that would lead us deeper within the underground chamber.'

Ahmed's eyes bulged at the statement.

'So there are two,' said Hazim with a mystified expression. 'Why wasn't the second key found in the same cave?' he asked.

'Because Alexander the Great never discovered that second key,' answered Youssef. 'I'm sure he spent a lifetime searching for it, but he would never have known it was hidden inside a tomb in the Valley of the Kings.'

A confused expression crossed Joey's face.

'Tutankhamun's tomb,' said Marie out loud, having put the pieces together in her head.

'That's correct. It was found thousands of years later by Howard Carter.'

'I don't understand,' said Ahmed. 'So you're saying it's hidden somewhere in Tutankhamun's collection?'

'That's exactly what I'm saying,' said Youssef with intense conviction.

'I'm sorry to burst your bubble,' said Hazim, throwing his hands wide to indicate the collection around them. 'But there's no such key here.'

Ignoring the man who ran the restoration department, Youssef suddenly smiled. 'I believe Alexander *did* somehow enter the Hall of Records inside the Sphinx, and that he added to the collection already there. Can you imagine what could be stored there from his own library in Alexandria? A treasure trove is waiting to be found, and I'll be the one to find it,' said Youssef, then gave a long pause as he glanced over his shoulder at the back of the room. 'My father never believed in me,' he muttered, almost as if to himself. 'He thought I would amount to nothing, and just live off my inheritance. I made a promise to myself that I was going to prove him wrong.'

He paused once more, then followed this with a statement that shook Joey to his core.

'Tonight the quest begins ... Tonight it's my time to shine ... Tonight I will possess both keys.'

Chapter 10

Joey's jaw dropped. He suddenly knew without a doubt that it was Youssef who had killed his estranged uncle. He cursed himself for not trusting his initial instinct the first moment he had sized Youssef up. Boyce moved forward, his eyes narrowed, his face contorted with rage. He stopped in his tracks when the barrel of a matte black Heckler & Koch, held by one of the security guards, was pushed hard up against the back of his neck. Joey suddenly noticed that the other security guard had disappeared.

'No!' screamed Marie, her eyes widening with distress.

'What's going on?' asked Ahmed, turning pale with dismay. He was looking at Abdul as though he had betrayed him. 'This is preposterous,' he said, although it sounded more like a plea.

Joey tried to think fast. What was he to do? he thought. His mind seemed frozen with shock. He eyed the group, feeling as though the scene was playing out in slow motion.

'Now, let's not do anything crazy,' said Hazim, facing the armed man. 'Abdul, why are you doing this? Where is Muhammad?'

'I'm sorry, my friend,' answered Abdul. 'I got an offer I couldn't refuse.'

While Abdul held the weapon firmly against the teen's head, Nader advanced. Abdul extracted a second gun that was tucked into his belt and handed it over to the bigger man, who grabbed it and waited for instructions.

'The tools are behind the colossal statue of Akhenaten in room three,' Abdul told Nader. 'He's positioned near the window and is the one with his left hand missing. You got that?'

Nader nodded and dashed out of the room, leaving his two associates in total control.

'I can't believe this is happening to us again,' blurted Joey, gazing into his girlfriend's petrified hazel eyes. He took a step forward, clenching his fists, but was immediately stopped by Abdul, who covered both Joey and Boyce with the gun, keeping them in check.

'So, you used my boss's influence to arrange a private meeting and take control of this museum,' said Boyce, slowly shifting his head away from the barrel of the gun at his neck. 'What's this going to achieve?'

Youssef adjusted his expensive suit jacket and said in the same, casual tone, 'Within this room I will find the second key that will lead me to the last secret chamber described in the stela.'

'I can assure you there's no key in this room,' said Ahmed with his hands out in supplication. 'I know every part of this museum. It's not here.'

Youssef drew a fake smile. 'The key is hidden in Tutankhamun's death mask, or as I have come to understand it, in Nefertiti's funeral mask.'

'That's absurd,' said Hazim, also standing beside Ahmed with his arms raised in surrender.

'The gold mask is not of the boy king,' said Youssef, giving the Egyptian experts their very own history lesson. 'It belonged to his heretic queen mother. Look at it,' he said, gesturing toward it. 'The protective covering appears feminine. The ears have earring holes in them. This was not a common practice for male Pharaohs back in those days.'

Youssef turned to the restorations manager, who stood with frightened, bulging eyes, thinking hard. 'When analyzing Tut's mask, didn't your team discover a cartouche that appeared to have been removed?'

'Yes ... but—' said Hazim, however Youssef interrupted him.

'The concealed stamp was traced to another name: *Ankhkheprure Neferneferuaten,* which translates to Queen Nefertiti,' Youssef explained. 'You see, Nefertiti concealed the key with her son to keep a secret hidden away, so that it could only be found by *thee who is worthy to find it.*'

'What secret?' asked Joey.

'That's what I want to find out,' replied Youssef condescendingly, with an expression that suggested he thought Joey was an idiot.

'Why do you think the key is within the death mask?' asked Marie.

'The last line on the rose granite stela read, *[mask symbol] inscribed to a map for the afterlife will show the way.* This is why Alexander the Great had no idea. The map he is referring to was a guide to finding it. The spell that is etched on the back of Tutankhamun's mask is pointing the way. It is the same spell that was written on the rose granite stela and was intended for the protection of the mask. It's way too much of a coincidence not to be true.'

'But, where on the mask is the key?' asked Ahmed, shaking with emotion. 'I don't understand.'

'The only place it could be hidden is inside the beard,' suggested Marie in a soft voice, as if to herself, then glanced quickly at Youssef, realizing she had probably helped him inadvertently.

Youssef nodded his head and his smile continued to widen. 'That's why I want to take you with me tonight, Ms Martino. You think outside the square. As soon as Benjamin shared with me your discovery in Cyprus, I knew I needed to have you on my team. All it took was one email pretending to be Benjamin and it lured you over here.'

'You're not taking her anywhere,' Joey said, stepping forward until he was forced to a standstill when he heard Abdul's gun being cocked.

'Hang on, didn't an employee knock the beard off the mask by accident during a lightbulb change a few years ago?' said Marie curiously, but Joey knew her well enough to guess that she was trying to distract the gunman.

'Yes, that's true,' said Hazim. 'I led the team in that restoration. The mask had been hastily glued back on with epoxy. We had employed a German-Egyptian party of experts to fix the problem. They scraped off the epoxy, removed the beard and reattached it using beeswax, a natural substance found throughout ancient Egypt. But we detected nothing in the beard at the time.'

'That's because you weren't looking for anything,' said Youssef disdainfully.

'I cannot allow you to damage this priceless artefact,' protested the director, moving his body in front of the glass box. 'I will not allow it. This mask represents Egypt's history.'

'Move out of the way, old man,' Youssef ordered, all pretense of a smile now gone.

'But we just told you, the beard was removed and glued back on,' said Hazim, pleading for mercy. 'No key was found!'

'I will be the judge of that,' said Youssef impudently.

The tension in the air was escalating and Joey knew things weren't going to end well when Youssef started pushing the smaller Ahmed away from the glass cabinet. Joey calmed his racing thoughts, focusing his mind on the problem at hand. His eyes darted over to the security guard Abdul, who was still carrying his pistol and controlling the room, and that's when he spotted Boyce's tingling fingers.

Boyce tucked his right hand behind his back and moved his fingers ferociously like an octopus's tentacles, attracting Joey's attention. He held them out wide like a starfish, pumped them closed, then opened his hand again to show four fingers. He then repeated the sequence, closing another one off, to three. He was counting down to when they were going to simultaneously spring an attack on the armed man.

A memory crept into Joey's mind.

They were in Switzerland. Boyce had stepped in front of a loaded pistol and put his life in danger. Joey had known that the boy was brave then, but now that he worked for the French Intelligence Agency, Joey knew that Boyce wasn't going to stand there and do nothing. If he was planning an attack, Joey knew he needed to be ready to help.

Two …

Boyce pumped his fingers closed.

One …

Boyce reacted swiftly, lifting the weapon with his left hand and followed in quick with a right hook that connected with Abdul's face. Surprised and taken off guard, Abdul pressed the trigger, firing off a single gunshot that rang out and hit the nearest wall, causing everyone to drop to the floor to avoid any crossfire.

Instantaneously, Joey charged at Abdul like a line blocker in the Super Bowl defending his turf, his shoulder crashing squarely into the man's sternum, winding him and knocking the gun out of his hand, sending it spinning into a dark corner as Abdul sailed backwards through the air and landed hard on his back.

A struggle ensued in the dimly lit room among the precious relics.

Abdul scrabbled to his feet and managed to wrap his arms around Boyce's throat, crushing his carotid artery. Joey dived on top of Abdul with a chokehold of his own, squeezing his neck with enough of an iron palm that the guard was forced to release the teenager, who sucked in desperate breaths as the air flowed into his lungs once more.

Working as a team, they restrained Abdul. It seemed their impromptu plan had worked. But their small victory was soon cut short by the loud rippling sound of gunfire slicing through the air, sending the director of the museum plummeting to the floor.

Chapter 11

The director's head jolted backwards, his eyes rolling back in his head, and his entire body went rigid. With his face a mask of confusion and a red hole blossoming in his forehead, his diminutive frame hit the hard surface like a heavy bag of potatoes, and he lay facing the ceiling of the establishment he had worked most of his life to protect and restore. He was a true Egyptian who was proud of his heritage and what his people had achieved. Now, he gazed sightlessly upward, his life's work forever finished.

'Oh my God!' whimpered Marie, taking cover with Hazim by her side.

Youssef stood calmly as the smoke from his gun's barrel drifted into the air. He too was carrying a nine-inch VP series Heckler & Koch pistol, most likely one of the latest models. Growing up in a family of crime, German-built firearms had come up in discussions on a regular basis, so Joey knew they were a rugged, reliable, accurate and ergonomic weapon that was as sexy as a thin shirt on a cold day. Or at least, that was what he'd been told.

The puzzle occupying Joey's mind now was how

Youssef had entered the building armed. The metal detector must have been switched off when it was his turn for a pat-down by his inside man, he realized.

'Why did you kill him?' said Hazim in a whisper, his tone grief-stricken as the lifeless director's blood oozed out onto the floor.

At that moment, Nader re-entered the room carrying over his shoulder a dark canvas backpack. He looked at Youssef, a dumbfounded look on his face. 'What in the hell is going on?' he said in a deep, gruff voice. 'I thought we were going to leave no mess behind?'

'Well, plans change,' uttered the man running the show menacingly, and he pointed his Glock over at Boyce and Joey, who were still restraining Abdul. 'You two, move over there, now!' he shouted. His voice boomed out in the silent room. 'Try anything like that again and you all die.'

Guided by Youssef's deadly weapon, Joey let go of Abdul and together with Boyce they rejoined Marie and Hazim, who were facing Youssef with their backs toward the nearest wall.

'Sit down,' commanded Youssef.

Joey, Boyce, Marie and Hazim obliged.

'There are hundreds of cameras in this museum,' said Hazim. 'You'll get caught. There's no hiding what you have done tonight.'

Youssef flashed an evil grin but ignored the comment. Instead, he ordered his men to get to work. Abdul picked himself off the cold floor and gave Joey a long death stare, cutting a sharp finger across his neck, which made Joey swallow uncomfortably.

He then approached the glass cabinet surrounding Tutankhamun's mask and went around to the back, where ten vertical and two horizontal lines of Egyptian hieroglyphs were inscribed. The spell: *the map for the afterlife that will show the way.*

Nader's imposing figure kneeled down beside Abdul and he dug his hand into the backpack, extracting what seemed to be a laminated piece of A4 paper, a spray can, a cordless drill with a Phillips head attachment and a solid, heavy-looking cube-like object.

Following Abdul's instructions, Nader used the drill to unscrew the four timber screws on the molded panel on the back of the cabinet. Moments later, the fascia board was detached and Nader leaned it up against the nearest wall, revealing the cabinet's inner cavity, which held a mass of blue Ethernet cables, computer scanners and transmitters with red flashing lights.

'Multiple alarm systems,' complained Nader before turning away to cough uncontrollably.

'I told you,' warned Hazim. 'You won't be able to remove the mask without triggering the alarm.'

'Shut up, you!' said Youssef, profound scorn and loathing in his voice. 'We're aware of that.'

Hazim sank backwards on the wall, shaking his head in disbelief.

Abdul picked up the spray bottle and showered the inside of the cabinet, revealing two green laser lines that bisected each other in a giant X pattern that would have been invisible to the naked eye. He carefully moved the weighted object past the lasers and sat it against a scanner pad. Cautiously, he snaked his hand back out and sprayed the can once more.

The sensors were deactivated.

It became clear to Joey that Abdul had inserted a hefty magnet to trick the system into bypassing the infrared beams.

'Okay, you're free to remove these two screws,' Abdul said, pointing to them. 'Be careful, though; do not touch anything else, especially that magnet, or it's game over.'

Nader flashed an uneasy glance at his boss, who was keeping a close eye on the captives.

'Take your time,' said Youssef encouragingly. 'We have this entire place to ourselves.'

Minutes later the integrated base that held Tutankhamun's death mask slowly slid downward, stopping two inches short of the magnet. The precious gold face of the boy king was exposed for all to see, outside of its protective glass shell.

'Now what?' said Hazim softly, shaking his head.

'What's wrong?' Joey asked him.

'If they extract the mask an alarm will go off. There are multiple hidden alarms and triggers attached to it that even I'm not aware of.'

Youssef heard Hazim's statement and stalked over with a hint of madness in his eyes, holding his gun's ergonomic grip tightly. 'Who said I was going to extract the entire mask?' he said with a sneer.

'He's going to snap off the beard,' said Marie, her horror at the thought evident in her voice.

'No! He can't,' said Hazim.

'You can keep your precious death mask,' joked Youssef, and gave the order in Arabic.

The expression on Hazim's face was one of appalled anguish before he turned his head away, unable to watch.

Abdul slowly wrapped a strong fist around the mask's beard. He squeezed his lips together in concentration, then, keeping his movements precise and controlled, he snapped off the beard with relative ease. Joey recalled that it was only glued on with beeswax.

The security guard carefully handed Youssef the narrow gold beard, inlaid with deep-blue, semiprecious stones. Youssef weighed it in his hand before he began to examine it for the cavity that was meant to contain the second key.

Everyone's eyes were trained on him as he studied his prize. Joey hoped he would not come up empty, because that would very likely end in dire consequences for them all. If he found the key, there might be a chance Youssef would leave the rest of the mask untouched, and Joey and his friends could offer their expertise to help finding this last secret chamber. That was what Joey kept telling himself, anyway, as he tried to prepare for the slaughter to come.

Joey's heart pounded thuddingly in his chest. Their lives depended on this ancient goatee and a riddle written thousands of years ago. But this had been a puzzle that not even his well-educated dead uncle had been capable of solving, so he felt hope drain away with every passing moment.

* * *

Youssef stuck his index finger deep inside the empty cavity and dug it around in a circular motion, but he found nothing. His face bore an expression of surprise and anger rolled into one.

'I told you before,' said Hazim tiredly. 'There's no key.'

Youssef examined the pipe-like cavity and noticed a paper-thin groove that was just above where the upright curve at the bottom of the goatee began. He tugged on it.

Hazim cringed.

Using greater force, Youssef ascertained there was movement when he twisted it in a clockwise direction.

'Please be careful with it,' warned Hazim again, although he fell silent when he was once more threatened with the barrel of Nader's gun.

Youssef carefully and slowly turned the base of the goatee, which spun like a layer of a Rubik's Cube. After a third quarter-turn, a familiar shape sprang out of a concealed position in the beard's inner cavity that was still connected to the famous goatee. There was no mistaking it: it was much smaller than the first key, but it was otherwise a perfect replica of the tri-spiral motif he already possessed. It looked other-worldly, its intricate carvings seemingly created by laser-cut machinery that didn't exist in those times.

A smile bloomed on Youssef's face. 'The key!' he uttered with glee, unable to hide his delight that he had been correct all along.

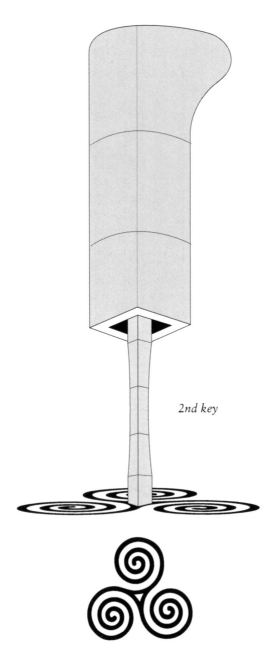

2nd key

Chapter 12

Joey watched Youssef grin as he held on to the key as though it were a holy relic. To him, it clearly didn't matter that he had murdered Joey's uncle and the director of the Cairo Museum. He seemed even to have enjoyed it. The stage was now set, the wheels in motion. Joey knew Youssef wouldn't stop until he had discovered what had lay sealed for thousands of years.

Fearful that he and his friends would be expendable, Joey got cautiously to his feet and kept a close eye on Marie, who stared right back with the same worried look she had given him before he'd dropped the real *Mona Lisa* in the fire in front of the famous Louvre pyramid.

'Okay, as planned,' ordered Youssef, tucking the key carefully into his suit pocket before rubbing his hands together in that classic way villains do. 'Let's clean up. Nothing happened here tonight.'

Hazim frowned in confusion. It was clear to Joey that he was wondering how all this could possibly be kept a secret. How would this end for Hazim, and would he live to tell the tale? Would any of them?

Nader continued to follow Abdul's quiet instructions. He pushed the base of Tutankhamun's mask back up into its original housing, exposing it once again for all to see within its glass case. After securing it with the two timber screws, he removed the magnet and screwed the wooden panel back in place. The only difference now was that the goatee-less gold mask stood in all its shiny glory with a gaping hole in its chin.

Nader shoved the magnet, drill and spray can back into the backpack, while Abdul stuck the laminated sheet of paper on the lower end of the boxed glass.

It read: *After our previous attempt to glue on the Pharaoh's beard using beeswax, the precious piece has fallen off again. It is currently within the restoration department and in due time will be reunited with Tutankhamun's death mask. Thank you for your cooperation, director of Egyptian Museum, Ahmed Daher.*

* * *

Joey, Marie, Boyce and Hazim were escorted out of the building through a secret back entrance known only to the workers, and guided over to a white van with *Cairo Museum Artefacts* advertised on its side. They were directed to climb inside the carpeted van through its rear doors, then made to sit across from each other. Wedged inside the windowless carriage was a green-colored circular saw, two pairs of steel-capped boots and one reasonably sized black duffle bag that appeared full.

'What's that God-awful stench?' asked Boyce, bringing his shirt up to cover his nose.

'This van is used for transporting ancient artefacts

and rotten old timber sarcophaguses, not to mention thousand-year-old mummies,' said Hazim. 'It's hard to get the smell out because of the carpet. Trust me, we've tried.'

Leaving the rear door open, Nader removed the two pairs of boots and headed for the driver's seat, while Youssef covered the captives with his handgun. Through the glass panel between the cargo area and the driver's compartment, Joey watched Nader discard his formal attire, revealing a black t-shirt that outlined his bulging biceps and a pair of charcoal work pants. Before taking the wheel, Nader reached over into the glove compartment and took out a cigarette pack. He tapped one out and stared at it with an expression that suggested they had been parted for far too long.

Moments later Abdul came into view, carrying the director's body on his shoulders, and threw him into the van like a piece of meat. Marie covered her mouth, gagging, although she couldn't stop staring at the poor dead man's corpse in front of her.

Abdul climbed in after him and wedged himself up next to Marie, his pistol aimed at her rib cage just in case Boyce or Joey wanted to be brave again.

'Careful with that,' said Marie coldly, adjusting herself as Youssef slammed the door shut and then strolled to the front of the vehicle, where he too discarded his suit to reveal a white t-shirt and comfortable brown work pants. Transferring the precious key from his suit to his pants pocket, he slid into the passenger's seat and put on his new boots.

Opening the glove compartment, he extracted a

watch and slapped it onto his wrist. It appeared to be some kind of GPS reader. That was the moment when Youssef noticed Joey staring at him through the glass barrier between them, so he turned to train his gun back at the captives as if to say, *I'm watching you.*

* * *

Crossing the Qasr El Nil Bridge in the darkness, Joey wondered how the night was going to unfold. Would he survive or would he end up dead like the man at his feet?

'Where are you taking us?' asked Hazim as the vehicle hit a pothole in the road, causing everyone to bounce up and down.

'We're headed for the Giza plateau,' said Youssef confidently. 'Let's see if all this was a bunch of bullshit or not. And maybe by the time the sun rises again I will be the man who uncovered the greatest treasure trove in the history of the world.'

'You are nothing but a murderer,' Marie blurted, her eyes fuming with hatred.

'Why are you taking us?' asked Joey, knowing the answer to his question, but asking it anyway. They were witnesses to murder. Youssef was far too smart to just let them go, but Joey wanted to know what this lunatic was planning.

'I was never the brains in my partnership with Benjamin,' said Youssef, looking back from his position.

'Clearly,' quipped Marie under her breath, which elicited a smile from Boyce.

'Yes, I was the investor. But don't forget it was I who discovered the whereabouts of the last key. I was the one who orchestrated this entire night to perfection. I know the three of you have worked well together in the past. Your presence here is no accident. As soon as I called Julien, I knew Boyce would be sent to America to collect you two. Everyone in this van is here because I wanted it to be that way.'

Youssef caught his breath.

'The thing is, ancient chambers such as the one I hope to find are often booby-trapped to prevent the wrong people entering them. I certainly don't intend to find that out the hard way.'

'So we're the test dummies who'll go first,' said Boyce angrily.

'Exactly,' said Youssef. 'Either you come and see where these underground chambers lead us, or I can easily pull the car over to the side of the road and have you all assassinated right now.'

'No, we would love to join you on the quest,' Hazim said quickly, speaking for everyone, his voice shaking.

Chapter 13

After a twenty-minute drive, the Pyramids of Giza rose up before them into the night sky. The amazing sight framed by the front window of the van gave them the feeling of being transported back in time to a vast desert landscape once ruled by the ancient Pharaohs. To witness such a place was breathtaking to say the least. The structures were so colossal in size that the occupants of the van couldn't crane their necks far enough to see their apexes. Joey couldn't find the words to convey the sense of size and grandeur the Pyramids embodied. All three triangular-shaped cones stood like mighty sentinels, dominating the landscape as they rose silently in the dark sky.

The van bounced up and down as they turned

onto the flat causeway that led to the Great Sphinx of Giza. The sound of the crushed rocks and loose sand underneath the tires filled the night as they came to a stop at their destination. Nader escorted the captives out of the vehicle at gunpoint, and they all looked up to see the enormous mythical limestone creature with the body of a lion and the head of a human still a fair distance away. Joey hoped fervently that the statue would give up its secrets easily, or they would all end up dead like the Pharaohs before them.

'Anyone tries anything funny and you'll die here with the ancestors,' said Youssef, ushering the troops along with his firearm.

A cigarette resting on his lips, Nader extracted the duffle bag from the back of the van while Abdul carried the circular saw.

'I told you we would see the Pyramids up close and in person,' said Boyce dryly, but then flashed a boyish grin that never got old.

'Yes, you did.' Joey rolled his eyes. 'But I wasn't expecting to be chaperoned by men with guns.'

'What's a holiday without a bit of adventure?' Boyce quipped.

Marie shook her head but smiled, then took off her high heels, which were making it difficult for her to walk on the uneven terrain. Joey looked worriedly at her bare feet and the dry sand beneath, which was littered with sharp slivers of limestone rock.

'And you said I could trust you,' Joey said to Boyce, continuing the banter, his eyes trained all the while on the impressive sight before him. 'Come to Egypt, you said. It'll be A-okay. Can I ever travel to a destination without someone trying to kill me? Sometimes I wonder why I even leave my beach club.'

Even though their current situation had definitely not been in the plan, the three shared a brief smile. This wasn't the first time they had been through a traumatic incident, and their calmness was born of experience. On the other hand, Hazim darted his head from left to right, breathing shallowly, and clearly very frightened.

Marie pulled Joey aside and carefully whispered in his ear so as not to be overheard.

'Be ready. If an opportunity presents itself to turn the tables back in our favor, we have to take it. Tonight there'll come a time when we'll need to *dance*.' She emphasized this last word.

Joey agreed with a nod and replied, 'Dance, I totally understand.'

Youssef turned suddenly, peering at them through the gloom. They walked on in silence.

'I would've thought this site would be flooded with people, even in the evening,' commented Joey, taking in the Sphinx and Khufu's Great Pyramid of Giza, the largest of the three Pyramids, which towered in the distance. Although Khafre's and Menkaure's Pyramids were certainly impressive monuments, only one was known as the Great one.

'It's a dangerous area,' reported Hazim. 'Sadly, many robberies and murders happen here, especially at nighttime.'

'What about in the day?' Joey asked curiously as he took in the desert before him. When he looked one way, he could see nothing but sand and rock, but in the other direction, the city skyline dominated, overwhelming the desert with its array of blazing lights. The view was a startling blend of modern and ancient.

'In the day, it's okay if you're on a tour,' said Hazim. 'Don't forget that Egypt is a relatively underdeveloped country with no real economy, and the majority of the population is poor. You'll most likely get harassed by kids selling souvenirs.'

'That's right,' Marie agreed, stepping carefully around the rough ground in front of her. 'A friend of mine visited the Pyramids a couple of years ago and said the tour buses were safe zones. No one other than the group was allowed to enter this area, to protect the tourists from constant beggars. She said a poor young Egyptian boy tried to sell the members on the bus pyramid souvenirs and was scared away by men with whips.'

Joey raised an eyebrow, unable to comprehend the unfairness of the poverty so many people had to endure, coming as he did from a background of wealth and opportunity.

Reaching the feet of the Sphinx, Joey saw that a deck was laid out, as Youssef had mentioned back in the museum. Joey felt a humbling sensation as he stood between the lion-creature's massive paws, each twice his height and longer than a city bus. Carved from a single stone, the creature gave the impression that it was ready to lunge viciously at any intruder, taunting them, daring them to come nearer the necropolis of Giza.

It was then that Joey noticed a young, barefoot male dressed in shorts and a ripped t-shirt approaching from the north. Cursing under his breath, Youssef swung his gun around and aimed it at the youth. The boy stopped in his tracks, eyes on the weapon, and, realizing these were not men to mess with, he turned on his tail and ran back the way he had come.

Lowering his gun slowly, Youssef turned back to the task at hand. 'Right here,' he instructed Abdul, pointing to a spot near the Sphinx's right paw, after establishing the position with his GPS watch.

How long has this plan been predetermined? wondered Joey.

Abdul started up his battery-operated circular saw and cut into the timbers with ease. The sound of the machine was loud but brief as it sliced through the boards like butter to reveal an opening wide enough to enter.

Nader planted the duffle bag in the sand and unzipped it to reveal a plethora of exploration tools: plenty of tactical flashlights for everyone, five yellow firemen's helmets, safety vests, utility belts, climbing rope, two crowbars, a snorkel set, three sets of underwater goggles, a small foldable shovel, a small-sized backpack, a pistol and the first tri-spiral key stolen from Benjamin's safe.

The high-visibility vests were passed around and everyone was handed their own flashlight as well as a helmet, leaving Joey and Boyce without.

'Hey, where's ours?' asked Joey.

'Sorry, not enough to go around,' said Abdul who extracted the VP40 semiautomatic pistol, having lost his weapon inside the Louvre. He then strapped on a utility belt filled with pocket holes carrying LED light sticks and flares.

'Boyce, you go first,' ordered Youssef.

'What is it with me going first?' said Boyce. He took off his navy suit jacket and left it on the timber deck, then rolled up his white-sleeved shirt and shouldered his way into the his-vis vest. He glanced inside the hole, six flashlights showing the way. He used his upper-body strength to lower himself and then jumped the rest of the way. The sound of rocks scrunching underfoot announced his landing.

'I'm in,' he said once he was on safe ground. 'It's extremely dark down here.'

Joey went next, flashlight first, his sneakers crunching the soft sand underfoot. Small, loose stones littered the entire floor. He glanced upward to see the starry sky behind Hazim, who was not dressed for this kind of thing. The older man began to descend. Joey circled the cave with his flashlight, cutting through the darkness, then came to a halt.

Boyce was on his knees, digging into the dry sand with his bare hands.

'What are you doing?' whispered Joey so the others above would not be able to hear.

'Move the flashlight,' Boyce quickly responded.

Joey jerked the light the other way. Boyce had extracted some kind of tracking device from within his car keys. Joey grinned. The hope of being rescued gave him the strength to fight on. The tiny yellow flashing beacon slowly disappeared as Boyce concealed it within the debris of broken limestone rocks.

Help was on its way. The trick was to stay alive long enough for someone to reach them.

Chapter 14

As soon as Hazim cleared the jump, Nader flicked his cigarette away before squeezing his heavy frame through the hole, like a beast that belonged with the Anubis warriors of the past. Abdul was next, carrying the hefty duffle bag, followed by Marie, who was hampered by her formal evening gown and stumbled onto all fours in the cold sand. She squirmed and fell on her side in the dress, which was fast becoming ruined in this environment.

Youssef was the last to enter, and the steely expression on his face let them know he was ready to make history. His eyes followed the six rays of light that were trained up against one of the limestone walls.

'We found the symbol,' said Nader solemnly.

'You were right,' Marie confirmed, following the curved lines inside the grooves with her flashlight.

'There is definitely a deep indentation here.'

Youssef's eyes darted around the cave. He then turned to face Abdul and demanded, 'Bring the key.'

Joey, Boyce, Marie, and Hazim all kept quiet, patiently aiming their light sources at the spiral symbol, which, they gathered, was some kind of doorway.

Abdul unzipped the duffle bag and took out the solid, carved piece of meteorite. With it in his hand, he proceeded to the smoothly rendered wall. It took him a couple of goes trying different positions for the key before he successfully managed to slide it comfortably in place. It now lay flush with the symbol's surface.

'Turn it,' Youssef instructed.

Abdul rotated it clockwise, and after a quarter-turn, a sharp bang was heard somewhere beneath the floor on which they stood. What followed was the sound of sand pouring out of some aperture somewhere within the complex.

'Can you hear that?' Boyce whispered nervously. He frantically searched for the source with his flashlight, but to no avail.

A moment later a flat limestone section near where Marie stood, about the size of a household door, began to descend. Marie jumped and shifted hurriedly to safe ground as the sand around the lowering surface cascaded southward like a showering waterfall.

'The entrance!' said Youssef grandly, his voice filled with passion.

The single solid stone moved at a snail's pace. Eventually the group peered over the lip to see a box-shaped room about eight feet below them.

'Let's go. Boyce, you're up,' Youssef ordered again.

'I must have a sign on my forehead,' sighed Boyce, inspecting the drop first with his flashlight before climbing down into the blackness.

At that point Youssef warned his men in their native Arabic to keep a watchful eye on the American. He knew Joey was unpredictable and dangerous, and Joey had nearly ruined everything by besting the security guard back at the museum. Youssef wanted to make sure that would never happen in here. He knew that to be able to keep his hostages under his complete control, he needed to teach Joey a lesson and make an example of him. This would show the rest of them who was running the show, before they progressed deeper into the underground labyrinth.

Once Boyce disappeared into the void, Abdul switched off his flashlight and crept up to Joey unseen. Quickly, he used the handle of his pistol to strike at the back of his head.

Joey howled in pain as he fell to his knees, grasping the back of his skull with his right hand.

'No!' Marie screamed as her boyfriend hit the floor.

'What's going on?' asked Boyce down below, hearing Joey's cry for help.

'What did you do that for?' Joey cried, his expression one of pain and anger.

Marie pushed Abdul out of the way and gathered Joey in her arms. Joey was overcome with dizziness and couldn't help but sway from side to side. Moving his hand away from his wound, Joey flashed the stream of light onto his palm to reveal a gush of blood. Steaming with rage, he clumsily rose to his feet, ready to fight the bearded Arab, but Marie held him back.

'Let it go,' she warned as Abdul and Nader stood there, waiting to react.

Youssef chuckled. 'That's just a small reminder,' he told the pair smugly. 'You try anything down here and we'll not hesitate to put a hole in someone. Do I make myself clear?'

Joey nodded reluctantly and called down to Boyce between gritted teeth, 'Everything's okay.'

'Well … it's not okay down here,' Boyce replied, his tone full of concern.

'What's wrong?' asked Marie.

'There's nothing down here. It's a dead end.'

'You.' Youssef pointed vehemently to the American. 'Go help your friend. Come up empty and someone up here will die.'

'What do you mean someone will die?' asked Hazim, who had kept quiet the entire time.

'So this is how we're going to play the game down here tonight,' said Joey, who turned to Marie and caressed her on the shoulder. 'I'll be right back,' he said, trying to sound optimistic.

'The key led us down to this hole,' Marie assured him with confidence. 'There must be a way forward somewhere. The ingenious mechanism needed to move that heavy piece of limestone was not put in place for nothing.'

'She's right,' concurred Youssef. 'This room must lead to someplace.'

* * *

Joey positioned himself at the lip of the hole and jumped to the lower level, once again landing on the soft sand on its surface. Five powerful LED military flashlights shone down from above as Youssef scrutinized the two in the pit-like room. They searched in the darkness for cavities or access points that could lead them further within. Joey knew that there had to be an underground network of tunnels nearby, as they were known to be found throughout the Giza plateau.

'Keep searching,' said Joey as he rubbed his hand up against the limestone wall.

'There's nothing here,' replied Boyce, defeated.

Youssef muttered something in Arabic.

They both heard the sound of Nader's semiautomatic being cocked, causing Joey's adrenaline to spike. He didn't need to understand the words to know that he had to find an entrance or death would soon be upon one of them.

'The floor,' Joey suggested, pointing his flashlight at the thick sandy surface beneath them, and creating a wavy riverbed effect of light and shadow.

Boyce was first to his knees, clearing armfuls of dry sand to one side, while Joey studied his progress. The dry sand was about two inches deep and moved with ease.

'There's nothing here,' Boyce said, exposing nothing but solid limestone footings.

'Here, use the shovel,' said Abdul as he threw the tool down to their level, almost hitting Joey in the process.

'There has to be something,' Joey said, falling to his knees to help. Leaving his flashlight to one side, he took up the small foldable shovel and dug desperately in all directions.

Ploughing through the sand, he suddenly saw a piece of granite through the sand, distinguished from the limestone base by its white, pink and gray textured coloring.

'That's it,' Youssef said exultantly. 'It's the same rose granite as the stela Benjamin found.'

'Let's clear it out, find the edges,' said Boyce.

After brushing back the sand from the rectangular surface, they uncovered a symbol engraved in the stone. It was the same tri-spiral design that had led them here, but it was also accompanied by a familiar cartouche.

'Nefertiti!' Youssef said, identifying it. 'We meet again. This past year I have been infatuated by this queen. I knew she was the link to a long-lost secret, and now I'm a step closer to finding out what it is.'

Kneeling opposite each other, Joey and Boyce dug their fingers along the perimeter of the stone. Joey glanced upward, his expression one of relief as the beam from his discarded flashlight illuminated his face. 'I feel cold air,' he said.

'I feel it too,' said Boyce. 'We need a crowbar down here.'

After an abrupt Arabic conversation took place, Abdul joined them, carrying the duffle bag filled with supplies. Joey stood up, his body ready to react, and he eyeballed the creep who had struck him not so long ago. His fists tightened, and he wanted nothing more than to end the security guard in this tiny space where he could not escape.

'Don't even think about it,' warned Youssef, watching it all unfold from above as if he were the puppeteer. 'Don't forget, I have your precious girlfriend up here.'

Swallowing his rage, Joey turned his eyes back to the task at hand.

'Hazim, go and help, make yourself useful,' said Youssef, playfully waving the gun in his direction.

'I will, just please don't shoot,' Hazim responded. Still dressed in his tailored dark suit, gray tie and shiny leather boots, he climbed awkwardly over the edge and down into the box-like room.

Two crowbars were wedged into the groove lines Boyce and Joey had already dug out. Abdul controlled one end, while Joey held the other. Leveraging their weight, they managed to lift the granite chunk of rock to reveal a cavity that would lead them further into the unknown. Boyce and Hazim helped them gain momentum, and they eventually pushed the heavy slab upright and tipped it over on itself to uncover steps that disappeared into the darkness.

Chapter 15

The temperature dropped as Joey entered the underground chamber, sending a violent chill down his spine. His flashlight carved a saber-like beam through the darkness, illuminating the precipitous stone steps before him. The loose, undisturbed sand now skimmed to the side as he continued his slow, careful descent.

Boyce was by his side, mirroring his every move, casting the small circle of flickering orange light onto the stairs in front of them. Reaching the final step, they saw a perfectly square, compact tunnel sloping steadily downward into the gloom, its walls seemingly hand-carved from solid limestone.

'Boy, I hope the air that's been trapped down here doesn't make us sick,' said Joey, taking in the corridor that seemed to disappear past where their flashlights reached.

'You're not going to start calling me that again, are ya?' Boyce chuckled and shook his head.

Joey smiled brazenly at how easy it was to toy with his young friend.

'As long as we don't disturb a cursed mummy,' intervened Hazim, appearing behind them, his own flashlight shaking in his hand. 'We don't want to end up dead like Howard Carter, do we?'

'I'll keep that in mind,' said Joey with raised eyebrows.

Abdul came fast on Hazim's heels, and once again flashed his beam of light onto Joey, clearly watching his every move.

'Get it out of my face before I shove it where the sun don't shine,' said Joey tightly as he glanced up to see his girlfriend being manhandled down the steps by Nader.

'Don't you ever put your hands on me again,' Marie uttered defiantly, shaking him off and putting as much distance between them as she could.

'Or you'll what?' replied Nader. Quick as a flash he reached out and grabbed her wrist, twisting it backwards and causing Marie to drop her flashlight and fall to her knees with a cry of pain.

Abdul grinned, satisfied.

Joey surged forward, the darkness camouflaging his face, which he knew would be red with suppressed rage. He faced up to Nader, a man too tall and too strong, whose one punch could end him, but he wasn't going to stand there and watch his girl be treated this way.

Nader reacted with a deprecating laugh, but didn't budge. 'Continue to move,' he responded, 'and I'll break her wrist.'

Joey eyed him out for a moment. His street smarts wanted to show the bully he wasn't one to back down, no matter the consequences, but he couldn't do that to Marie. Nader was too unpredictable.

At that moment Youssef appeared out of the darkness, and the moment of tension was broken. Joey slowly reached over and took Marie's other hand, then stepped backwards, taking her with him.

'Let's move, people,' Youssef commanded. 'Time to make history.'

Abdul slid a glow stick out of his utility belt and cracked it to life, causing a flood of green to surround them, then tossed it as hard as he could down the corridor to help show the way.

Retrieving her flashlight, Marie headed into the tunnel first, Joey right by her side. He held her tight up against his torso with his free hand, wanting to assure her they would get through this and that he would do whatever he had to, to see them safely out the other side.

The passageway, barely ten feet high, had a slight decline to it, so the further they walked into the vast tunnel system beneath the Sphinx, the deeper below ground they descended. Joey felt uneasy, not liking the confined space, as they continued down the mysterious underground shaft, wondering all the while what could be lurking at the end of it. The air inside was stale and musty, and made it difficult to breathe.

They soon reached the glow stick Abdul had thrown, which turned everyone's clothing a bright fluorescent green. He picked it up and threw it again.

Up until that point, the limestone walls had seemed lifeless and barren. Another fifteen feet in and they suddenly came to life with drawings rich in color, even after having been undisturbed for God knew how long.

Two Corinthian columns drawn on either side of the tunnel marked the start of the artwork, that seemed to flow endlessly away down the passageway. Walking through it was like gazing up at the Sistine Chapel in all its glory.

'This is amazing,' Marie gasped, shining her flashlight at the breathtaking images before her.

Joey knew his girlfriend. Being an art connoisseur, she couldn't help but become absorbed in the artwork in spite of their circumstances; even he could see the workmanship was impeccable. The images depicted a battle scene: the prominent Pyramids at Giza stood proud among war elephants and men holding their swords up high, victorious. At the forefront was a warrior riding a horse, wearing a helmet that symbolized his power, most probably the king of the time.

Further along, an enormous sun motif was displayed. The ornate yellow image had sixteen separate pieces forming the sunrays, each of which extended outward to a sharp point.

'Isn't that …?' said Boyce out loud, gesturing to it.

Joey knew exactly what Boyce was thinking. He remembered that symbol like it was only yesterday. But his thoughts were cut short when Marie manically flashed her light left and right. It appeared she had discovered something.

'What is it, babe?' Joey asked, following the direction of her flashlight to where a shadow of a horse was drawn on the opposite wall.

'These drawings are Greek,' she said. 'You're right, Boyce, that sun symbol represents Alexander the Great, as we found out not so long ago. This amazing combat scene shows his victories at war, from which he went on to conquer most of the known world.'

Through his fear, even Hazim managed a smile when he spotted the Greek language written with the imagery that explained the story in question. 'Marie is correct,' he said. 'That horse you see featured on the wall is Bucephalus. It belonged to Alexander the Great. The tale tells us of how Alexander broke in the wild horse when he was only a teenager by turning the horse's head toward the sun, understanding that Bucephalus was simply afraid of his own shadow.'

'Why are there images from Greek history deep inside the Sphinx?' asked Boyce, looking from Hazim to Marie.

'You're forgetting that Greeks under Alexander and his successor, Ptolemy, ruled Egypt for nearly three hundred years,' stated Hazim proudly. 'This period became known as the Ptolemaic dynasty, which ended with Cleopatra's rule, the last Pharaoh, before it became a province of the then recently established Roman Empire. Greeks in Egypt is not a new thing.'

'So this would explain why the key to enter this place was discovered in a cave meant for the Greek king,' said Joey, putting the puzzle pieces together. 'He must have found this place when he took control of the Middle East.'

'I like where you're going with this,' interrupted Youssef, his voice dripping with sarcasm. 'This is exactly what I told Benjamin, who was too chickenshit to act. If Alexander did enter this place, can you imagine what he could have hidden down here?'

'What are you hoping to find?' asked Hazim, darting his eyes over to the ceiling in front of him and avoiding Youssef's gaze.

'The famous Library of Alexandria and all its treasures, for one,' said Youssef. 'My name will be recorded in the history books,' he continued. 'I'll be known as the man who discovered the biggest archeological find of the century.'

'Let's just hope there isn't a dead mummy down here that wants to kill us all,' scoffed Boyce, throwing a wink at Joey.

'Man, you watch way too many movies,' said Joey, which put a smile on Marie's face.

'Okay, enough fun and games, let's move on,' ordered Abdul.

The paintings intensified as they strolled deeper, filled with what appeared to be more Greek writing and religious symbols, and the vibe turned eerie. The artwork made it seem like they were walking within a church adorned with stained glass windows.

But then it changed again. What soon followed were hieroglyphics etched into the limestone, the artwork now Egyptian in nature. It was as if the deeper they went, the older the civilization the illustrations represented. Hundreds of side-profile men and women with elongated heads massed the walls, handing offerings to their gods. The sun image was always a focal point as they prayed and worshiped it.

About three hundred and fifty feet into the subterranean solid bedrock, they finally reached the end of the tunnel, where their stream of flashlight beams now disappeared into blackness. While Joey couldn't see beyond the range of his flashlight, he sensed that he was about to enter a vast internal space.

Abdul stepped forward holding what looked like an orange-colored kid's toy, which he pointed upward. A moment later a dazzling incandescent flare shot high into the air, illuminating the way.

Joey's jaw dropped, and he stared in amazement. He flashed a smile in Marie's direction, and his girlfriend reciprocated with a joyous grin. A flight of steps in front of them led to a long, expansive but narrow room that dwarfed the entire party. He then peered over to Youssef, who was standing speechless, flashing his torch aimlessly, and said, 'It looks like we've found your Hall of Records.'

Chapter 16

With the used flare showing only part of the way, Abdul stepped forward, unclipped four light sticks from his utility belt and cracked them to life, heaving them into the various dark corners to reveal sections of the amazing vista of engineering and craftsmanship.

Pockets of emerald green lit up the surrounding walls with enough light to guide them through, but not enough to see the full extent of the subterranean cave.

'This place is enormous,' Marie said, shining her flashlight beam high and low, near and into the distance, clearly elated by the sight.

Hazim raised his head in wonder, lost for words, staring unblinkingly, humbled by the grandness and scale of the view before him. The legend was true: the Hall of Records, a term originally coined by Edgar Cayce, an American mystic, was real. So many stories had been written about this possible underground passage beneath the Sphinx, but all they had been until this moment were rumors. As a man devoting his life's work to ancient Egypt, Hazim had always admired the men and women in the trenches who searched for secret tombs and were not afraid to get their hands dirty. The tables had now turned for him, but under dire circumstances. And in spite of his fear, he wasn't disappointed, as he felt he was finally living and breathing the once thriving civilization he had always longed to know better.

Joey was the first to stumble across a three-foot-high stone wall with a peculiar barrel resting atop it on its side. 'Why was this left here?' he asked.

'Might have wine inside,' joked Boyce, guiding his light around the object's circular timber frame where some drawings along its side had faded. 'I wonder how two-thousand-year-old vino tastes?'

'That's no wine barrel,' said Hazim, looking at the upper surface of the low stone wall, which had a V-shaped groove cut into it. The short wall seemed to run the entire length of the long hall, and disappeared into the darkness. 'I've seen this before,' he muttered.

Hazim leaned over and ran his flashlight down the V-shaped channel, then touched some loose pieces of wood in the groove. 'Does that smell like oil to you?' he asked the others.

'It does. I bet that's what's in the barrel,' Marie replied.

Moments later, Joey found a meter-long solid piece of timber lying on the floor. All eyes turned to him as he moved swiftly. He removed his bright yellow vest and wrapped it around one end of the stick, nice and tight. Facing the spigot on the barrel, he prised it open with the sharp pointy end. The liquid flowed with ease like a lazy river down the single pathway of stone, which appeared to have been constructed on a gentle slope. It filled up the groove as it was intended thousands of years ago, soaking the charred timbers that lay in its path.

The smell of a car mechanic's workshop perfumed the room.

'You were right,' said Joey as Youssef observed with a watchful eye. 'It's definitely oil.'

'Can we borrow your lighter?' Hazim asked the smoker in the group, seeing for the first time that his knowledge of the ancient world might help keep him around longer than the others. He realized that staying quiet wasn't the answer; he needed to speak up and help in the hope that it would save him.

'You lose it, you die,' Nader stated in an ice-cold voice that made Hazim swallow uncomfortably as he handed it over to Joey, who gave him a nod, clearly understanding what had to be done.

The fluorescent fabric at the end of Joey's stick was now saturated in oil, and after a quick flick of the lighter – *whoom!* It burst into flames.

'Don't even think of trying anything funny,' warned Abdul, backing away from Joey with his gun aimed at his head.

Joey stepped up to the wall and touched his burning torch to the V-shaped groove and, just as if they were watching a *Tomb Raider* movie, the fire caught and began to stretch away from them, revealing more of the hall as it disappeared into the darkness that they'd become accustomed to and illuminated it.

The so-called Hall of Records was in view.

The vast chamber was the size of a football field, three stories high, but with a narrow thirty-foot width.

Two pairs of monolithic pillars, strategically placed in the center of the room, divided the area into sections. Its ingenious design was to stop your line of sight, until you walked around them.

As they headed toward the large pillars, the group was confronted by two colossal figures carved into the limestone bedrock, bearing witness on them on either side. They were a man and woman who were on their knees with hands over their heads, and they towered over the humans beneath them. Their presence made Hazim feel as though he were entering a place of biblical importance, like St Peter's Basilica in the Vatican. Hazim gazed up at the craftsmanship as the fire from below made them feel otherworldly.

'What are they doing?' asked Boyce quietly.

'It appears they are making an offering to their god,' said Hazim, now taking the lead as the most educated person there.

'Their faces are familiar,' said Marie, her eyes darting from one to the other.

'That's because you've seen them before,' replied Hazim. 'That's Akhenaten and his beautiful wife, Nefertiti, with their famous elongated heads.'

'Wasn't he the Pharaoh who stopped the worship of multiple pagan gods to follow what he believed was the one true god?' Marie followed.

'That's correct, Atum the sun god, but he was punished for it later on,' said Hazim. 'His image and name were chiseled from his monuments and his temples were dismantled.'

'I guess he was lucky they didn't find and destroy

this place,' said Joey, continuing to gaze up in wonder, his hastily constructed torch illuminating the details.

Hazim didn't reply to Joey's comment, as he was deep in thought, wondering why the two statues were erected inside the Sphinx. They were from the eighteenth dynasty, he knew; what was their connection with this place? It didn't make any sense, as Khafre was said to have built the Sphinx in the earlier fourth dynasty.

The second set of pillars was now in full view, each ten feet wide with a five-foot gap on either side to walk through. Youssef edged ahead of the group and disappeared around them, while Abdul and Nader brought up the rear.

'I found it,' Youssef shouted with exhilaration.

Hearing the excitement in his voice, they all jogged enthusiastically around the pillar to see Youssef's elated face.

'Oh my God,' Marie said, slowing to a complete stop, her eyes wide and mouth ajar as she tried to comprehend what she was seeing.

'Pinch me, 'cause I think I'm in a dream,' said Boyce, a bemused expression creeping across his face.

'This ain't no dream, boy,' said Joey, pausing himself to take a moment. 'Now, that's something you don't see every day.'

A treasure trove was amassed before them, its smooth shiny surfaces reflecting the flames from Joey's torch. The pile was about the size of an Olympic swimming pool. Crown jewels, diamonds, silver plates, Egyptian statues, chalices and countless sacred artefacts had been scattered in one place. It was as if every important piece of jewelry and sculpture that had been found and collected throughout the ages was dumped here, making it a breathtakingly stupendous sight to behold.

The entire group stood speechless for a moment, mesmerized.

Then the sound of a triumphant shout erupted from the rear as Nader and Abdul could no longer contain themselves. 'We hit the jackpot,' shouted Nader, who unexpectedly smiled, uncharacteristic for a man who always kept a down-turned expression on his face.

'Woohoo!' called out Abdul, pumping his fists into the air and probably thinking he would never need to work another day in his life. He sprinted over to a life-size Anubis sculpture to hug it admiringly.

Hazim advanced, tucking his flashlight into a pocket before digging his hands into a chest filled with coins. 'These are ancient Greek and Roman,' he said in awe as they cascaded out of the palm of his hand.

'Look at this place,' Youssef yelled victoriously, his boot up against a shiny sculpture of a black cat, which Joey knew would have been idolized and considered sacred within the ancient Egyptian culture. He turned to Joey and gestured to his surroundings. 'Your uncle screwed up big time, kid. He could have shared all this with me.'

Joey ignored the remark and headed toward Marie, who was sitting on a gold throne that dwarfed her petite frame, her bare feet swinging in a childlike manner, her polished nails highlighted by the jewels surrounding them. An ancient sword leaned against the side of the ceremonial chair. Its silver handle was decorated with images of scythed chariots engaged in battle. 'I wonder …' she said, picking it up while still sitting on the throne. 'Jeez, it's heavy, it must weigh thirty pounds.'

'That could be the blade that was used to conquer the world,' said Hazim as she struggled to hold it upright with disbelief. 'I think it belonged to Alexander the Great,' he said, watching it glisten with an ethereal power.

Abdul sauntered around the edge of the pile of loot and found a short blade whose handle was made from solid gold, stabbed into a wooden table. He extracted it from the timber, appraising the craftsmanship, and shoved it into his utility belt, which now held two knives.

His partner in crime, Nader, tucked an extravagant diamond necklace encrusted with blue sapphires into his pocket, not knowing that the precious piece could have belonged to the beautiful queen and ruler of Egypt, Cleopatra. However Joey noticed that the big man remained on guard, his eyes flitting often to Youssef; his top priority was to keep his boss safe.

While the group of six played in the midst of the treasure trove, Hazim scanned the room with a deep realization that the items they were touching had once been owned by important Pharaohs of ancient times. Turning his eye toward the back of the room, he spotted something among the glistening yellow that he knew was undoubtedly more valuable than anything else.

His adrenaline spiked.

He couldn't speak, he could only point the way. It was a find many people had been searching for all their lives. A find that he felt was far more important than the gold he was swimming in.

Chapter 17

A rotting twenty-foot-long timber bookshelf was covered in a netted mosquito canopy, stocked with what appeared to be ancient texts that sat atop one another. Hazim's heart was racing in his chest. The knowledge in his sights could possibly hold the answers to some of the world's most confounding historical mysteries.

He hurried over to it and flung aside the mosquito net at the same time as it caught Youssef's gaze.

Hazim took a deep breath, ignoring the others and blocking out the noises around him. In front of him were countless rolled papyrus scrolls, stone tablets and books that could possibly date back to the beginning of time. Taking a moment to comprehend what was in his sights, he noticed the cedar timber construction of the bookshelf, which would have been without doubt imported from Lebanon, a major distributor of the time.

Dusting away the cobwebs with his free hand and retrieving his flashlight from his pocket with the other, he identified many names and hieroglyphics that seemed to indicate a catalogue in some kind of chronological order from right to left.

It wasn't long before Marie, Joey, Boyce and Youssef joined the Cairo Museum restorer and expert in the field of antiquities as he ran his fingers along the carved timber plaques. All the while Nader and Abdul continued with their shopping spree, filling up their pockets with priceless pieces that would fetch hundreds of thousands of dollars on the Egyptian black market.

'I think this is part of the Library of Alexandria that wasn't destroyed,' said Hazim, a sense of pride and joy in his voice at sharing such a find. 'Look!' He pointed to a plaque adorned with Greek writing. It clearly read, *Megas Alexandros.*

'I think this entire shelf is dedicated to the king and conqueror, Alexander the Great.'

Marie nodded and leaned forward curiously as Hazim proceeded to sort carefully through the scrolls, pulling out one written in Greek calligraphy, and another of many words that came from a Hellenic origin. Luckily for them it was one of four languages he spoke fluently.

At this point Youssef extracted his Heckler & Koch and aimed it carefully at Hazim, while Joey held his burning torch over the paper to assist with an abundance of light.

'Read it,' growled Youssef.

'It's a letter from Alexander the Great's father, King Philip II of Macedon,' said Hazim shakily, quickly scanning the document. He cleared his throat and continued. 'It's addressed to one of the greatest philosophers of all time, Aristotle, who is being asked to be his thirteen-year-old son's personal tutor. The king offers him a handsome salary to move to the town of Mieza, deep in the Macedonian countryside, and says he wants his young prince to learn from the best.'

'Wow, what an amazing find,' said Marie in astonishment.

'Sure is,' said Hazim, putting it back on the pile and rolling open another like it was Christmas. He unfurled the scroll to its edge, revealing beautiful painted aqua blues on the thick creamy parchment. It appeared to be a drawing of concentric islands separated by broad moats and linked by a canal that penetrated to the center. πόλη της Ατλαντίδας was written as the heading.

'What is this place?' asked Boyce curiously.

Youssef leaned in, his eyes fixed on the page.

'It's a sketch of the city of Atlantis,' replied Hazim. 'This must also be part of Plato's dialogues, the *Timaeus* and the *Critias* that were written in 330 B.C.'

'Does it tell us where it can be found?' asked Joey.

'Sadly, no,' said Hazim.

'You don't think the lost city is down here somewhere?' said Marie, only half joking.

'I guess we'll find out soon enough,' Hazim replied, then continued to search along the long cedar bookcase, only stopping when he saw a triangle-shaped emblem of a pyramid. 'Here we go,' he breathed.

On the shelf lay a flat stone tablet the size of a laptop. He held it in his hands and ran his fingers across it to remove the dust that had built up over the years.

Marie sneezed, covering her mouth with the back of her palm.

'It's the architectural blueprints for the seventh wonder of the ancient world,' said Hazim wonderingly, mesmerized by the find of intricately carved diagrams and measurements.

'The actual plans?' said Youssef, sounding excited as he tucked his weapon into the back of his work pants and moved in closer to see for himself. 'Anything out of the ordinary?' he asked.

'Yes,' said Hazim, pausing to assess the find. 'The pyramid appears to have been built with two ramps,' he said. 'One external slope that was used to construct the lower third that was later destroyed, then its limestone blocks were taken through a second, internal ramp for the higher levels of the structure that were assembled inside the pyramid. It states here that the external incline plane was six feet wide with a grade of seven per cent.'

'So this tablet is definitive proof of its construction,' said Boyce.

'Or at least proof that they planned to do it this way. Believe me, it's going to upset a lot of people in our field when they find out. Many who have sworn their theories were correct.'

'What else can we find?' asked Youssef, all but rubbing his hands together with glee.

Hazim placed the ten-pound tablet of stone back where he found it and moved his finger once again along the shelves, naming the hieroglyphics he recognized.

'That's Ramses II ... Akhenaten ... Khufu ...'

'Go to the last Egyptian symbol,' Youssef instructed.

'That's Menes, also known as Narmer.'

'Who's that?' asked Joey.

'He was the first Pharaoh to unite Upper and Lower Egypt and the founder of the first dynasty,' said Hazim, unrolling the three-thousand-year-old papyrus. But they soon saw that it was half perished, and nearly completely illegible. 'I'm sorry, I can't read this,' he said.

'But we can,' Youssef said with a sinister smile, digging out his cell phone from his pants pocket. 'Now you will all understand why Joey's uncle needed me as a partner. I spent a fortune building an app that would translate the oldest of ancient hieroglyphics. It uses the phone's inbuilt camera and light to scan the hieroglyphics before translating them back in English.'

Youssef approached Hazim, who was still holding the frail papyrus in his hand, and ran his phone over the column, scanning the broken text as it would have been read.

'Nifty device,' said Joey grudgingly.

By his side, Boyce eyed Youssef's weapon, which was only a hand's reach away.

The passage was scanned in seconds and after Youssef pressed the 'finish scan' button in the app, a female voice with a British accent began to emit from the phone's speaker.

'*After thousands of years, today we stand as one and will live together as a unified society, both Upper and Lower Egypt. I have inherited the throne and crown from our creators, the oldest gods to walk the land. Peace will be*—'

'What the hell?' were the first words out of Boyce's mouth.

'It's incomplete, but it tells us how he unified the country under his rule,' said Hazim. 'The rest of it is a bit weird; I don't think your app is completely accurate.'

'Maybe a word here or there is out,' said Youssef, readjusting his weapon. 'But trust me, it's pretty close. Try another one.'

Hazim picked Hotepsekhemwy, a Pharaoh dating back to the second dynasty 2840 B.C. The papyrus was just as frail and damaged as the previous one, but more readable. Youssef repeated the scan with his cell phone and the female voice once again began to translate.

'*A thunderous power from the gods was unleashed around the Aur. Its tragedy on the land and crops revealed to our people the God of the Afterlife, Anubis, carved by our ancestors from solid stone.*'

Hazim took a minute to digest the audio translation.

'*Aur*, what's that?' Marie asked.

'It means black,' answered Hazim. 'It comes from the phrase "black soil", which is how the ancient Egyptians referred to the river Nile. Around September of each year the Nile would flood, which was a wonderful thing because it brought in rich black soil and renewed the farmlands.'

'*Carved by our ancestors from solid stone,*' repeated Youssef. 'Is this talking about the Sphinx?'

'It has to be,' responded Hazim, deep in thought. 'This is an amazing discovery. This means it was sculpted by a pre-dynastic civilization much older than we once thought. It would indicate that the fourth dynasty Pharaoh Khafre didn't construct it as many

Egyptologists would have you think, as it predates the first pyramid by thousands of years. It would suggest that it was only restored and reshaped during his reign.'

'According to this, it was also shaped as a dog, not as a lion,' said Joey, and Hazim nodded back in agreement.

'I have no doubt that it was Anubis,' said Hazim. 'The Egyptians were too fastidious to get the proportions wrong, like it is now.'

'We've only been sifting through this library a short while and look how much we have already uncovered,' said Youssef, his eyes gleaming. 'These scrolls will change history as we know it.'

At that moment Abdul interrupted the group, his voice containing fear and excitement rolled into one. 'Um, boss, I think you need to see this.'

'It better be good, because the Library of Alexandria is at the top of my list,' Youssef growled.

'Trust me, I think you'll want to see this,' he repeated.

Nader was there to round everyone up; it seemed important. He pushed them all forward and around the last pillars to see what the fuss was all about. Hazim turned one more time to face the archive of text, wondering what could be more significant than that small section of space within the Hall of Records.

But little could have prepared him for the shock of what lay before him. Turning back to see what Abdul was pointing at, he faced the God Anubis and the two sarcophagi resting at his feet.

Chapter 18

The sculpture was Sphinx-like, shaped in the body of Anubis, the God of the Afterlife, and carved out of solid black granite. It towered over them as the fire still burning in the low wall channel on the room's right-hand side caused the mirrored surface to reflect back at them. In between its detailed paws a set of stairs descended but seemed to go nowhere, a dead end of stone.

At the feet of the guardian rested two funeral boxes, which appeared to have been from two different time periods. One had a humble timber frame, while the other was a solid curved stone sarcophagus that most certainly had been made for someone of immense importance.

'It's breathtaking,' Marie said, walking slowly forward past the two coffins to touch the smooth cold surface that was Anubis's paw.

Hazim felt mixed emotions. He trailed behind Marie and also laid his hands on the black granite, transfixed by the craftsmanship. This evening was both one of the worst and best nights of his life rolled into one. Touching this amazing structure, he felt alive, and for a brief moment he forgot he was being held captive at gunpoint. Today he wasn't organizing restorations within the museum or giving talks to students on school visits, he was walking in the steps of his ancestors, who had once ruled this fascinating place.

Joey, Boyce and Nader grazed their fingers against the two sarcophagi before reaching Hazim and Marie, all wearing dumbfounded expressions.

'What I want to know,' said Youssef to his audience as he came up the rear, 'is what's the dog of the underworld guarding? Somewhere here must be the entrance to the secret chamber.'

'Guarding …' repeated Hazim, pausing as that word struck a nerve. 'Yes! … It all makes sense now. I've been wondering this whole time why Akhenaten and Nefertiti were represented inside this structure. Their timelines didn't correlate.'

'Why are they?' asked Boyce, tilting his head upward to face the enormous granite animal, still in awe.

'We have clearly established from the Hotepsekhemwy

text that the limestone Sphinx on the Giza plateau was always Anubis in its original form, like the statue you see in front of you,' said Hazim, eyeballing everyone in front of him to make sure they understood.

'Where are you going with this?' asked Marie.

'Now you know how I feel.' Joey gave her a grin. 'You're usually the one who knows everything.'

'Be quiet, you.' Marie said playfully, shrugging off the criticism.

'Akhenaten and Nefertiti's son, King Tutankhamun, is the missing link to all this,' continued Hazim. 'For some reason Nefertiti wanted to hide this place from existence, so she secreted a key where no one would be able to find it.'

'Yes, inside Tutankhamun's death mask, we all got that,' said Youssef, aiming his flashlight at the god in front of him where the decorative neck-plate resided.

'Did you know that at the entrance guarding the treasures of Tutankhamun's tomb stood a black Anubis shrine that faced westward?' Hazim said.

'I still don't see the connection between all this,' Joey said, flinging his palms in the air in a gesture of confusion.

'I'm getting to it,' said Hazim with the hint of a smile. 'They also found inside his tomb a pyramidion, which depicted the god Anubis sitting on a box that looked strangely like the Arc of the Covenant, and it had an inscription on it.'

'Sorry to be the dumb one here,' said Joey, raising his right hand like a student at school. 'What's a pyramidion?'

Marie interrupted, 'It's the capstone piece that sits on top of a pyramid.'

'That's correct,' said Hazim, nodding. 'And when the imprint was translated it read: "aNEBES VARTI" which means The Gates of Heaven, and "ARAJINA SHKIp-RiTA" which is The Box or Coffin of Orion.'

An enormous smile erupted upon Hazim's face, but his audience didn't share the same excitement. 'Don't you get it?' he exclaimed. 'The symbolism could not be any more perfect for the Sphinx, being Anubis, who guarded the three Pyramids to the Gates of Heaven in the form of Orion's belt.'

'So … what you're saying is that the theory that the Pyramids were built in the line of the star constellation Orion is justified, then,' said Marie, catching up a little quicker than the others. 'How about the Sphinx in all this? What was its purpose?'

'I'm glad you asked. The Sphinx is aligned to the rising sun on the spring equinox, the day representing rebirth, and who is the god of resurrection?'

'Anubis,' answered Boyce.

'When you say it like that, it all fits together nicely,' added Joey.

Youssef turned to face the two coffins, and called out when he saw a distinctive marking on one of them. Up against the side of the timber coffin was a red-painted cross.

'Perhaps a Knight Templar,' Hazim hazarded.

Whoever had marked the burial box was in a rush as there was evidence of more paint scattered across the sandy floor.

Youssef ordered the coffin to be opened, reminding Hazim once again that this wasn't going to be a pleasant scavenger hunt.

Nader took away Joey's fire stick and passed him a crowbar, gesturing for him to get to work, while the kidnappers stood back and let their slaves do their dirty bidding.

Hazim, Boyce, and Marie watched on.

'I thought we said we weren't going to mess with the dead,' said Joey uncomfortably. By the expression on his face, he seemed afraid, and he wasn't the only one.

'Have you seen the *Mummy* movies?' asked Boyce,

who playfully answered his own question. 'It never ends well for the people who muck around with the deceased.'

'There's nothing to worry about,' Hazim reassured them as they surrounded the sarcophagus. 'I deal with mummies on a regular basis, we're okay.'

'Hurry up!' Youssef barked.

Joey dug the crowbar forcefully into the coffin and jacked up the lid, removing whatever old screws were holding it in place. Hazim helped grab hold of one side while Boyce held the other, and together they levered the cover off and let it fall on the sandy stone floor.

'Well, it's no Egyptian mummy,' Hazim informed them, studying the contents of the coffin. There was no sacrificial wrapping of linen cloth and no coating in resin to keep the threat of moist air away.

It was just a skeleton of a man wearing simple clothing: a sleeveless white cotton tunic that reached to the knees, held together by a cincture that could be loosened or tightened. On the feet were sandals with wooden soles that were fastened with straps of leather. The hands were folded on the skeleton's chest, clasping an object wrapped in a blue cloth.

'Who do you think he is?' asked Marie.

'It could be anyone,' replied Hazim as he carefully searched the inside of the box, knowing that most ancient civilizations etched a name within the sarcophagus so that its 'resident' could be identified.

'Surely he must have been someone of importance, to be placed here,' said Joey.

Hazim's eyes jolted to a single spot. He'd found what he was searching for. He leaned forward and hovered over the corpse, tracing a carved marking with his finger.

'What is it?' asked Marie.

'It's a picture of a lion with wings,' retorted Hazim.

'It can't be,' Boyce said, scanning the tattoo on his own wrist that bore the same mark.

Joey sighed with satisfaction.

'I don't understand,' said Hazim, not recognizing the importance even though he had studied Theology at Cambridge.

'I think the man you are looking at could be St Mark,' said Joey, sounding excited now.

'How can that be, when his body is in the Basilica in Venice?'

'So we've been told,' said Marie, continuing to stare curiously at the man.

'It's a very long story,' said Boyce, moving forward to remove the wrapped item in the skeleton's hands. He apologized to the dead man who could have been St Mark the Evangelist, the man who'd died as a martyr while being dragged through the streets of Alexandria. The man who was honored with the Patriarchal Cathedral Basilica, commonly known as St Mark's Basilica in Venice, which was said to house his dead remains.

Boyce carefully plied the man's fingers apart to take possession of something that could be of historical importance. Hazim felt like every fiber of his being was tingling with anticipation. Adrenaline coursed through his veins at the thought of what this religious man might have been protecting. He bounced on the balls of his feet and rubbed his hands together as Boyce held it up high for all to see.

It was a translucent agate cup, mostly colored in a deep red, but with flickers of green, gold and black. Its diameter was three and a half inches with a total height of five inches.

'The Holy Chalice,' blurted out Boyce, mesmerized by the possibilities.

'The cup used at the Last Supper?' Youssef said in disbelief.

'It can't be the Holy Grail?' questioned Marie, trying to make sense of it.

'We're standing in front of an enormous granite statue of Anubis in the style of the Sphinx,' said Joey dryly. 'Anything is possible.'

Hazim heard the men running the show speak quickly together in their native Arabic tongue. He watched as Nader's imposing frame sauntered forward, his evil stare and size threatening. Nader held his hand out to Boyce. Intimidated by the man, Boyce reluctantly gave him the cup and watched him stroll back to Youssef, who respectfully gazed upon it in awe.

A grin spread over Youssef's face, displaying his over-whitened teeth, as he took the chalice with gleaming, greedy eyes. There was no disputing it, he had hit the jackpot, but something in Hazim's gut was telling him this was just the beginning.

Chapter 19

Joey took a moment to process the evening as Youssef packed the precious agate cup into a canvas backpack he pulled from within the duffle bag and strapped over his own shoulders.

What a night it had been, Joey thought. They had uncovered so much of Egypt's mysterious past, not least the fact that the great Sphinx of Giza in its original form had been in the shape of Anubis, the guard dog of the afterlife.

They had ventured inside the mind-blowing Hall of Records to discover a vast treasure trove that would have made even the riches in Tutankhamun's tomb seem inferior. Here, they'd stumbled across what they thought was part of the Library of Alexandria. And they'd found a skeleton that could possibly be St Mark the Evangelist, who held a cup that most likely was the Holy Grail.

Joey saw an opportunity to grab Boyce by the elbow and move him ever so slightly closer so he could whisper in his ear without being overheard. 'How long will it take before help arrives?' he asked.

'I have no idea,' said Boyce, still facing the opposite

direction so as not to be seen colluding.

'We're running out of things to discover,' whispered Joey. 'They might kill us all now.'

'I don't think so,' Boyce responded, trying not to move his lips.

'How can you be so sure?'

'They won't kill us until we help them find the last chamber.'

'I just hope your boss and his troops get here soon, 'cause we're running out of time,' Joey murmured as Nader stepped forward, placed a heavy hand on his shoulder to split the two of them apart, before directing them to the next sarcophagus.

'This one now,' he said shortly.

Standing on the same side of the coffin, Joey, Hazim and Boyce prepared to slide the stone cover plate across while everyone else stood and watched.

'This thing weighs a ton,' grimaced Joey as the three of them struggled to get any movement at all.

Nader shook his head in displeasure and approached the lid on the opposite side. His expression was one of both concentration and anger as, with grunt-fueled force, he gained some traction, gritting his teeth, muscles bulging, and the solid cover scraped against the hollow base.

Now Joey and the others had some success of their own as they tried a zigzag, you-go-I-go pattern. The top end would move, followed by the bottom end, and they gained momentum with each heave, until finally the lid fell off its perch and hit the ground with a loud thump.

Youssef and Marie quickly trained their flashlights on the red linen covering that was draped over almost the entire anthropoid coffin, blue glass beads sprinkled across it ritualistically. The face of the casket, however, was left bare, revealing that it was made of pure gold and inlaid with semiprecious stones.

'It's just like Tutankhamun's innermost sarcophagus,' Marie suggested, glancing at the man who had previously discussed this fact back at the Cairo Museum.

Hazim nodded but had a bewildered look on his face as he guided his flashlight to the core, which was just over six feet tall, and removed the linen cloth.

'What's that black stuff?' asked Abdul, now the only one armed, and ready to fire if circumstance called for it.

'That pitch-black layer was an anointing liquid or perfume poured during the burial ceremony,' answered Hazim, reaching in to touch it.

At that moment Joey observed another smug grin growing on Youssef's face, which infuriated him, making him want nothing more than to knock their captor unconscious. This murderous lunatic would soon be idolized and praised in Egypt for single-handedly discovering not one, but an array of archeological gems, an accolade that should have been awarded to Joey's dead uncle.

'Whose sarcophagus is it?' Boyce asked, scanning his flashlight from top to bottom.

Hazim inspected the feet and inhaled when he found a cartouche. 'It's Nefertiti,' he uttered with awe in his voice. 'The queen mother of the boy Pharaoh.'

'Nefertiti?' mouthed Marie, eyes wide. 'What a find!'

'Open it,' Youssef demanded, intrigued.

'Hang on, I'll show you how.' Hazim stepped forward and climbed inside the hollow stone shell, which was just big enough to encircle the box-like container. 'We need two people on either side,' instructed Hazim. 'If it's like Tutankhamun's, the top part can be removed using its gold handles.'

Joey slid across to help Hazim, while Boyce and Nader lifted the other side.

They raised the gilded frame in the form of a mummified Osiris holding scepters in crossed hands and carefully placed it on its side.

Disdain flashed across Youssef's face. 'It's empty?'

'Not entirely,' grimaced Joey, finding that a dark granite stela the size of a medium computer monitor and etched in hieroglyphics lay within.

Hazim reached in, and with his right hand dusted away the dirt. He ran his index finger along the symbols to unearth another cartouche. 'Akhenaten,' he said out loud, backing away with a puzzled expression.

'I thought you said it read Nefertiti,' asked Abdul.

'Here, scan the text,' said Youssef, handing Hazim his phone. 'It might tell us how to enter the secret chamber.'

Hazim accepted the cell phone and, with the app activated, skimmed the hieroglyphics guided by the inbuilt light, which again initiated the automated female voice.

'Akhenaten, son of the great king, was appointed Pharaoh and ruler of the round-headed ones. In his fifth year of reign, he was instructed to change the worship of the people to the one and only true god

[Atum]. This was not accepted with open arms and an uprising soon followed with temples destroyed and vandalized. Fearing his father's wrath, he made a pact with his queen [Nefertiti] to save the life of their future king [Tutankhamun] and reinstated all the pagan gods back to the people. But there was no escaping the fury to come, so to hide a secret only shared to the few that were worthy, the doors were sealed and hidden within the Walk of Souls to never be found, because he who opens the door will end life as we know it.'

The voice stopped and Marie was the first to break the silence. 'Hidden within the Walk of Souls?' she said uneasily. 'What could be so dangerous that it would end life as we know it?'

'I'm starting to believe the key you have to this secret chamber will lead us to something man wasn't supposed to find,' warned Hazim.

Marie coughed expectantly.

'Sorry, I meant to say man or *woman* wasn't supposed to find,' he quickly corrected.

'Could it be some kind of toxic virus?' asked Boyce.

'We haven't even found the entrance,' said Youssef, putting things in perspective. 'And there's panic already.'

'That's because there could be aliens buried inside or something like that,' Joey added.

Nader shrugged his shoulders. He seemed to be concerned as well, but he was a man who did as he was told so he stood waiting to be directed.

'Boss, who cares about this chamber?' stated Abdul defiantly. 'We have the treasure.'

'I'm not in it for the money,' Youssef muttered as all eyes turned on him.

'So what you're saying is that the Hall of Records, Library of Alexandria, St Mark and the Cup of Christ ain't enough for you?' said Joey with a wry smile.

'One thing you should know about me, Joey, is that I don't settle for second best!' Youssef frowned, visibly agitated. 'And if I did, you four would be already dead. Is that what you want? Do you want to die?'

'No,' said Hazim quickly, answering on everyone's behalf.

'You're going to kill us anyway,' retorted Joey. 'This place was hidden for a reason. That sacred key you hold in your pocket was meant to have been never found. Aren't you afraid to discover what lies beyond when the warning on the tablet is clearly saying we shouldn't?'

Youssef took out Tutankhamun's goatee and held it in his hands. He twisted it, releasing the sacred key from within. For a moment he waited and took in the intricate patterns that covered the key. 'I understand your concern,' he said, peering in Joey's direction. 'But this key was never destroyed. It was found and tonight we *must* find the door that fits it. We must! It's simple,' he said with a malicious grin, taking a moment to make sure he got his point across, and retrieving his gun from behind his back. 'Find me that entrance, or else the four of you will die right now.'

Chapter 20

Leaving the sarcophagus, Joey turned to face the enormous black granite Anubis that was almost half the size of its limestone twin guarding the Giza plateau. Time was running out. He knew the only way to stay alive was to assist the man he despised until help arrived. His priority now shifted to finding the elusive keyhole, or he would end up dead like the skeleton in the wooden casket.

Joey was always a glass-half-full kind of guy, but the possibility that he would not find the doorway crept into his mind. Yes, not so long ago in Paris he had found himself up against trained soldiers and he'd survived, but this time was different. The man running the show was no dumb army man following orders. He had his own agenda and was intelligent and witty, making him exceedingly more dangerous. His unpredictable and calculating nature had played everyone right from the beginning.

Joey's flashlight hit all the dark crevices not lit up by the burning flames still ablaze in the low grooved wall. The overwhelming heat emanating from the fire caused sweat to trickle down his forehead and he was not the only one experiencing discomfort. Marie's neckline was damp with perspiration and the cotton shirt his young friend wore was clinging to his body.

With guns pointed at his head, Joey peered between the jackal's paws.

'Hang on,' he said out loud for all to hear.

Everyone turned to Joey, who moved right up to the statue to take a closer inspection. Five giant stone steps descended, leading him to a short narrow passageway that stopped at a dead end; nothing but solid granite in front of him which formed part of the chest of Anubis. 'It has to be here,' he muttered to himself, his exploring hands rubbing up against the slab, dusting away the cobwebs that had built up. 'Why else build these steps? They must serve a purpose.'

At that moment, he spotted a giant timber lever. The thrilling sensation that rushed through him as he pulled it down was quickly met with confused disappointment as nothing happened. There was more to this than met the eye, but what was he missing?

Hazim, Marie and Boyce approached Joey while Youssef, Nader and Abdul stood and watched from afar.

Joey continued his search, flashing his torch up at the black granite that bore a reflective sheen. Ten feet up, a slender ledge protruded outward, like an architrave of a doorway. He followed the seam that butted two enormous pieces against each other. At the base of its construction the cracks caused by the heavy load were apparent.

'Find anything?' asked Boyce, tapping Joey's sweaty shoulder.

Joey shook his head in disappointment. 'Only a lever that doesn't seem to work over there.'

Hazim observed it warily with a raised brow.

'Don't worry, we'll find it,' said Marie, optimistic as always.

'And if we don't?' said Joey, swinging to face his girl.

Marie reached out and embraced him before lovingly grabbing hold of his face. 'The weight is not all on your shoulders,' she said as they stared into each other's eyes. 'Together we'll work it out, like we always do.'

'Hazim, is there anything you might know historically that might help us?' asked Boyce.

'Well,' said Hazim, fisting a hammer punch on the solid construction before him. 'This is Aswan granite, found hundreds of miles to the south. The only other place with this much granite would be at the Serapeum of Saqqara, a necropolis found near Memphis. It is believed to have been built sometime around 1300 B.C.E., by Ramses II.'

'What was there?' asked Joey, hoping he could trigger a spark in the expert.

'They discovered twenty-five megalithic stone boxes weighing around one hundred tons each. The way these containers were shaped has left researchers puzzled to this day. We're talking about an ancient society with primitive tools that could cut perfect rectangles into the solid granite, with ninety-degree angles and polished surfaces.' He paused for a moment. 'Now, looking at this structure with its superb curve lines and smoothness,' he said, tracing his finger in the air at the dog's impeccable face, 'this must have been created by the same people.'

Someone coughed behind them and everyone spun incredulously, as it wasn't the cough they had become accustomed to with Nader.

'Tick tock… time is passing,' Youssef informed them, tapping his Rolex with his gun.

'Is there anything else?' Joey asked Hazim, desperation building in his voice. 'How about the Sphinx? If this is a replica, were there any tunnels found on the structure?'

'Yes, actually there were,' said Hazim. 'An old photo was taken in a hot air balloon before the Sphinx had been excavated and restored. A hole appeared on its head.'

'Okay, move over,' said Joey, who took a small run up and leaped onto the left leg of the beast and pushed himself up.

'Be careful,' said Marie as he struggled up Anubis's limbs. The God-like creature of the underworld looked down upon him, as though these intruders from the twenty-first century didn't belong in this ancient world. The dark granite encompassed most of its body except for certain parts that Joey now saw were completely covered in gold; its frowning eyes, pointy upright ears, and neck plate that draped down to where he would begin his climb.

Up close, the glistening orange caught his attention, as it was covered in ancient indented text that must have told a story. Joey used the deeply carved hieroglyphics as hand and footholds as he clambered up the Anubis monument like a child ascending a tall tree. As he advanced, the adrenaline once again coursed through him.

After a precarious climb, he finally reached the animal's neckline, where the collar wrapped around itself, revealing a hollow symbol. Joey smiled with relief.

After taking a moment to regroup he shouted, 'I found it!' knowing for a brief second that he had saved everyone. It was a small win but a welcome one.

Marie applauded and cheered from down below.

'Give him the key,' Youssef interrupted, handing it to Abdul, who then gave it to Boyce. Boyce scrambled up to join Joey.

Waiting for Boyce to arrive, Joey glanced over the Hall of Records in its entirety. Its grandness stretched away from him, built to last the test of time. The boy he admired like a little brother soon joined him, carrying the key in his hand. He seemed so out of place dressed in his navy-blue suit and fighting to gain an adequate footing with his pointy brown leather shoes. Joey couldn't help but grin.

'Hey, Boy?' said Joey, as lightheartedly as he could. 'I can't believe this trip, man. You got me climbing up this freaking giant dog?'

'Yeah,' said Boyce, now by Joey's side. 'I'm sorry it turned out like it did.'

'It's not your fault.'

'No, it's yours,' quickly retorted Boyce, causing the crease lines to appear on Joey's forehead.

'Hey, what do you mean, my fault?'

Boyce handed him the key and said, 'All this

craziness is because another one of your family members is involved.' The youth glanced up at Joey and grinned. 'You wouldn't happen to have any other relatives you're not aware of, would you?'

Joey smiled and nodded his head. If it weren't for his long-lost uncle, they never would have visited Egypt.

'Boy, you crack me up.'

'It's Boyce! It's a good name, stop calling me Boy.'

'Does it even have a meaning?'

'Actually, it does.'

'Go on, this is going to be good.'

'It means *lives near the wood*, derived from the French word *bois* meaning wood.'

Joey blew out a cough of laughter as he carefully took the key and placed it into the hollow in Anubis's collar plate. 'Wood,' he mocked the teen as he rotated the key clockwise a quarter-turn. A clicking sound rang out, only to be overshadowed by a stronger jarring bang from deep within the statue.

'What was that?' asked Joey with suddenly terrified eyes.

'No idea,' Boyce replied.

It seemed like something had been set in motion. First came the sound of a solid object scraping up against something else, followed by a flood of pouring sand.

Marie moved her flashlight in the direction of the noise but saw nothing.

'It seems to be cascading somewhere behind the statue,' she said. 'Joey, Boyce come down,' she warned just in case they were in any danger.

'Must be another counterbalancing system. Hopefully that will reveal a secret passage,' said Hazim. 'Like when we first entered inside the Sphinx and the stone slab began to descend.'

'If so, where's the entrance?' questioned Marie.

'The wooden lever,' Hazim remembered. 'Try it now.'

Marie pulled down on the enormous wooden lever and this time something transpired. An ear-shattering grinding sound of immense intensity shook the ground at their feet, causing Marie and Hazim to backpedal.

Between the paws of Anubis, the left granite piece with the cracked base started to move upward into itself. It climbed at a snail's pace into its own specially designed cavity, grinding against its twin, paving the way to a narrow but high cave labyrinth.

Hazim rubbed his hands together. They had just discovered the entrance to the last secret chamber.

The Walk of Souls.

Chapter 21

The Walk of Souls

Joey and Boyce scrambled down and leaped off the oversized paw to re-join the group still wearing the fireman helmets who were standing, waiting, peering into the dark and gloomy entrance that had been revealed.

'What do you think is hidden down there?' Marie asked, gazing with trepidation as the cool breath of the cave blew against her face.

'Let's find out,' said Youssef, who signaled with a jerk of his head so that they would move along.

Joey bravely took the lead and tentatively examined the new opening. The engineering and mathematics involved in lifting such a heavy object was mind-boggling. He was engulfed in chilling blackness as he entered the cave. Boyce and Joey cut through with their flashlights as the sound of crushed rocks scraped beneath their shoes.

Marie cringed as she watched her shadow dissolve into the darkness. She took each step with care as she struggled to find solid ground with her bare feet. The loose stones underfoot shifted, twisting her ankles one way and then the other. Silence descended on the group.

From the moment Marie had entered the Sphinx's tunnel system, she'd had soft Egyptian sand to walk on; now not so much. The floor was cold, rough and sharp in places. To make matters worse, suspiciously life-like noises could be heard scurrying in the shadows, causing multiple shivers to run down her spine.

They moved steadily deeper into the unexplored corridor, the leaders breaking through screens of cobwebs that seemed to drape between the side walls with their flashlights. Marie's eyes began to adjust to the absence of light, but even so she relied heavily on her hands out in front of her to feel the way, while Youssef and his team brought up the rear.

Alongside her was Hazim, who remained close, rubbing shoulders with her with each stride.

After a few dozen yards, the hallway widened into a tall limestone box with a single arch opening up ahead. Marie slid over to one side to accommodate the three men behind her and observed the peculiar space she was in. Although the large stones were beautifully cut and set, there was no trace of writing anywhere.

Abdul cracked a glow stick and tossed it at their feet. It immediately emitted an eerie yellow glare that revealed an important feature that they had missed in the dark.

Marie took in a short, sharp breath.

'Wow, are those human skulls?' said Boyce, readjusting his flashlight beam. 'There must be hundreds of them. What is this place?'

In an instant, a thought flooded Marie's mind and she aimed her flashlight beam once again to the ground. An overwhelming realization washed over her. She had been walking on crushed human remains this entire time. Unrecognizable broken pieces of bone were scattered everywhere, making her feel sick to the stomach.

'I have a bad feeling about this,' warned Joey, shaking his head.

'It's definitely not something you see every day,' said Boyce with a grimace. 'Why would someone do this?'

'Maybe it's Nefertiti's *warning to thee who decides to enter,*' said Marie, regaining her composure.

'I think these people were unsuccessful in the Walk of Souls,' said Hazim, biting his bottom lip. 'I think Marie is right, this is a warning. We should head back. Let's not be stupid and continue on this route.'

'No one is going back until we find out what's down here,' said Youssef in a cold, somber tone. 'We are not going to let a few skulls frighten us.'

'A few skulls?' winced Boyce. 'More like hundreds.'

'This is no joke, Youssef,' pleaded Marie. 'We could all be in grave danger, yourself included. There'll be booby traps.'

Hazim shook his head and took several steps back toward the warmth of the burning flames still flickering at the end of the snake-like corridor.

'Stop!' Youssef grunted.

Hazim ignored the warning.

'If he takes one more step, kill him,' ordered Youssef.

'No!' Marie pleaded.

Hazim froze and snapped around. Abdul extended his right arm, a Heckler & Koch at the end of it ready to incur its wrath upon him.

'You can't shoot me,' said Hazim. 'I'm too valuable to you down here.'

'You're right, your expertise is unquestionable,' said Youssef. 'But listen carefully, because I'm not going to repeat myself again. With your help or without, we'll find what is down here. Your choice is simple; do you want to live or die?'

'Don't be stupid, Hazim,' Marie exhorted and gestured hurriedly for him to backtrack.

'Now keep going,' ordered Youssef.

Nader immediately reacted and turned his own gun on Joey, the one person who could start a revolt. He gestured with the gun for Joey to continue through the creepy tunnel with its cobblestone-like walls. Joey did as he was told. However, as he approached the passage, the stone beneath one foot sank slightly into floor beneath the scatter of broken bones.

Marie was the first person who noticed the startled expression on her boyfriend's face.

'A trigger stone of some sort,' he gasped.

What followed was the sound of a hefty boulder as it came crashing down, fast and hard, ending with a loud thump.

It blocked their only exit back to the Hall of Records. They would have to go forward into the unknown darkness.

To make matters worse, a howling cry of unbearable pain filled the room.

Hazim had been in the wrong place at the wrong time. The man's foot had snapped like a toothpick as the solid mass of limestone crashed onto it.

Marie's heart raced out of control as she turned to see Hazim trying to yank his foot free, tugging savagely with grinding teeth, tearing away the likelihood that he would ever walk again. A scream of horrific torture erupted as he managed to peel it free.

Marie approached the trembling man lying on the carpet of shattered bones. She moved her flashlight up to his face; it was the expression of a man in immense pain, his skin pale and clammy as his pointy leather shoe flopped aimlessly straight down. 'We need to get him to a doctor,' she said, horrified at the sight of him as she began to wipe away the sweat from his face.

Youssef stood there with an impassive scowl.

'Good luck with that,' joked Abdul.

'We're stuck in here now,' said Nader as he tried to budge the stone, but it looked as if it were there to stay.

'What now?' asked Boyce, his face worried.

Abdul spoke in Arabic and after an intense discussion with his team, it seemed as though they had concurred on something.

'We move forward,' said Youssef with a lack of compassion in his voice, as Hazim continued to moan in agony. 'Leave him here,' he said evenly. 'He was stupid enough to try to ditch the group and punished for it.'

'We can't just abandon him here,' Marie breathed. 'He could go into shock.'

'You leave me with no choice, then,' said Youssef,

raising his Glock and aiming it at the wounded man who would slow them down.

'No! Wait,' said Joey, raising his arms and using his body as a shield. 'Stop, I'll carry him. I'm the one who stepped on the trigger stone, it's my responsibility.'

Youssef hesitantly agreed after he considered that Hazim could still be useful to him as long as he remained conscious, and allowed Joey to heave the man up from the floor.

'Hang on, man, don't you die on me,' said Joey, resting Hazim's dead weight on his shoulder, while helping him hop on his strong leg.

A sadness flowed through Marie as she watched Hazim struggle with the pain, knowing that he probably would not make it through the night without immediate medical attention. The journey into the Walk of Souls was just about to begin.

Chapter 22

Hazim's moans of agony continued as they entered a narrow void that stretched away into the darkness. They trudged carefully with flashlights guiding the way, alert to any hazard, with the now familiar sound of bones being crushed under their weight a constant companion. One hundred feet in, the hallway widened into a larger area that resembled the apse of St Peter's Basilica.

'Stop!' shouted Boyce, almost losing his footing as he raised his hands wide on either side to warn of danger.

Marie briskly walked to the front to see what the fuss was all about, but Boyce stopped her from going any further.

'It's a trap,' Boyce alerted.

Understanding the warning, Marie peered into the distance, her eyes following the thin stream of light from her flashlight to a seventy-foot devil's drop that fell straight down. If one were to fall into it, and miraculously survive the fall, hundreds of deadly arrows that were pointed upward from the floor ensured certain death.

Without uttering a word, Marie massaged her

friend's shoulders as if to say, 'Well caught.' If it weren't for Boyce paying attention, she would have been next to plummet to her death after him.

'So, it seems the fun and games have just begun,' Marie sighed, then started looking for a way to get across safely.

'What's the hold-up?' asked Youssef, pushing his way forward with Nader beside him.

'There is a massive hole in front of us,' advised Boyce, directing his torch onto twelve tree-like pillars rising from the cavity and separated by nothing but air. 'We'll need to jump across these like stepping stones.'

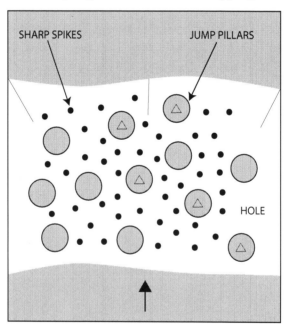

'So why aren't we jumping?' replied Nader, his deep voice echoing in the empty space.

'It can't be that easy,' said Marie, pondering for a

moment and noticing as she did so hundreds of skeletal remains at the bottom of the pit. Something didn't feel right and she knew she needed to be smart if they had any chance of getting through their adventure in one piece.

Joining them at the edge of the pit, Abdul lit a flare and held it aloft, illuminating the stone walls that encircled them. He tossed the incandescent light over to the opposite side, where its light showed a thirteen-foot-wide ledge that led to an ominous narrow opening that disappeared into the shadow.

'I have an idea,' Marie said, turning to tread back into the narrow tunnel. Flashing her torch along the cobblestone-rendered wall, she stopped to kneel feet away from Youssef, who now aimed his gun at her, suspicious of her actions.

'What are you doing?' he asked her.

'You have to trust me,' she responded, using the back end of her seven-inch flashlight to pound against the wall, setting free a sizeable rock that fell to the ground. She picked it up, weighed it in her hands and decided it would be enough to do the job she had in mind.

Walking back past Joey, she noticed the concern in his eyes as he shook his head imperceptibly and struggled to hold up Hazim's trembling frame. Marie sent him what she hoped was a reassuring look and headed back to the front of the group, knowing time was of the essence. With a calculated underarm throw, she landed the cobblestone onto the nearest stepping stone–like pillar, which was so narrow it would barely fit two pairs of shoes side by side.

Instantly, the entire vertical shaft plunged downward, taking the rock with it, like a filled bath with its plug removed draining away. The sound of the dislodged stone breaking into pieces as it tumbled, colliding with anything in its wake, rang through the cavern until it abruptly came to a stop.

'How did you know?' asked Boyce with a solemn and fearful expression.

'I didn't,' replied Marie, using her wrist to rub off the sweat that had been building up on her forehead. 'We need to stay sharp.'

Boyce agreed with a nod.

From the front, Nader coughed and targeted his own flashlight at one of the closest pillars in a rhythmic circular motion. 'Do you see it?' he said in a low voice.

It was faint but noticeable; a triangular-shaped pyramid that was carved into the horizontal surface of the pillar. Continuing the search, Nader found four other pillars similarly inscribed, leading to the ledge on the far side.

'This could indicate the safe way across,' he said, coughing again throatily, making Marie look away.

'I think you might be right,' said Boyce. 'We'll need another stone to test your theory.'

Abdul obliged, using the heel on his steel-capped boot to kick free two more cobblestone rocks from the corridor. He then handed them to Marie, who lined up to take a throw at the first pillar bearing the pyramid pattern.

Uneasiness crept over Marie at playing good with these criminals, but she knew they needed to work as a team if they had any chance of survival.

Marie's first toss was short and missed the platform, rattling once more down to the base of the cavernous hole. Taking her time with the next stone, she landed it with perfect precision, and much to her delight the pillar remained strong and sturdy, not moving an inch.

Marie exhaled a long, elated breath.

'We have our way across,' said Boyce enthusiastically.

Nader said a few words in Arabic that made his friends chuckle, most probably something along the lines of yes, he was the muscle, but he also possessed the brains.

Boyce, being the youngest and the lightest, decided to go first before Youssef could dictate anything. Stepping up to the edge of the pit, he signaled the cross on his chest for luck and prepared to leap to the first step three feet away.

'Be careful not to slip on the stone I threw,' advised Marie.

'You can do it, bro,' encouraged Joey, still holding on to Hazim.

Boyce jumped to the first pillar, avoiding the small rock already there, stretching his hands to the side to maintain stability. Bending down, he picked up the cobblestone and threw it on to the next pillar that bore the triangular symbol, just to make sure this was no coincidence. A clever idea, Marie thought, to make sure they were on the right track.

It worked. The pillar didn't budge. Reaching the second jump stone, this time Boyce despatched the stone off the edge so it wouldn't interfere with the rest of the group's passage, and comfortably took the next three jumps with ease to reach the other side.

Marie's cheer was short-lived when she turned to see Hazim, barely able to stand on his own without Joey's assistance. His body shook uncontrollably as he clung to Joey, who was trying to comfort the man as best he could. Joey helped Hazim sit down against the cobblestone wall so they could formulate a plan.

'We have no choice but to leave Hazim here. We'll come back for him later,' Youssef urged.

Marie shook her head firmly. 'We can't just leave him here. Hang on, we have rope. I saw it in your duffle bag. Let's use it to get him across.'

Youssef stared at her disdainfully, before glancing over to Nader and speaking in Arabic.

'What are you saying?' she hissed.

Nader dropped the duffle bag and Abdul picked it up before he and Youssef hurried across the pillars to the other side, leaving them at the mercy of the gorilla in front of them.

'Move!' Nader commanded in an ice-cold voice. He stepped forward, using his imposing frame to nudge her away from Hazim and Joey and toward the steep drop. 'Go, or you die,' he gestured.

'Leave her alone,' Joey responded fearfully. 'Stop pushing her.' He tried to grab hold of Nader's shoulder.

Nader turned, grabbed Joey by his shirt and lifting him off his feet as if merely doing bicep curls, and tossed him forcefully back over to where Hazim sat resting. The force bowled them both over among the debris of broken bone fragments, which grazed Joey's forearms as he raised them to protect his face.

'Stop it!' Marie screamed at the top of her lungs. She clenched her fists, wanting to attack the giant, but she knew it would be pointless.

All of a sudden a hand grabbed her wrist.

'It's okay,' Hazim said in a crackling voice, adjusting himself back against the cold surface. 'Go, I'll only slow you down.'

'You need medical help,' she said, her voice cracking with emotion. 'I can't have that on my conscience.'

Nader shook his head in annoyance, before uttering something in Arabic over to Youssef, who answered with such menace, Marie knew it was not good, despite her not speaking a word of the language. And when she spotted Hazim's reaction to it, dread and despair filled her.

'No!' he mouthed with wet, fearful eyes, and he raised an arm in supplication.

'What's going on?' asked Joey, scrambling to his feet. 'What did he say?' he asked Hazim.

Before the antiquities expert had time to explain, Nader drew his Glock pistol and fired a single shot at Hazim's good leg, sending him rolling to one side screaming as he tried to put pressure on his wound to stem the bleeding. Nader then turned aggressively to Marie and growled, 'I will count to five. If you're not over the other side by then, the next bullet will be into your boyfriend's head.'

Marie's eyes widened in shock.

He started the count.

'One … Two … Three …'

'All right! I'll go!' Marie jumped across the obstacle as tears ran down her face. Youssef and Abdul's eyes followed her every move. She felt responsible for Hazim's pending death as Boyce came to comfort her with a hug on the other side, telling her it was okay and that she had done the right thing.

* * *

'You next,' Nader growled at Joey.

Joey apologized to Hazim as he rose unsteadily to his feet with a sprained hand, caused from when Nader had thrown him. He was unable to hide the discomfort on his face. He walked slowly over to the edge of the pit, ignoring Nader's triumphant leer.

Still rattled from Nader's assault and his injured hand, Joey misjudged the second pillar and slipped.

'Oh my God,' Marie gasped.

In the nick of time, he managed to clasp onto the edge of the pillar with the fingertips of his good hand, avoiding the seventy-foot drop as his legs scraped to find a footing. With upper-body strength that he'd built up from his time surfing the break at Venice Beach, he clambered back to the top. As he exhaled deeply with relief, he turned to see Nader's unamused expression. The big man shouted expletives at him to carry on. Joey composed himself and leaped across to where Marie and Boyce were waiting with open arms.

Nader was the last to make the leap, leaving Hazim to fight his own death. His heavy size-sixteen boots found the first pylon and he steadied himself.

'Come on, man,' said Youssef irritably. 'This has taken long enough already.'

Nader prepared himself for the second jump. His solid stature made it seem harder than it really was to soar across. His next target was in sight, and he made it, but then he suddenly gave a bellow of agony. His left leg had twisted on landing, while the momentum of his hefty frame carried him inexorably forward.

Everyone bar Joey turned to witness the excruciating desperation of a frightened man fighting to keep his balance as he swung his arms out of control, only to fall backwards, screaming, into the deep, dark abyss.

Chapter 23

The sound of horror echoed for a couple of seconds. Nader's body twirled and jerked aimlessly, swimming in midair, before it landed with a loud thump. The towering giant with the annoying smoker's cough had fallen to his demise. Five sharp arrows protruded from his neck and chest, sealing his fate.

Suddenly, a sinister problem faced the man running the show. The death of one of his own was unfortunate, but it had also quickly changed the playing field. Youssef shot a poisonous look at Joey, who tried to play it cool, but Youssef wasn't buying into his charm. He had known Joey had had something to do with the 'accident' the moment he'd turned to look the other way.

'You killed Nader!' Youssef shouted, his burning rage clear in his voice. He whipped out his Heckler & Koch and aimed it at the American, his hand shaking.

Gobsmacked at this turn of events, Marie and Boyce stood stock-still, wearing the same perplexed expression.

'I don't know what you're talking about,' retorted Joey, holding his hands up in surrender.

'When you tripped earlier on that same pillar

Nader fell from, it was all part of your plan, wasn't it?' Youssef scowled. 'It was all a ruse so you could plant a trap. I saw how Nader reacted when his foot landed. You put something on the pillar so he would lose his balance.'

'No.'

'Yes,' Youssef said grimly, stalking over to the cliff face to see his old friend splayed on his back, mutilated by the sharp arrows, his mouth and eyes still wide open, the horror of knowing he was about to be impaled to death written all over his frozen face.

Even though Nader was paid to be the muscle, he was always a man Youssef thought he could rely on, always there for him like a shadow when he needed someone to do the dirty work. He was a loyal friend and now, in the blink of an eye, he was gone.

Youssef took a moment and paced, thinking aloud. 'Two of us and three of them,' he muttered to himself. The captives' odds had now improved dramatically. He turned to Abdul and delivered a message in Arabic, his words calm and in control, but with a clear objective. Joey was always going to be a problem. He had that American I'm-better-than-you attitude and smugness Youssef so hated. Something drastic needed to be done to show the other two who was running things down here.

Youssef steadied his gun hand, keeping his weapon trained on Joey.

'Don't do anything foolish,' Marie begged. 'Joey just told you he had nothing to do with Nader's death.'

Joey stared at the Glock with bleak eyes, his

expression much like a trapped fox in the henhouse. Then, with lightning speed, Abdul extracted the gilded blade that had been tucked away in his utility belt and slashed Joey across his outer right thigh. The deep gash sent him to his knees, squirming as he tried to stem the gush of blood with hands that were quickly turning red.

'Ahh, it burns!' he cried out, looking around desperately for something or someone to provide aid for the wound.

Marie sobbed and Boyce tried to help, but was warned away when Alexander the Great's blade was turned toward him, Joey's fresh crimson blood shining along its edge as the culprit tilted it sideways and looked at himself in the reflection.

'After all these years it's still sharp,' Abdul said with a pretentious smile as he hovered over Joey, who continued to apply pressure on his wound. 'What you did to Nader was uncalled for,' he said, positioning himself behind Joey to rub the blade slowly up against his neck near his carotid artery.

Joey froze and visibly gulped in a deep breath, but was too traumatized to exhale it back out. He shut his eyes and waited for the killing blow to come, as though he was a lead character in *Game of Thrones* who'd thought his time would never come, but then it always does.

Marie reacted instinctively to this new danger, placing her petite frame between Abdul and Joey, pleading for mercy, while Boyce continued to eye the knife, knowing that if he moved Joey was as good as dead.

In the heat of the moment, Abdul grabbed Marie forcefully by the arm and bent it backwards, then shoved her to the hard limestone floor, causing her to graze her hands and knees. She fell onto her side and her black dress tore, exposing her dark undergarments, which caused Abdul to smirk and leer openly.

This infuriated Joey, who responded with a loud roar and tackled Abdul near the edge of the drop, winding him and knocking the knife down into the darkness alongside Nader's mangled body.

Abdul snarled and gritted his teeth. 'You lost my sword,' he barked, and the struggle intensified. They were now rolling and throwing blows at each other in a frenzy, like a street fight.

Joey freed his right hand and came in hard at Abdul's face, who reacted and rolled out of the way. Now on his feet, Abdul extracted the second knife from his utility belt and spun it round like a nunchaku. Joey was weaponless. He clenched his fists, his only defense mechanism, and prepared to protect himself from the wrath to come.

'Stop!' Marie intervened, once again placing herself between the two men. 'I swear, if you kill Joey, I will not help you, and you're going to need my assistance,' she called out to Youssef. 'Don't forget we're trapped down here, don't be stupid, man. We're going to need each other. There'll be more booby traps.'

Youssef took in Marie's plea as he pursed his lips in thought. She was right, they were stuck and he needed her help. He wondered belatedly if it had been a mistake to have entered further into this cave. The warnings were there, but he had chosen to ignore them. He had already found the Hall of Records and its treasures, a discovery that would give him the recognition he so desired. To any other man this would have been enough, but it was about more than greed for him; this was personal. He wanted to prove to himself that he was not the failure his father had branded him. He was not just a trust-fund baby, but a man who was going to be remembered as one of the greatest archeologists in history. He had no choice now but to move forward with the goal he had set out to achieve, and for that to come to fruition he accepted that he may need to be lenient with his hostages.

Youssef spoke to Abdul in Arabic and stopped the attack.

'Joey is too dangerous to be kept alive,' reiterated Abdul, not liking this decision but understanding the reasoning.

'If we let you live, will you promise to obey?' Youssef asked Joey, as he stepped away from the fuming Abdul.

'Yes,' Joey answered, defeated.

Youssef turned to Marie. 'You're right, Ms Martino, we need to work together, but if anyone tries anything funny I will shoot first and ask questions later, do you understand what I'm telling you?' He eyeballed the three captives, who nodded their heads in compliance.

'We need to stop your bleeding,' said Boyce, turning to Joey and ripping the sleeve from his shirt. He tied it carefully but firmly around Joey's thigh. 'We can't have you losing too much blood, can we?'

Joey thanked his friend and said, 'You'll make a good husband one day.'

'You first,' Boyce replied jokingly.

Marie decided to take the lead and she moved toward the opening that led away from the ledge and stopped there, waiting for them to move as a single unit.

'Are we ready?' she asked.

'As ready as we'll ever be,' muttered Joey.

'Eyes and ears to the ground,' repeated Boyce as Marie took that all-important first step.

* * *

They had already made history that evening by finding the Hall of Records and its many treasures. Now, they were about to penetrate deeper into a place hidden away by Tutankhamun's mother, Nefertiti. The one big question remained. What rested at the end of the Walk of Souls, and why was it so damn important that it needed to be kept secret and sealed away for an eternity? The answer had to lie beyond the ominous doorway that had lain undisturbed for thousands of years.

Chapter 24

In the dark passageway, the only sound that met Marie's straining ears was the echo of footsteps created by her team as they plodded deeper within. Her flashlight beam seemed puny in the blackness as she led the group, bent forward to be able to pass beneath the low stone ceiling. The tunnel was perfectly square, but as it continued, it widened until they were able to walk upright.

After a few minutes they came into a tall, narrow cavity. It was an impressive sight to behold, similar to the grand gallery within the Great Pyramid. It rose up about twenty-eight feet and stretched away into the darkness for about a hundred yards. The walls were made of solid limestone blocks that were smooth to the touch, but it was so narrow that if you stretched your upper torso outward you could almost tap the opposite wall.

'This can't be what it seems,' said Marie, shining her flashlight aimlessly with each uneasy step, not knowing what could be lurking up ahead. Why had they built such a narrow entrance, she thought, looking up to take in the room's height. Was it constructed this way just for the grandness, or was this another one of Nefertiti's agonizing tests that needed to be overcome?

Breathless, Abdul came up alongside Marie and took the lead. He took another light stick out of the duffle bag and held it aloft to help guide the way. Boyce followed behind them, Youssef behind him, and in last position was Joey, who kept close so as not to break the configuration.

Twenty feet inside the mammoth corridor they saw a tombstone that rose up from the ground. It seemed to be positioned directly in the center of the void. Marie stepped closer to examine it.

'I found something,' breathed Marie, kneeling to examine the low structure.

Emblazoned on its smooth surface was an image of three triangular pyramids taken from a top-view perspective. Beneath the images was some text in what could have been an old Egyptian dialect, but she wasn't certain, as this wasn't her field of study.

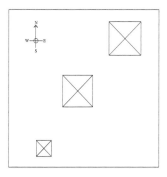

'What does this mean?' asked Abdul, warning the others to stop by holding a solid fist up in the air, as if he was at war and the people behind him were his troops.

'I don't know,' replied Marie, biting her bottom lip. 'If we had Hazim with us he could have been of more assistance.' She cast an accusing look at their captors. 'But you had to shoot him and leave him behind.'

Abdul shrugged his shoulders as if to say he didn't care.

'What's the hold-up?' asked Youssef, stepping forward to see what they were staring at.

'I think these triangles represent the Pyramids at Giza, but the symbols below . . . I don't know,' she muttered, as Youssef flashed his light on it to see for himself.

'Definitely not Egyptian,' he said. 'Maybe pre-dynastic.'

'Or alien text,' interjected Boyce sarcastically, making Joey grin.

Marie noticed Joey's smirk. He always wore a smile, but it had been a rare sight since he'd sustained his injuries. So to see him like that even for a brief moment was special and reassuring.

'Do you think your app could translate it?' Marie asked.

'I don't know what good it will be, it's just a bunch of dots with lines.'

'Hang on, there are heaps of other stones like this one down here,' Abdul informed them, throwing his light stick past the first stone and onto the distant floor. 'Hundreds of them.'

Youssef nodded his head as if to say he concurred.

Marie sprang up from her knees.

Abdul cracked another light stick and tossed it down the long room, illuminating more of the walkway. The group saw a plethora of drawings at their feet that were lit up in a green-colored hue. Square, limestone floor tiles stretched away from them, each with its own unique pre-dynastic pattern that repeated unevenly throughout the display.

'Don't move,' Marie hissed in warning, noticing a connection.

Abdul froze in mid-stride and backtracked, waiting for instructions.

'What is it, babe?' asked Joey.

'I think I know what this is,' Marie said evenly.

All eyes turned to her.

'The image on this tombstone thing depicts the three Pyramids at Giza and the alignment to the star constellation Orion.'

Hazim had earlier described the symbolic meaning between the Pyramids and the way they were constructed in the form of Orion's belt and it was still fresh in her mind. Orion was perhaps the most famous constellation viewed from all around the world and mentioned by Homer, Virgil and even in the Bible.

'These symbols are star constellations in their simplest formation,' she continued. 'A terrestrial map of the three stars.'

She did not know them all, but she recognized fifteen of them: Aquarius, Aquila, Aries, Canis Major, Cassiopeia, Cygnus, Gemini, Leo, Lyra, Orion, Pisces, Scorpius, Taurus, Ursa Major and Ursa Minor.

She pointed and said, 'That's the symbol Orion, I'm certain of it.'

'So, we are meant to decipher the correct connection and utilize it as a guide to step across this field,' said Youssef excitedly.

'That's what I'm thinking,' said Marie, nodding her head. 'But we have to stay on the path and not deviate, and most importantly stick close together.'

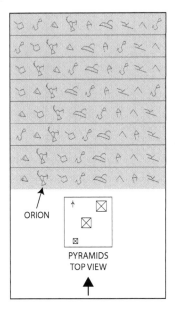

'I knew you would be of tremendous use,' Youssef breathed, ushering everyone back to their original positions and waiting for Marie to start the chain.

She took the first hesitant step onto the Orion square tile, being careful not to overstep the lines. The group followed as she moved in a zigzag pattern at a snail's pace. Her mind was constantly thinking and analyzing, but a glance up at the ceiling introduced a new problem. She realized that the stone ceiling was in fact resting on giant rollers. Huge rollers on both sides were spaced out along the narrow cavern. This started a panic that ran right through her, but she tried not to share it with everyone else, hoping not to cause unnecessary hysteria. If released, she reasoned, the enormous slab of granite from above would crush them like bugs. However, it was not the only problem they faced. The ceiling contained hundreds of rectangular-shaped holes the size of soft drink cans.

'What are they?' Boyce asked, following her gaze, his voice filled with dread. 'I'm too young to die.'

'You sure picked the correct career path,' joked Joey.

'Don't worry about them,' said Marie as lightly as she could. 'Just watch your step.'

On the ground she now noticed indented shapes, as though something heavy had stamped its mark on it. To have made an impression in the solid limestone, that something would have to have been extremely hard and punched down from overhead with immense force.

At that moment an excruciating, grinding racket echoed around them.

'What the hell?' uttered Boyce, turning his head left and right in search of the source.

'What did you do?' asked Marie, frantically craning her neck to see, her eyes enormous and petrified.

'Nothing,' Boyce called.

'This doesn't sound good,' Joey screeched at the rear.

'Oh my God! The ceiling is moving down on us!' warned Marie, taken aback by the events that were unfolding. 'Quickly!' she shouted, picking up the pace as the ceiling, weighing God knew what, began to rumble southward.

And so everyone reacted with haste as the entire ceiling of the chamber lowered above them in a single piece, like a giant hydraulic press. They followed the leader, dancing across in Marie's footsteps. At one section the pattern ran diagonal and in another straight, and at some spots you had to leap over a whole line of tiles knowing you couldn't miss the jump or hell would be unleashed.

The space above them had now halved.

And that's when the panic set in properly and multiplied, as Abdul tripped and pushed up against an incorrect symbol, which caused numerous solid panels of granite to come crashing down all around them while the ceiling continued its descent. Glancing behind him, Joey saw that the falling panels had blocked the entrance, so there was no going back.

Bang … Bang … Bang …

The ceiling was now only about fourteen feet above their heads.

Marie didn't waste any time. Her heart pounded in her chest as she forced herself to stay focused and jumped from square to square. She could feel the four men staring at her back with worried eyes, swiftly copying her every stride. Their flashlights ping-ponged to each square they needed to land on, as well as up to the descending ceiling.

'We're going to need to move faster,' Boyce called out through gritted teeth.

'For once I agree with you, little man,' said Youssef, squeezing himself forward past Boyce and bettering his chances, but stepping off the pattern just for a moment.

'Ahh, come on,' Boyce chirped out of frustration as a loud grinding sound now screeched from above.

'You're going to kill us all!' he cried out.

'Fuck!' screamed Joey as he dodged a set of vertical panels that slammed down inches from his face. 'Hey, just remember I'm at the back! What you do affects me.'

The wall was only ten feet above them now.

'Holy shit,' yelled Marie, stopping abruptly. 'I can't identify the Orion symbol anymore. The last hundred or so feet have completely weathered away.'

'We have no choice,' shouted Joey. 'Just make a run for it … Move! … We're gonna become pancakes if we don't.'

With no other choice open to her, Marie took off like an Olympic runner at the starting blocks and everyone else followed. Inevitably, they stumbled all over the wrong symbols, unleashing their worst nightmare.

With bang after bang, the solid panels dropped harder and faster, and they were now joined by sharp spikes, which lanced down about half a foot from other holes in the descending ceiling, to deliver the ultimate blow.

'We're going to be shish kebabs,' said Boyce now, bending forward as he ran.

The ceiling slab was seven feet above them.

Six.

Marie was the first to jump to safety on a narrow ledge that abutted the end of the press about to crush whoever was left behind. She knew it was going to be tight for the last one out, the most important person in her life.

The granite slab continued to rumble downward.

Youssef jumped to his freedom, Boyce following seconds before Abdul.

Five feet remained until the slab would crush Joey, unless the sharp arrows got to him first. Joey flung himself into a Spiderman position, on all fours, as the ceiling relentlessly descended with each second.

A spike grazed his shoulders, causing his face to contort with discomfort, so he dropped even lower to crawl, with his elbows pushing his body along.

Four feet.

The cage was closing in, sealing off any viable exit.

Three.

The opening was up ahead, not far now.

Two.

With his exit window fast diminishing and the sharp spikes now inches away, he Superman-dived onward, freeing his head and chest, and continued to scuttle through like a lizard.

In the nick of time he made it and the ceiling slab collided with the floor with a loud *boom*. Except that he didn't land near them. Marie turned in despair as she realized that Joey had flung himself out so hard, that he had slipped down what she now saw was a steep, dark vertical drop.

Chapter 25

Boyce catapulted to the edge to meet Marie, whose face had the panicked desperation of a mother who had lost her child. They both aimed their flashlights into the darkness below. The hole Joey had fallen into was circular, about thirty feet wide, with high stepping stones that ran down inside the perimeter in a spiral fashion. The steps were wide enough for a single-file formation but there was no rail, so slipping would lead you to a sheer drop down the central cavity.

'Are you two just going to stand there or are ya gonna give me a hand?' a voice said from fifteen feet below in the gloom.

Marie gasped with relief and delight and instantly diverted her flashlight to the source of his voice, to find him signaling with his hands. Joey was lying on his back; he had miraculously managed to land on one of the stepping stones.

Marie didn't waste any time.

Her flashlight lit up the space, bathing the entire cavern in an orange glow. Her naked feet found her footing among the loose stones littering the floor as she hurried down the stepping-stone stairs to where Joey rested. When she reached him, they locked together in a fierce embrace.

Boyce had never witnessed as much love between a man and a woman as he had seen between Joey and Marie. Even though the two of them had come from completely different backgrounds, they were perfect for one another. Marie complemented Joey as much as he complemented her. She possessed the brains while he possessed the street smarts, and together they gelled as one unstoppable force. Even in this awful situation, Boyce was reassured by the thought.

Boyce climbed down to Joey, who was still in Marie's arms, and patted him on the shoulder. 'Glad to see you're still with us, JP,' said Boyce with a cheeky smile. 'Thought we'd lost you there for a minute.'

'Thanks, Boy,' said Joey as Marie helped him up to his feet. 'I thought I was a goner too.' He stretched and arched his back, trying to smile, but Boyce noticed the grim set of his lips and the pained look on his face. The fall had hurt him more than he was willing to admit. 'Two more inches and I would have gone over. Man, I was lucky.'

'This isn't exactly the first time you've survived a fall,' joked Boyce. 'Remember the time in Switzerland when we crashed into the freezing lake?'

Joey shot his friend a half-smile and nodded.

'Lucky is your middle name.'

'What do you think is down here anyway?' said Marie, peeking over the edge.

'Probably end-of-the-world shit,' said Boyce.

'So the usual,' said Joey, playing along.

But the levity couldn't last. Above them, Youssef leaned over to see down into the cavity.

'It seems like we only have one way to go,' Youssef said, beginning his own descent. 'Let's find out where this leads us.'

'I would have been happier if he'd fallen to his death,' said Abdul behind his boss, loud enough to be heard.

Joey scanned upward and shook his head in disgust. 'Did you hear that bastard?'

'Don't worry about him,' said Boyce, trying to lift his spirits. 'Let's concern ourselves with getting through this Walk of Souls.' He lowered his voice so the idiots fast approaching would not hear. 'Let's just hope Julien isn't far away.'

'And what if he doesn't turn up?'

'He warned me not to use the emergency beacon unless I was in grave danger,' said Boyce quickly. 'Trust me, he's coming.'

Youssef and Abdul now joined them at the same platform, and Youssef pointed his flashlight beam at the wall next to them, which had on it a symbol which was identical to that etched onto the key. 'Look at this. We must be on the right path,' he said.

'You're right,' agreed Marie, also training her light onto it. 'Maybe it's a guide that we need to follow. Keep your eyes open.'

Joey tightened the binding over his wounded thigh, and Abdul smirked.

'I'll go first,' offered Boyce by way of distraction. The less they had to be close together, the better for everybody. In his now very dirty navy suit pants, brown leather shoes and untucked white shirt that was missing a sleeve, he landed on the next step with ease and everyone followed as per their now usual order.

They moved further and further down the strange vertical well-like passage, which seemed to get narrower as they went. The smell was musty and as they went deeper, the sound of dripping water could be heard.

All of a sudden from above came a loud jarring sound, which echoed in the space around them.

All heads tilted upward.

'It must be the ceiling moving back into place,' Marie surmised.

Abdul lit up another glow stick, ignoring the commotion, and tossed it over the edge. It fell fast and the walls illuminated a pipe-like stone shaft that dropped a fair distance.

Splonk ...

The light stick landed in water, and the green light slowly disappeared as it sank fast.

'There's water in here,' said Joey, limping behind Boyce with his flashlight trained over the edge. 'Who would've thought ... in the desert?'

'Why do you find that unusual?' asked Youssef, comfortably bringing up the rear.

''Cause it's the desert,' Joey replied sarcastically.

'There are over one hundred shafts cut into the limestone bedrock like this one all over the Giza plateau that were thought to bring in water from the river Nile. Some lead to tunnels that travel north to south and some east to west, with some being miles long. Also, don't forget, thousands of years ago this place wasn't a desert, it was a tropical oasis, and the river Nile was not in the same place as it is now.'

'I just can't comprehend that all these labyrinths and tunnels were constructed just to bring in water; they're too complex,' said Marie, turning her head to question Youssef. 'There has to be some other explanation.'

'For once we agree on something,' said Youssef. 'One theory is that rather than being tombs, the Pyramids were machines that generated energy by breaking water into hydrogen and oxygen ... long before the Pharaohs.'

'If that is correct, why were they creating energy?' said Marie. 'What were they up to?'

'Perhaps that's one thing we'll find out,' said Youssef. 'Once we find this secret chamber.'

After a few close calls that almost sent them over the edge, Boyce and his team reached the bottom of the well-like abyss. However it wasn't the true bottom; the stones at their feet continued, but now they simply disappeared down into a frigid pool of stagnant water.

'Looks like we're going swimming,' said Boyce, and waited for Youssef to respond.

'No, Boyce,' said Youssef sharply. '*You'll* be going swimming. We need to see if there's a way through first.'

'I thought you would say that,' Boyce replied with a roll of the eyes.

Abdul slammed the duffle bag he was carrying down at Boyce's Windsor Smiths, causing a loud thump at the water's edge. He handed him a snorkeling mask and some light sticks to help him see, in addition to the flashlight he already possessed.

Boyce slipped off his expensive leather shoes and cotton socks, but left his ripped shirt and suit pants on. Fitting his mask carefully, he tiptoed over to dip a toe in the freezing water.

'Be right back,' he said confidently, before he took a deep breath and leaped into the dark abyss, feet-first. A cold shiver ran up his spine as his entire body was submerged into the murky water. As he swam down further, he snapped an LED light stick and the shape of the underwater structure came into view in a ghostly shade of green. Boyce followed the steps, which continued to spiral southward, tapering off at the bottom where they met a colossal and distinctive man-made opening or doorway that was closed off by hundreds of giant stones. It was as if this had been done on purpose to hide what was behind it.

Boyce thought about the earlier discussion regarding Queen Nefertiti and her promise to her husband to keep this place a secret for the protection of their only son. It rattled in his consciousness as he appreciated the extraordinary lengths that had been gone to to achieve that goal.

Approaching the gargantuan wall of rubble, he found an opening the size of a washing machine, which was a walk in the park compared to what he had needed to swim through in Cyprus, so with his gulp of oxygen starting to burn a hole in his neck, he decided to go for it. Guided by his waterproof flashlight, his arms brushed by the rough surface of the rocks as he squeezed through to the other side.

Boyce found himself in a sort of cave, the floor of which was covered with what seemed to be broken squares of a metallic material that he couldn't identify. Boyce thought it weird but continued forward, his lungs burning now.

Then, in the distance, Boyce made out two blurry sets of giant stone feet that Boyce assumed belonged to two enormous statues. An underwater stairway sat in the center of the cave, inviting him to swim upward. In search of the air he so longed for, his head broke the surface and he sucked in his first desperate breath. Lungs heaving, it took a few moments for him to focus. But when he did, all he could manage was a gasp.

Chapter 26

A circle of light appeared in the dark pool of water, brightening with each second as it neared. Boyce broke the surface and took in a deep breath, then turned to where Joey and Marie stood and flashed them a Herculean grin.

'What did you find?' Youssef asked quickly.

'You'll have to come see for yourself,' said Boyce with a new chirpiness as he stepped upon solid ground, his soaked clothes sticking to him. 'There's a huge man-made grotto with giant statues at the end of this. It looks like Nefertiti had the entrance sealed, but you can still swim through a section of the debris.'

'How long is the swim to reach the cave?' asked Marie, pinching her chin nervously.

'You'll be okay, Marie, just take a really deep breath,' said Boyce encouragingly. 'Probably the same distance as the tunnel we swam in Cyprus, but not as tight.'

'Yippee.' Marie gestured with sarcasm, fist-pumping her hand in the air. She couldn't hide her lack of enthusiasm for the swim. It didn't help that she was dressed inappropriately.

'Before we go,' said Abdul, digging his hand into

the duffle bag and retrieving the rope. 'You carry this,' he said, forcefully pushing the rope, which was tied in a knot, down hard on Joey's shoulders. Joey returned Abdul's stare with bloodshot eyes, then leaned in and pushed him back, and they both once again faced each other toe to toe, eye to eye.

Youssef's quick response in his own language seemed to quell Abdul's ghastly expression.

'Stop this macho crap,' Marie warned Abdul. 'Remember we need to play nicely together.' She turned to Joey and nudged him aside. 'Now's not the time,' she murmured.

'But your time will come,' said Abdul with a somber laugh, as he zipped up his bag of supplies.

'So will yours,' retorted Joey with pent-up anger, even as Marie placed her arms around him.

'How many pairs of goggles do we have left?' Youssef asked Abdul.

Abdul said, 'Three,' and distributed two of them to Marie and Youssef. 'None for you,' he said to Joey with a vicious smile, in another attempt to get under his skin.

The few who wore fireman helmets tossed them to the ground and prepared themselves to plunge into the abyss. Everyone but Marie and Boyce left their shoes on.

Marie cringed as she tested the water at her feet.

'Okay, lead the way, Boyce,' said Youssef, securing his gun and phone into a waterproof zip lock bag. 'Marie, you follow him and, Joey, you come in last after Abdul.'

Boyce entered first.

Marie inhaled a deep breath of the musty air around her, shut her eyes to focus and followed her friend's escort with a splash.

The world went eerily silent.

Down here, her senses were altered and the sounds seemed slower, softer. Marie kicked deeper, feeling the pressure against her dress as she propelled herself forward. The water was colder than she had anticipated, but then, she supposed, they were deep underground now. She trailed Boyce closely, carefully keeping clear of his flailing feet.

The green LED light stick that Boyce was carrying lit up the bottom like a Christmas tree, which made him easy to follow. She could also see Youssef's flashlight beam shining from behind. In front of her loomed a wall made haphazardly of colossal stones of all different sizes. She watched Boyce point to a section and realized this was the hole he had mentioned previously. She nodded her head and observed him swim through it like a dolphin gliding in the water. It was her turn. She held both hands together in a diving pose and forced her way through with a fluttering kick to avoid the walls. Exiting on the other side, Boyce had started his ascent.

Her lungs desperate now for oxygen, Marie only glimpsed the floor for a brief moment, noticing that it glinted as if made of metal, before she swam upward as fast as she could.

She burst out of the water, filling her lungs with the oxygen her body so longed for. Only now did she notice that she was flanked on either side by massive human feet, which rose above the water line, framing a stairway between them.

Boyce waited for her to join him where the depth became waist high.

'Oh my God,' she gasped, easing her way toward the steps and glancing upward in wonder at the crystal-like ceiling that created a natural and ethereal shimmer in this dark place.

Youssef was not far behind, and soon he was spitting out water as he too reached the surface. The submerged stone steps led them to a fifty-foot-long sandy beach area. At the end of this pathway was a ramp leading to a raised platform that led further into another cavern.

On the sandy beach on all four corners were enormous scary-looking granite statues of Anubis, each with elevated scepters, like in a scene from *Braveheart*, as if cheering before they attacked. The guardians of the underworld seemed to be protecting this place. Marie felt as if they were Christians and they were being baptized in the water they had just come out of, or being tested to see if they were worthy of being here.

Abdul and Joey broke out of the water alongside them and took in lungfuls of air, two body lengths from each other, as Marie adjusted her black gown and squeezed out the water weighing her down.

'Be careful,' warned Marie as she joined Boyce and Youssef with relief on the soft sand. She couldn't help smiling at the warm, familiar feeling beneath her toes.

'It's okay,' Boyce assured her.

Youssef strode forward, his eyes to the ground, heading for the cave's entrance.

But twenty steps further and Marie's relief turned to despair, for at that moment she felt her legs start to go from under her. Looking down with her flashlight in hand, she saw sand seemingly begin to pile at her feet.

Boyce let out a vicious curse in French.

Youssef sighed.

Marie's feet were already half covered. The sand was actually sucking at her feet. She began to struggle.

'It can't be,' Marie said, as her legs sank further. In only a moment she was waist deep in sand. It was as if someone had grasped her ankles from below and was pulling her under. 'Quicksand,' she said, and panic bloomed in her chest. She had seen this in the movies but had never thought in a million years that she would become a victim of it. 'How stupid am I?'

Boyce, too, was trapped, and struggled against the sand as it swallowed him further and faster. He was now chest deep. 'What do we do?' he pleaded, trying to swim out of its grip, but looking like he was fast losing the battle.

'Don't move,' commanded Youssef, holding his hands up to keep his balance. 'The more you struggle, the more you sink. Stay still.'

'Um, babe,' Marie called with a soft but fearful tone. 'Are you there? We kind of need your help! Now would be better than later.'

LAST SECRET CHAMBER

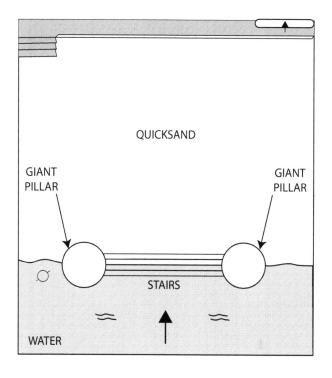

Chapter 27

Joey entered the holy inner sanctum of Nefertiti's deadly labyrinth. After hearing Marie's distressed call, he'd swum to the steps and hurried up them to see the three of them being swallowed up by the quicksand.

Even though they were holding deadly still, they sank further and further.

Abdul reacted swiftly, wading out of the water in the direction of his boss, but Joey stopped him at the sand's edge with a heavy hand pressed against his chest.

'Don't be stupid, man,' said Joey. 'It's quicksand. If you walk over there, you'll be sucked down too.'

'I have to help Youssef,' Abdul responded in an angry voice, as though Boyce and Marie meant nothing.

'This is just another test,' said Joey firmly. 'We need to think.'

'Think, my ass.'

'Joey!' Marie cried. 'Quick!'

'The rope,' Abdul said suddenly, grabbing it off Joey's shoulder and tossing it over to the one person he cared for.

Youssef managed to grasp hold with both hands. Abdul braced himself on the stone steps, his body half submerged in water, and tugged on the line, but strangely this only made the situation worse.

As Abdul pulled, Youssef sank deeper into the soupy mixture of sand and water.

'Stop!' warned Joey. 'You're just pushing him under. You need to get to higher ground to wrench them out.'

Joey gestured over to a ledge on the other side that was like a giant viewing platform with a curved granite balustrade.

'How do we get across if we can't walk on the sand?' said Abdul, frowning, the wrinkles on his face deepening further.

'I don't know,' said Joey, trying to think fast as he surveyed the site before him. He ran his hands through his wet blond locks.

'Time is running out,' said Youssef, and for the first time they all heard a note of fear in his voice. His head and neck were all that remained above the sand as he endeavored to keep still so he would not go under. 'Quickly!'

Marie whimpered as the shoulder straps from her black dress were now completely consumed. To her side, Boyce shut his mouth as his chin rested atop the goopy, sandy surface, but his grim expression said all that needed to be said.

'Hang on, guys I'm working on it. If you go under, hold your breath and leave your hands up over your head,' said Joey, taking another glance at the Anubis figures before him with their raised scepters. Turning to Abdul, he said, 'I don't think these statues are just here for decoration. I think they serve another purpose.'

Abdul only shrugged.

In a rush, Joey moved to study the enormous sculpture to his right, encircling it with his hands, then gliding them across its smooth surface. The distressed sighs from the others continued, gradually becoming more desperate.

'Hurry, Joey,' Marie called.

Finding nothing out of the ordinary, Joey darted over to his left and his eyes came alive.

'The spiral symbol,' he uttered loud enough for all to hear. 'It's on the feet of Anubis.'

'Follow it,' Marie blurted, before shutting her lips as she sank down to the tip of her nose, her eyeballs now resting just above the mud and flicking left to right in panic.

'There has to be something here . . .' said Joey, investigating.

'How's this symbol going to help us?' asked Abdul, not convinced. 'You have just killed your friends.'

'This is another test we must pass,' Joey reminded him, scanning the stone steps from above with his flashlight. 'It must be concealed under the water.'

'What is?' said Abdul, his eyes wavering wildly.

Joey didn't respond; instead he dived down at the feet of the giant Anubis warrior. When the bubbles subsided, he spotted a circular wheel a little larger than the size of a bus's steering wheel. To his right he also saw that the statue of the half-man, half-dog was resting on some sort of rotisserie-like construction.

Joey exited the water, screaming, 'It's here! Abdul, come quickly.'

At this point, Youssef was down to his eyebrows and all you could see was his thick curly hair floating on top. He would have taken his last breath and the others were just about to take theirs.

Joey and Abdul plunged down to the circle, where they took hold of opposing ends and began to turn the ancient wheel clockwise. Joey ground his teeth as he used every bit of strength he could muster, bubbles escaping from his mouth all the while. It was hard at first, but with the two of them working together in perfect unison it started to move more easily.

With the motion continuing, Joey could see from below that the Egyptian god near him had rotated.

It was a confirmation that all this had indeed been constructed for a reason.

Needing a quick breath of air, Joey swam up to see what effect their efforts were having. To his surprise, the four Anubis statues now all faced each other, and their long scepters were now lowered and crossed against one another, making it easy to climb across.

The way they were supposed to have navigated.

Meanwhile, in the sand below, he could only see three sets of hands sticking out from the quicksand waiting to be rescued.

They had gone under. Time was up.

After a quick glance, Joey dived back down again and found Abdul still turning the apparatus on his own. He was a machine, strong and determined. His eyes were shut as he struggled to turn the last bit to lock it into place. Joey knew there was an underlying reason for Abdul's need to save Youssef. Aside from the fact that they would outnumber him three to one should Youssef die, Abdul wasn't so stupid as to do all this for nothing. There was some sort of payment at the end of this that was going to set him up for life, Joey felt sure. So it was imperative for Abdul to keep the businessman safe and breathing.

The wheel locked into place.

Abdul was the first out of the water, gasping for air. With no time to waste, Joey grabbed the rope left on the ground and placed it around his shoulder before free-climbing up the Anubis statue and across the solid scepters. Wrapping his feet around the extended scepter and hanging beneath it, he shimmied his way across.

'Climb up and stay at the crossroads of the four rods,' Joey instructed Abdul. 'I will pass you the rope from here. Circle it on your end so we can hook them out.'

'Okay, I understand where you are going with this,' said Abdul, who watched Joey rush up to the viewing platform.

Joey could see the entire scene before him, including the flailing hands needing immediate assistance. Working as fast as he could, he used the solid granite railing and wrapped the rope around it, erecting a sort of pulley system. On the other side, he tied a noose and tossed it to Abdul, who caught it with his free hand and flung it over the scepter as instructed, before proceeding to Youssef's extended hands.

'Tell me when,' said Joey, ready to pull now with two anchor points that would help take the load.

Abdul looped the knot over Youssef's outstretched hands, and as he tugged the rope it squeezed tight against his wrists.

'I've got him,' he shouted.

Working as a team, they fished the businessman out from the quicksand in long, heaving pulls. His entire body was consumed in mud as he began to gasp for air in relief. Up at the scepter he selfishly took his time, throwing his leg over the pole that would assist to slide him to safety.

'Quick,' warned Joey. 'Marie and Boyce don't have much time.'

'Climb to the other side, sir,' said Abdul, also turning to do the same.

'Wait!' Joey screamed. 'You can't just leave them here. Help me, please!'

While straddling the granite scepter that was used in ancient Egypt to show power, Youssef faced Abdul and asked him to save Marie.

'She's proven herself to be a good asset, and her expertise and passion for art and history would be beneficial in moving forward,' he said coldly.

Abdul agreed with a reluctant nod and removed the lasso from Youssef's hands before attempting to fish Marie out from the semi-liquid surface.

'I can't get both hands around the rope,' Abdul squirmed from above.

'Just grab one, then,' Joey urged. 'Do it now!'

He caught Marie's right wrist and gave Joey the order to pull.

Marie emerged wheezing for air as she spat muddy sand out of her mouth. 'Boyce!' she croaked, swinging aimlessly about.

'It's too late for him,' said Abdul. 'I'm sorry, we must move on.'

'Try to grab him, Marie,' Joey yelled, not listening to the idiot.

Turning to face the quicksand, Marie reacted and stretched for the teen's limp hand, as it was about to disappear completely from sight.

She caught it, and somehow Boyce held on to her, and together they managed to hoist him out. Boyce's face was pale with a bluish tinge from lack of oxygen. His mouth opened wide and his head arched backwards as he inhaled the welcome breath of air.

'Don't let go, babe,' Joey urged.

Marie struggled to hold on to the teen's one hundred and thirty pounds with her weaker arm, but she held tight as they ascended. If she let go from this height he would sink faster than a boat with a hole in its hull. Reluctantly, Abdul helped lift them both up to safety and one by one they all slid across the scepter, unharmed.

Joey embraced his sandy friends, who wore speechless expressions and were too emotionally drained to be able to talk.

'You look like dead mummies,' he joked, giving them both another bear hug. Their appearance now seemed perfectly appropriate for the spooky cave they were about to enter next.

Chapter 28

Without the need to hurry on into the next cave, they all stopped and rested at the viewing platform in contemplative silence. This was the closest they had come to death, and the gravity of the situation seemed to have occurred to all of them. Marie found comfort in the arms of her boyfriend, who rubbed her back and assured her that everything was going to be okay, even though they both knew it probably wouldn't be. Youssef and Abdul stood close, muttering something in Arabic, presumably a discussion on how they were going to maintain control within the group.

Boyce knew there would come a time when they would turn on them. At this moment they were flying blind and required their assistance, but that wasn't going to last forever. They were still two ruthless killers out for themselves, choosing who would live and who would die. And the fact that they had planned to leave him to suffocate in the quicksand was the final blow, even though it didn't really surprise him. If it hadn't been for Marie's unselfish act earlier on – and Joey's – it would have been game over, he would have vanished from existence, lost in an ancient cave until the next brave soul discovered it.

Struggling for air beneath the liquid sand that had consumed him, he had heard everything from above. The fact that Abdul and Youssef had had no intention of rescuing him had caused anger to rush right through him. He shut his eyes, fuming with so many mixed emotions. He pressed his fists hard up against each other on the granite balustrade in front of him. Then, with a violent, uncontrollable rage shaking him, he turned and rushed at Youssef with an animal-like roar.

Caught by surprise, Joey yelled at the top of his lungs as Boyce stormed by.

Marie's mouth dropped.

Abdul saw Boyce's charge and reacted with urgency, pushing aside his boss so he wouldn't be in the path of what was coming. Boyce flung a killer swing at Abdul, but was deflected and thrown down hard on the cold stone. Boyce panted as he rose from the ground, his jaw clenched, and prepared himself for a second attack, knowing the consequences could possibly end his life, but he didn't care.

Lucky for him Joey was there to stop any physical damage he might have wrought. The American's athletic frame held him firm, extinguishing the youth's wild onslaught.

'It's not worth it, bro,' said Joey, staring him in the eyes, trying to reason with him.

'They were going to leave me there,' sobbed Boyce. Just the thought made him want to vomit. 'We can't trust anything they say.'

Joey embraced the young Frenchman, pulling him into his chest, while Boyce wept into his friend's wet t-shirt. 'We'll get through this,' Joey said lovingly, like an older brother would.

'Come on. I'm waiting for you,' provoked Abdul, trying to give him an excuse, already hovering his hand over his gun's holster. 'I dare you.'

'Don't worry, you will get yours,' Joey told him with a deadly stare. 'Mark my words.'

Boyce knew his friend and what he was capable of too well. He was the son of the man who had been the most feared gangster in America before he died. Even though Joey didn't act tough, it was embedded in his DNA. To incur his wrath was a foolish move, as Boyce had discovered when they were up against extremely dangerous military operatives on their trip to Paris. Those men had not lived to tell the tale. When the time was right he knew Joey was going to erupt and have his vengeance. God help them when it happened.

'Well, that was unexpected,' said Youssef, adjusting his shirt. 'Are we going to have a problem?'

'How did you expect Boyce to react?' said Marie in an authoritative tone. 'You said we were in this together. We agreed we needed to work as a team to get through these obstacles. But we learned here that you only keep up your end of the bargain when it suits you.'

'No one can be left behind,' said Joey, getting to the heart of the situation.

'You're right,' said Youssef, showing himself from out of the shadows. His face was lit up by Joey's flashlight.

Abdul wrinkled his nose in disgust and stepped back to let him speak.

'From now on everyone in this team will be treated with the same respect.' He extended his hand toward Boyce.

Boyce shook his head disbelievingly at the man who had planned and orchestrated this entire day meticulously. How could he be trusted? Every bone in his body was evil and vindictive. He had killed Joey's uncle, and the Cairo Museum director, and had left Hazim to die an excruciating, lonely death, with no remorse. They were just puppets in his narcissistic game until he got what he wanted.

Boyce ignored the man's hand and proceeded past him to the cave that would take them further into the unknown. In his peripheral vision, he saw Youssef slowly raising his gun, and paused.

Marie sighed at the sight.

Boyce felt a shiver of fear as he turned in slow motion to face the armed man, hoping he hadn't made a foolish mistake by offending him.

'Let it go,' Marie said, pushing Youssef's gun hand gently southward, away from Boyce's torso. 'It's been a long night. Another death would be completely needless at this point, so can we at least pretend to be civil from now on?'

Youssef reluctantly withdrew his weapon.

Boyce exhaled a sigh of relief, took a moment, then continued into the barely lit tunnel, hemmed in by a perfectly arching sandstone construction.

Joey and Marie kept close behind him and the assholes, ironically, fell in at the rear.

The entrance was designed to look like gaping jaws.

Inside, a glistening wetness trickled down the walls and Boyce could hear the sound of dripping water and felt it under his toes. The tubular passage angled downward, and when he flashed his light on the side walls, Boyce observed horizontal scratch lines that traveled as far as the flashlight could illuminate.

'Watch your step, Boyce,' warned Marie, moving her flashlight across the slippery surface beneath her naked feet, then up to the granite structures on either side that also disappeared into the dark void.

'Looks like a rail track,' said Joey, following the tunnel southward. 'I have a really bad feeling about this one and it feels kind of familiar to me.'

'What do you mean?' asked Youssef evenly.

'The tunnel is circular and steep,' said Joey, before pausing. 'Why? I'm scared a huge boulder is gonna roll us over from behind like in—'

'*Raiders of the Lost Ark*,' said Marie, finishing his sentence and flashing him a nervous smile.

Everyone froze and turned their heads to make sure that wasn't going to happen, and then observed the granite track in question more closely.

Eventually Boyce continued forward. One hundred feet in they began to see alcoves on either side of the passage. Each long rectangular space was enough to fit two bodies comfortably.

'What is this place?' asked Abdul in a trepidatious whisper.

'Look at this,' Boyce called, shining his beam into one of the alcoves. The symbol that seemed to be showing them the way in this Walk of Souls was engraved inside, on the back wall. 'What does this mean?' he said anxiously.

'Here, let me take the lead,' said Marie, who stepped forward and began to study the symbol intently. She knew it had been placed in this spot for a reason, having shown the way on multiple occasions previously.

Stepping into the alcove, she rubbed her hand down the back of the stone wall, which felt cold to the touch, and massaged around its corners in search of a secret passageway but came up short.

It seemed it was nothing but an empty void.

With no choice but to continue, they pressed on down the tunnel until they came to a throng of alcoves that were spaced evenly apart, about ten feet from each other. Some displayed the symbol and some did not. Marie calculated that there was a symbol in every fifth cavity. Then the impossible happened.

The tunnel floor dropped from under them.

Screams of panic erupted from the group as they struggled back to their feet.

It had only been a short fall, but when Marie turned back to face the track, it was as if the tunnel had become steeper and they were at the bottom of it.

'Joey, I hate to say this, but I think your original thoughts about this tunnel might be right,' said Marie grimly.

Out of nowhere, an ominous rumbling sound was heard and felt vibrating through the granite.

Everyone spun around.

'Ahh, shit!' said Joey, looking back up the tunnel. 'Here it comes.'

'Everyone, find an alcove NOW!' ordered Marie.

Right behind them a huge boulder came roaring downward, perfectly form-fitted to the passageway and guided by the scratch marks in the walls. Youssef and Abdul darted into the first alcove with the key symbol etched into the wall as the massive rock came crashing by, obliterating everything in its path.

Boyce stumbled and tripped, and Joey only just managed to scoop him up and shove him into another hole bearing the same mark before the boulder rumbled past. Joey held the youth tight in his arms as they escaped the treacherous death that would have been certain had they not acted so fast.

Marie was inadvertently left alone as she sprinted for her life in her bare feet. To make matters increasingly more challenging, she noticed that every cavity without a symbol inside it had begun to extend outward to form a solid wall, providing no protection.

They were death traps if you decided to use them for cover.

Her heartbeat raced out of control as she now searched for the sign that was going to save her. All of the alcoves on both sides seemed to be closing.

Her flashlight danced wildly. Until she found that all-important hole she could duck into, all she could do was run for it. She bolted faster than she had ever run before. Even her former schoolgirl self, who had won the state hundred-meter sprint, couldn't have kept up with her now. She had one purpose, and it wasn't to win a stupid medal that would be thrown in a cupboard to collect dust; she was running for her life.

There were no more alcoves. The only refuge was an exit up ahead where the track banked to the right. She could feel the boulder gaining on her. If she fell, she was dead. It was as simple as that. Suddenly she saw that hundreds of vine-like ropes loomed out from an opening to the left of where the tunnel angled right. This was going to be her move, her only chance of survival.

Six feet until the jump …

Her breathing was so labored she was beginning to see stars.

Three …

She could feel the rush of air behind her as the boulder neared.

One …

She angled her leap to the left, letting go of her torch to reach out with both hands.

The huge rock rushed by like a roller-coaster car and disappeared into the darkness to the right. Mid-flight, Marie felt the wind at her back. Looking down, she could now see that the vines continued to fall for at least a hundred feet. It was a long jump and it felt like an eternity. She lunged for the nearest vine, gripping on with all her might as it swung wildly back and forth before it slowed to a stop.

Having survived imminent danger by the skin of her teeth, Marie exhaled the breath she'd been holding after she had jumped. She strangled the vine with her feet, trying to catch her breath, slow her racing heartbeat and calm her terror-filled mind. After a few minutes she looked around, trying to decide her best course of action. She couldn't make her way back to the tunnel. The only way was down. Slowly she free-climbed downward. The vines stopped short of the ground, but the jump wasn't life-threatening. She let go and was met with a splat as she landed. She felt a squirt of mud hit her legs and she slipped to her backside.

Her right toe had hit some sort of circular metal object. She dug down into the wet sand to discover it was her flashlight. She picked it up and flicked it on, grateful that it still worked. She flashed it to the wall in front of her and her mouth dropped.

She was staring at the biggest door she had ever seen.

Chapter 29

Limping down the corridor with flashlight in hand, Joey prayed that his girl had made it to safety. There was no sign of her, and he could only hope that she had escaped unharmed. Boyce, Youssef and Abdul followed with a more careful, steady pace, warily turning their heads every few seconds just in case.

Joey hobbled to an opening up ahead where the track banked to the right. He peered over the edge to see another drop consumed by darkness. Fearful thoughts looped around in his mind, until there was no room for anything else. Would he find her broken, breathing blood out of her dying mouth, or even worse, find her already dead? She was the one person in his life he needed by his side. She understood him. She was his rock and together they made an exceptional team.

Then and there, Joey made a pact with himself. If Marie didn't make it, he would unleash hell on the men who were responsible for destroying his happiness. He would tear them apart with his bare hands, even if they were carrying firearms. The bullets would not stop him. A black cloud seemed to hover over his subconscious, building a darkness within Joey that he knew would be hard to control.

He called out to her in the hope that she would answer before he released the beast from within.

'Marie!' he shouted. 'Please, tell me you're alive?'

Boyce reached him and laid a warm hand on his shoulder. Together they waited for a response.

'I'm okay!' he heard her call, and then he saw a dim light from below as she aimed her flashlight up at them. 'Down here.'

Relief like he'd never felt before washed over Joey.

'Are you hurt?' he called down.

'No,' she replied. 'Use the vines to climb down. You have to see this.'

Joey didn't waste any time. He took a step back and lunged at the nearest vine, which swayed back and forth as it took his weight. He wrapped his feet around it to release the tension in his arms, and once it came to a stop, he put one hand in front of the other and lowered himself to the bottom.

'You have to jump the rest of the way, babe.'

Joey let go, and his expensive sneakers found the sticky mud. Moments later, Marie rushed into his arms and he crushed her to him, the thought that he had almost lost her rattling him to the core.

'Are you okay?' he asked her, not wanting to move away from her enough to peer into her face.

'I am now,' she said, leaning her head against his chest, cherishing the moment.

A few moments later, Boyce, Abdul and Youssef jumped down from the vines above onto the muddy surface.

'How the hell are we going to climb back up?' uttered Abdul in disdain. 'We can't reach the vines from here.'

'Perhaps that was the point,' said Marie, releasing herself from Joey's embrace and shining her flashlight on the timber doors that dwarfed them. 'Look here!'

Abdul cracked a yellow light stick and the shaft came to life with an eerie, incandescent glow.

'What the hell do they have behind this giant door,' joked Boyce. 'King Kong?'

Marie chuckled. 'You never know. Nefertiti might have been hiding giants down here. Many legends have said they walked the earth a long time ago. It's even in the Bible.'

'Well, if it's in the Bible it must be true,' said Joey in jest.

'Behind this door,' said Youssef, gesturing dramatically with his hands. 'This must be it. What we've come all this way to find!'

'Open it,' ordered Abdul, his gun out once again and trained on Joey. 'Let's hope this is it, 'cause I'm running out of patience.'

Joey walked over to the thick timber doors, which, like the bookshelf in the Hall of Records, were also constructed from cedar from Lebanon. The doors were enormous, thirty feet high, and held closed by a giant metal brace, too highly elevated to reach. Connected at the end of the truss was a chunky rope that ran to the ground. Its purpose was simple; pull it down and the lever would lift up and unlock the entrance.

Joey didn't waste any time. He jumped up at the

rope and hung there in midair as the mechanism rose slightly. 'It needs more weight,' he said, swinging.

Boyce grabbed hold of the line beneath Joey and lifted himself up, tilting the latch vertically on a seventy-five-degree angle. One more body was required. Marie approached the bottom end after Joey and Boyce climbed up further to give her some space. Low to the ground, she hoisted her own weight inches from the earth.

The brace came free of its bracket, and before they all let go, Abdul stepped forward and shoved the door with his palms. The squeaky, rusted hinges squealed as the door creaked open. Marie, Boyce and Joey, in that order, let go of the rope, careful not to topple each other over, and stared in awe at the impressive sight before them.

Youssef forged ahead, flashing a million-dollar smile they had all seen far too many times that night. It seemed they had passed the test, making it through the Walk of Souls to reach the end of the line – the last secret chamber.

Chapter 30

Once through the doors, Abdul fired a flare into the dark void, illuminating the entire space. They soon saw that there were no further entries or exits; this was the absolute end. They were standing at one corner of a massive super-cavern, perfectly square.

Youssef took in the sight as he sauntered down a ramp, where he was confronted by two colossal obelisks. The tall, four-sided, narrow monuments tapered as they neared the ceiling. Each bore a name in hieroglyphics: Akhenaten and Nefertiti. Carved into the pointy-ended pillars, the king and queen's elongated heads worshiped the sun god above them as the rays descended over them. Each had their own obelisk, proving they had shared equal power during the eighteenth dynasty. The monuments stood proud in this megalithic structure, and Joey knew it was a rarity to find two standing together. Only one obelisk remained in Luxor, over three hundred miles south of Cairo; the other stood alone in the Place de la Concorde in Paris.

They advanced into the airport hangar–sized chamber in awed silence. Nearly eight hundred feet in length, about the size of three football fields laid end to end, its floor was covered by knee-deep water, giving it the appearance of a vast, flat lake. Protruding inches above the water's surface were a handful of low monoliths. Engraved on one of the horizontal smooth surfaces was a depiction of the body of a man with a jackal's head.

'Anubis,' said Youssef, keeping a distance, knowing there could be traps that would send him to the afterlife. He wasn't ready to take that journey, not yet.

Reaching the bottom of the ramp, the group allowed their eyes to adjust to the dim light provided by the flare, then looked around for any possible traps. Not seeing anything unusual, Youssef began wading through the water, his flashlight trained straight ahead of him.

In the center of the enormous cavern was a raised square platform flanked by stone stairs leading up to it from the water. At its core, rising up from the lake, dry and protected, was a focal point no one was expecting to find down here.

A stupendous view to say the least.

It was a perfectly rendered limestone pyramid.

'I have no words,' said Marie, trudging toward it, her fingers gliding over the water, her eyes widening with excitement and wonder.

'Who do you think built this?' asked Boyce, looking genuinely impressed by its grandness.

'God knows,' replied Joey, also in awe.

'Definitely not Khufu,' said Marie. 'There's no way he could have erected both in his life time.'

'He was supposedly the builder of the Great Pyramid,' said Boyce, answering his own question.

'Yep.' Marie nodded her head, deep in thought.

'This one has kept its rendered surface,' said Boyce.

'It sure has,' said Youssef wonderingly. 'The original polished white Tura limestone that is used for the finishing coat seems to have been protected down here away from Egypt's harsh climate.' He paused for a moment, gazing at it admiringly. 'This pyramid might even reveal who built it.'

'I have a funny question to ask,' said Boyce.

Joey rolled his eyes teasingly. 'Oh no, here we go.'

'Does this mean that this pyramid predates the one above ground? It would mean the Great Pyramid is not the oldest Wonder of the World, wouldn't it?'

'It's amazing how your mind works,' retorted Marie with a smirk. 'I guess it does,' she replied. 'But the hundred-million-dollar question you all should be asking, is how and why did they build this one down here? That's what I want to know! What is its purpose?'

Youssef nodded, agreeing with Marie.

Holding a light stick aloft, Abdul proceeded, and the shadows on the eastern side of the cavern revealed themselves to be a terrifying crocodilian head. In actual fact, there were two enormous dinosaur-sized open-mouthed crocodile profiles carved into the limestone rock. Quite a confronting sight to behold, thought Youssef, with their razor-sharp teeth on display as they rested above the shallow water. The tubular, dark mouth hole was like an amusement park waterslide ride, with controlled streams of liquid shooting out from the creatures' jaws.

A long, rectangular stone tablet flanked the scary-looking twins. A single hieroglyphic on it made Youssef sigh.

'That cartouche among the hieroglyphics bears the name of the Egyptian god Sobek,' he informed the others soberly. 'Sobek is the God of the Nile river, the place where this water would have come from.'

'They sure are huge aqueduct holes for such a small stream,' said Boyce, flashing his beam of light into the darkness of the first beast's mouth.

'I'm more concerned about the crocodiles that roam the river,' Youssef retorted, then paused for dramatic effect. 'The Nile is filled with them.'

A sudden panic struck everyone, including Abdul, and they aimed their flashlights frantically into the milky water around them. An object that could have been a crocodile waiting to strike and shred them to pieces was up ahead.

'It's just one of those rocks with an image on it,' warned Marie as Boyce flashed his beam onto the next tablet not far away. 'Don't touch anything and keep your eyes open. This may be nothing but it doesn't mean there are no other booby traps or dangers here.'

'Trust me, I'm not falling for that again,' said Joey, turning to smile at Marie. 'Remember in Cyprus when I stepped on the Poseidon symbol and the entire cave flooded?'

'We wouldn't want that, would we,' said Boyce, turning to face the crocodile heads once again.

No sooner had Boyce spoken, when a loud buzzing sound startled the group, and they all snapped their attention to the source. It was coming from Youssef's wristwatch. He checked the GPS coordinates on display and a shocked expression came across his face. Raising his head in amazement toward the stone-covered ceiling above, he turned his wrist to show the others the watch's display: 29.9792° N, 31.1342° E.

'What is it?' asked Marie.

Youssef was the first out of the water, clambering up the steps to the central pyramid. 'Believe it or not, folks,' he announced, pointing his torch skyward, 'we are now standing directly beneath the Great Pyramid of Giza.'

Quickly, he turned his flashlight back to the outer walls encircling them. 'I bet if we were to measure the length of the enclosure down here, it would be exactly seven hundred and fifty-six feet, just like the one above.'

They all took a moment to appreciate the enormity of the discovery.

To know that they were standing beneath a colossal foundation that was the belly of one of the Seven Wonders of the World was truly mind-bending and surreal, magical even.

'How can that be?' asked Joey, taking his first step up with squeaky wet shoes. 'Our engineers in the twenty-first century would have struggled to work out the logistics to keep all that dead weight from toppling into itself.'

'Tell me about it,' said Youssef. 'We are talking about 2.3 million stones, weighing between 2.5 and 15 tons each.'

'Maybe this inner pyramid will have the answers we seek,' Marie speculated, joining the rest of the group as they traveled up the stairs. 'And it might explain its true purpose and who was buried inside.'

'I told you before, these pyramids were not built to be someone's tomb,' said Youssef irritably, reaching the elevated platform. 'They're machines that generated energy.'

Abdul tossed his light stick at the leveled floor surrounding the fabled engineered structure. Its amber glow reflected against the smooth stone, exposing the structure's untainted surface. The pyramid rose a hundred and twenty feet above them, a quarter of the size of its bigger sibling above ground.

Youssef rubbed his four fingers on the sharp angled point where two of the faces met, marveling at its complexity, and extracted his cell phone. Everyone watched as he rested it upon the incline, using a leveling app to reveal what he had already come to understand.

He hinted a smile. 'It's 51° 50,' he said with conviction. 'These Egyptians don't do anything half-assed. It's also the same angle as the Great Pyramid above.'

Marie bent her neck backwards and aimed her beam at the pinnacle of the triangle. 'And look here,' she said with obvious excitement. 'The pyramidion is still intact.'

Boyce stood near Abdul as Youssef, Marie and Joey aimed their torches as one to gain a better line of sight. That's when they realized the capstone was a giant transparent crystal.

'Holy shit,' murmured Youssef, seeing what could

have been the largest crystal ever to have been quarried and cut to shape. 'Abdul, can you see this?' he said, gesturing to his friend, knowing that this alone would make them the kind of rich one could only dream about.

Abdul hesitantly approached the group. Like the others, he trained his flashlight beam on the pyramid's crystal capstone, and all of a sudden, like in an Indiana Jones movie, a stream of light bounced around the room. It rebounded on strategically placed mirrors, or highly polished discs that gave off an abundance of light, as though powered by electricity within the super-cavern.

'Oh my God,' mouthed Boyce, turning to look around the expansive cave.

'This technology can't be Egyptian,' said Joey, as the underground cavern came to life, revealing its true size as the shadows were banished.

The pyramid seemed even more ethereal with the lights on. The water was a transparent milky blue, displaying the rectangular footings, monoliths and obelisks.

Movement on the surface, golden with flashes of green, revealed a water boa, as it glided away from the light and sank to the bottom, out of sight.

No sign of crocodiles, though.

As soon as Youssef moved his flashlight's beam away from the crystal, the vast, empty space dimmed, so he raised his hand once more, and the light returned. 'It looks like we need four torches to keep this place lit,' he said as they continued to point upward.

Seconds later, Youssef spoke to Abdul in Arabic, which in turn caused Abdul to extract his firearm with his free hand.

Joey took a step back, fearful, his eyes filled with dread.

'Relax,' Youssef advised Joey. 'Boyce, come here and take my place while I search the pyramid for any hieroglyphics,' he said casually, swapping places with the youth.

Youssef could hardly contain his excitement. He began to search the perimeter of the room, his thoughts racing. He had made it through to the last secret chamber to find this unexpected wonder, but he still had so many unanswered questions. Why was it here? And what was inside it that could be so valuable to Nefertiti that she wanted it kept secret?

After reaching the far end of the chamber and turning back, he spotted something within the pyramid that stopped him in his tracks. It took a second or two for the new information to sink in, even though it was right before his eyes. His lips stretched wide into a triumphant grin.

'I found something,' he called out.

A rectangular doorway the size of a small backyard pool had been partially concealed by limestone bricks, but its discolored render in the newly lit-up chamber made it easy to identify the brick pattern. It seemed like the opening had been erected in a hurry, as the otherwise meticulous Egyptians would never have made such a mistake in its design.

Perhaps it was Nefertiti's last act to hide the secret she had promised to protect until her dying breath. Whatever was concealed inside was now within his grasp, and he knew exactly what needed to be done.

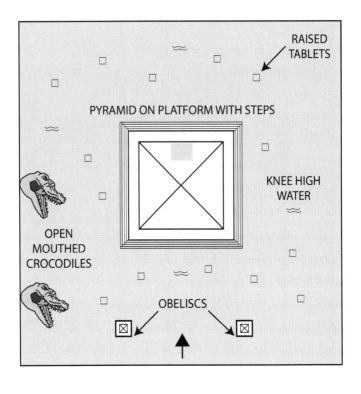

Chapter 31

Youssef's discovery gave Marie a nervous kind of energy that ran right through her body. She wanted to know what it was, but she also knew she needed to find another way to keep the cavern lit.

'What are you doing?' asked Joey as she moved away from the group.

Abdul's hand hovered over his nine-millimeter.

She leaned her flashlight against the pyramid in an upright position and the light dimmed for a brief moment.

'Hey,' Abdul grunted.

Marie adjusted the position of the flashlight until the yellow beam ran straight into the crystal capstone, and voilà, she was free to roam as she pleased.

'I'll be right back,' she said, taking off down the square platform, where at the corner edge, she found Youssef kicking at the discolored section he'd found in the wall. She identified the outline of shoebox-sized bricks that indicated where a doorway had once resided, and been bricked up. The render in this segment had crumbled away, clearly distinguishing the new from the old.

'We need to get inside,' Youssef breathed, persisting

with his forceful push-kicks but not making any progress. Marie had to smile inwardly. He was not the typical archeologist or Indiana Jones character that one would envisage among the tombs and ruins. He was the opposite: a clean-cut, self-controlled personality, who always reaped the rewards and used gophers to carry out the simplest of tasks for him.

Minutes later, Abdul, Joey and Boyce, having followed Marie's lead with their flashlights, joined them, and their eyebrows shot up at the sight.

'The entrance seems to have been covered up here,' Marie pointed out, moving closer to study the surface. She touched the soft render with her fingers. 'It doesn't have the same finish as the rest of it,' she said, turning to face Youssef. 'What did you call the substance the Egyptians used at the final polishing stage?'

'Tura limestone,' Youssef replied, before about-facing and mentioning something in Arabic to his accomplice, who stepped forward and extracted a knife from his utility belt.

Joey and Boyce braced themselves, giving him a wide berth, not wanting to cop the sharp end of his blade. Who knew what Abdul had just been instructed to do? The man was violent and unpredictable and had proved himself loyal to the man running the show, making him even more dangerous. He sauntered over to the wall where Marie was, his hand tightly closed around the handle of his knife, and the cold look on his face gave her chills.

Marie stepped away, petrified.

Then Abdul flipped the knife and jabbed his blade

between the bricks. His jagging motion was quick and hard and he ate into the mortar a bit at a time. After five minutes or so, the pointy edge found its way through.

'It's hollow,' he confirmed, continuing to dig around the first brick.

Once the block was loose, Abdul repositioned himself and used his upper body strength to push the single solid block inward with his shoulder. On his third nudge, the limestone piece fell to the ground and his arm was forced in with it, causing him to lose his balance and hit up against the wall. Pulling his body out with a grunt, he stood upright and peered into the hole for a brief moment. He frowned.

Now that the structure had been weakened, he used his steel-capped boot to hammer down around the opening, the bricks falling one after the other in a domino effect. Once the dust had subsided, a hole generous enough for a person to enter presented itself. Clearing the way forward, Abdul entered the well-lit chamber, stepping over the broken debris.

'Don't you think we should wait a while for the bad air to escape?' asked Boyce apprehensively. 'It's been sealed for a long time.'

'You have a point,' said Joey. 'Give it a moment.'

'Try to stop me,' Marie said, smiling at her friends, and they saw the first sign in a long while of her usual carefree and stubborn attitude. They had gone through hell to get to this very spot and she didn't want to just wait, as the anticipation was killing her. Without another thought, stale air or no stale air, she stepped into the fray, careful not to cut her exposed toes on the broken bricks.

Inside the pyramid, Marie glanced quickly around. It wasn't what she had expected at all. There were no tombs. No sarcophagi. No grand gallery and no gold treasures. It was hollow, like an enormous hall, the same pyramidal shape as the outside. She caught Abdul's eye and looked quickly away. She wanted nothing to do with that creep.

The base of the building was wide and square. Dolerite stones encircled its perimeter, like in graveyards of immense importance. At the pinnacle above, the bottom end of the crystal showed itself. It seemed built into the structure, like the stone in a diamond ring held in place with giant claws. The light filtered in from above and flashed a spotlight on a hollow wheel-shaped structure that was thirty feet tall with a slender depth of twenty inches. Its heavy-weighted construction was held upright by its indented limestone base, as though it was in its own man-made vice. The narrow material was solid and sturdy and had a gunmetal-gray appearance to it.

Either side of the circular structure sat two mysterious nine feet tall pyramids that were covered by custom-made Aswan timber helmets with handles.

Marie's eyes widened in puzzled thought, trying to make sense of it.

Youssef came through the hole in the wall, maneuvering over the bricks at his feet. Once through he stood speechless, lost for words. Marie could tell he, too, was trying to process what was in front of him.

'This better be worthwhile,' said Boyce, treading with caution over the debris, as he too entered the pyramid barefoot. 'If I die because of this bad air . . .' he muttered. Once through, he pinched his nose to avoid the awful smell. Then he too froze and stood speechless with a perplexed expression.

'What the hell?' were Joey's words when he entered the inner sanctum.

'It looks like we found what Nefertiti promised to hide,' answered Youssef, his eyes on the structure on the central platform. He took a step closer to examine it.

'What is this thing?' asked Abdul, dumbfounded, standing opposite Youssef.

Youssef didn't respond, obviously trying to make sense of it himself.

'Hang on, what's under these timber hats?' said Boyce, drawing everyone's attention away from the focal point in the room. With Joey's help they carefully lifted one of the hollow helmet-like cover plates to discover a dark, shiny black granite capstone covered in carved images.

Youssef's eyes widened.

'Help me with this one now,' asked Abdul to Joey to the twin that sat on the opposite side of the room.

Abdul raised the timber cover with Joey's help.

Sighs of astonishment erupted all around as they peered at the sight before them, the teen's discovery of the inferior pyramidion all but forgotten. This one glistened with a dominating yellow glow that evoked a pharaonic sense of royalty and power.

Youssef had just hit the mother lode of all treasures. 'The golden capstone,' he breathed. 'I can't believe it.'

One of the most revered objects in all of history, lost in time, was standing in front of them all. It was made entirely of gold and stood nine feet tall, the size required to have completed the Great Pyramid of Giza. It was inscribed with mysterious carvings and symbols, dominated by the right eye of Horus, an Egyptian symbol associated with the sun god, and called the Eye of Ra.

'Archeologists have been searching for the Great Pyramid's capstone forever and it has been down here all along,' said Marie. 'This is an enormous find.'

Youssef smiled knowingly back at her, as if to suggest that the steep price they'd all paid to come so far was justified by the find. Marie looked away, disgusted.

'So why isn't this sitting at the top of the pyramid?' asked Joey. 'Why is it here?'

'Akhenaten's sun cult, also known as the Cult of Amun-Ra, must have moved it here,' speculated Youssef, rubbing his hand over it like a child being given a precious gift on his birthday. 'They were the priests said to have placed the golden capstone on the apex of the pyramid, and so I assume they would have been the ones to take it down.'

'But why?' asked Joey, like an annoying child.

'I think I might know why,' said Boyce, gesturing to Marie to come over to where he remained hovering over his not-so-attractive granite pyramidion.

Marie approached Boyce with a puzzled expression, kneeled beside him on the limestone floor and took a look at what he was showing her. Four simple consecutive drawings were laid out in a vertical column sequence.

A man holding on to a box.

A long object in his hand.

A figure silhouetted against a circular light.

A line that ascends north from the apex of a pyramid.

Marie darted her eyes back to the hollow wheel-shaped structure, then turned to the group as she held in a smile. 'Maybe the gold capstone of the Great Pyramid of Giza is here because it has something to do with the Stargate that is staring us right in the face.'

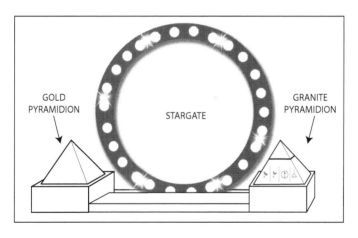

Chapter 32

'Stargate?' repeated Joey, rolling his eyes. 'I knew you would say that the moment I saw it. Come on, babe, this ain't no science fiction movie.'

'That's right,' said Boyce with a beaming smile. 'The one with James Spader and Kurt Russell.' His eyes darted over Marie and Joey. 'I love that film,' he breathed. 'You don't think this could teleport us to another star deep in space?'

'No, I don't,' said Joey with a shake of his head.

'Kalium Galaxy,' blurted Boyce in jest, remembering where they ended up traveling to in the nineties blockbuster. 'This one doesn't have any symbols on it, though, it's clean and sleek. How would we dial home?'

Joey shook his head again, as though he sometimes wondered if he was surrounded by idiots.

'If it were true,' said Youssef, admiring the alien-like construction. 'It would explain why Nefertiti wanted it kept a secret.' He turned to face the group, who wore mystified expressions. 'The answer to *are we alone in the universe* could be answered. Did our species come from someplace else or did we evolve from natural selection, like Charles Darwin mentioned in his book,

On the Origin of Species in 1859?' He took a breath, paused, then continued. 'Faith in the almighty God could be expunged and downgraded to myth. There is no greater discovery than the one we have at our fingertips, people. We must find out how to activate it.'

Marie ran her finger up the carved drawings on the granite capstone and stopped on the man holding a box. She paused for a moment and thought about the image. There was nothing inside this ancient pyramid that resembled any type of container. Struggling to solve the puzzle, she spotted a thin indented line that ran around the entire crest of the pyramidion. It caught her eye since the groove was deeper than any other on its hard surface.

'I think this top section might come off,' she said, just loud enough for Boyce to hear, as he was squatting next to her. She positioned her feet against the stone floor and leaned in to get a grip on the tip of the pyramid, in the hope that it would tilt or move out of place.

She thrust her weight forward and it moved. As she had guessed, a second piece sat camouflaged from above.

'There's a secret cavity underneath,' whispered Boyce excitedly.

Marie smiled back and nodded her head.

Inevitably, Youssef approached, as did Joey, while Abdul stayed with the golden capstone on the other side.

With their backs straight and their knees bent, Boyce helped Marie lift the crown end. They carried the granite cap piece, which must have weighed sixty pounds, to one side. With the cover plate removed, Marie peeked inside the inner cavity and found what she was searching for. She pulled the ornate chest out of the secret compartment and held it for all to see.

An etched cartouche was clearly visible; it most likely would have belonged to Akhenaten or Nefertiti. The box was stupendously valuable in itself. It was made from solid gold and inlaid with precious blue and green stones, just like the ones on Tutankhamun's death mask, or as they had come to understand tonight, the veil that was first constructed to fit his mother, Nefertiti.

On the face of the chest was an extractable rotating sun-disc puzzle piece. It was Akhenaten's symbol for invoking the one true monotheist god, Ra.

Marie turned it clockwise and heard the sound of a mechanism opening with a click. She flipped the lid backwards and found inside two peculiar spotted dolerite stones of different sizes. The purple-blue rock was thinner and shorter than its warmer red twin. They were beautiful and seemed to have been laser cut, shaved and sanded down to form perfectly shaped triangular prisms.

'Superman's kryptonite,' joked Boyce with a frown, waiting for Marie to answer.

Marie smiled and cupped the red stone in her hand for all to see. 'Look to see if you can find a hole that fits its shape,' she suggested, while peering over to the central structure. 'I think it might be a key of some sort.'

Boyce proceeded to investigate.

'Can we please stop with this bullshit already,' said Joey. 'There's no such thing as a Stargate. Teleportation is inconceivable.'

'After all you've seen tonight?' said Marie, always with an open mind.

'But you're talking about science fiction,' said Joey. 'Did you ever consider that this could be some type of weapon or bomb?'

'Looks like we're in the middle of a domestic,' said Abdul dryly. 'My money is on the female, she seems to have the balls in this relationship.'

'I found it,' shouted Boyce moments later, his voice one of both dread and happiness. 'The triangular gap is one-and-a-half inches wide.'

'Give the boy the larger red stone, then,' ordered Youssef, wanting to reassert his control over the situation.

'Hang on,' said Boyce, palms raised. 'Before we begin stuffing the holes with these rocks, don't you want to discuss the possibility that this is in fact a Stargate to another galaxy? We need to think this through rationally; if there is another advanced civilization out there we could be in grave danger. Nefertiti had this hidden down here for a reason. Maybe it wasn't ever meant to be found.'

'Not likely,' uttered Joey. 'If there was a far superior race out there, don't you think they would have come back to Earth already?'

'Let's find out,' said Youssef, who looked over to Boyce and gestured to him to go ahead.

Marie gave up the red stone and Boyce turned and approached the distinctive hole in the contraption. He carefully slid the stone into it and it clicked into place. He stepped back, waiting for a reaction.

Five seconds went by.

Ten.

Thirty.

'See, I told you!' Joey said in triumph, turning his back to the structure. But no sooner had these words come out of his mouth than a zapping sound buzzed around the device in the center of the room. It was faint at first, but it soon began to build in intensity.

Joey turned with fearful eyes.

Youssef took another step back.

Marie licked her lips, which had gone completely dry.

The red dolerite stone seemed to be working like a battery, which started an electromagnetic pulse. Short bursts of life in the form of lightning strikes hit the top of the golden capstone and then ran upward to the giant crystal directly above. It seemed like it was gathering and blending shimmering energy fields of power from the Great Pyramid's core structure. The trickled-out beams were thickening with an assortment of colors, mainly white, electric blue and turquoise.

The group stood well away, petrified and silent, as a rumbling sound coming from the ring shook the chamber with a deafening roar.

Shhh boom!

The Stargate blasted to life with a flash of cerulean light that illuminated every corner of the room. The glow was almost blinding and created a ghostly waterfall within its circumference. The dazzling power of the structure showed itself, making them feel small and insignificant. They had just ignited a portal to God knew where. It was as if the Great Pyramid above, dormant and mysterious for so many centuries, was doing what it had been designed to do all along.

Chapter 33

The DGSE commanding general Julien Bonnet was en route in his dark Aérospatiale SA 330 Puma helicopter. Swooping low over the Egyptian desert, blowing loose sand every which way as they approached the Giza plateau, Julien was following the emergency beacon activated by one of his men. He never abandoned a man in need. Never. Not in his earlier days leading his troops into battle, and not now while in command of the French Intelligence Agency. Boyce had become his youngest protégé after he had helped discover the location of Alexander the Great's resting place. The distress beacon was only to be used for an emergency. He had made that drastically clear. He knew Boyce had to be in mortal danger and so might his friend Youssef.

Sitting in the co-pilot's chair, he wore a helmet piece with a microphone over his thick snow-white hair, while four of his elite commandos sat in the rear armed and ready to deploy. Julien was in his seventies, and if it hadn't been for a distinctive scar on his temple, he would have been an attractive man for his age.

'The beacon is coming from the Sphinx,' he said in

accented English through his microphone to the pilot sitting next to him, who then banked left around the triplet of Pyramids.

The blades sliced through the thick air, but in the blink of an eye, everything changed. A dazzling straight laser beam of white light suddenly blasted into the night sky from the apex of the Great Pyramid with a roaring *boom!*

Julien was blinded by its intensity and power, and he sat dumbfounded, his mouth ajar. The cabin within the helicopter was now a fluorescent blue, as was the rest of Egypt, it seemed, as the pilot turned the chopper to face it and hover at a safe distance away. The sight was breathtaking, a once-in-a-lifetime event that needed to be appreciated and cherished.

Julien's eyes widened in wonder.

Then, as quickly as it had come alive, the beam of light was shut off like a computer that had had its plug tugged from its socket. The pitch-black sky once again occupied the heavens and there was complete darkness. It took a second for Julien's eyes to readjust from the bright-blue hue, and in that moment the helicopter's communication lights switched off, the control-panel console becoming a dark blur. It was immediately clear the engine had ceased as well, and the rotating blades began to slow.

Panic ensued in the cockpit as the pilot tried to reboot the systems, frantically switching notches on and off in the hope that it would come back to life.

Julien glanced at the city skyline in the distance and it was the same, nothing but blackness.

Egypt had been thrown into the dark ages.

'We're going down!' the pilot warned. 'Brace for impact.'

'No time, we need to jump,' called out Julien, taking off his helmet and opening his door. 'Now! Evacuate!'

Julien and the commandos leaped out of the helicopter in the nick of time, just as the chopper pitched to one side and dropped quickly to the ground, where a billowing fireball heralded its end. After a twenty-eight-foot drop, Julien's lean frame landed on the uneven sandy terrain. Bending his knees to take most of the impact, he used his forward momentum in a commando roll that ended with him coming up against a small limestone wall.

'I'm too old for this,' he grumbled as the flames of the chopper burned only feet away, the heat of the fire felt all over his now bruised and aching body.

All that remained was a mess of mangled metal.

He stood up holding his rib cage and was soon greeted by his team, who were in various states of pain and discomfort. One soldier had a gushing wound on his forehead, but he didn't seem to mind. Julien trained his people to push through the pain of injury and he was proud of the fact.

'You okay, sir?' asked his senior commando.

Julien looked at the four men, all carrying flashlights and hefting their bags over their shoulders, and his expression became one of distress. Someone was missing. 'Where's Victor?' he asked quietly. Their saddened faces and lowered heads said it all. Their pilot had gone down with his helicopter.

'What in the hell happened?' said one of the younger commandos.

'The pyramid must have produced some kind of EMP that wiped out all the power on the grid,' suggested Julien.

'The beacon is eight hundred and twenty yards down this slope,' informed the lead commando, holding the GPS tracking device he had pulled out from his pack. 'We have night-vision goggles to get us there.'

Julien nodded his head, accepted the gear and together with his team proceeded to the Sphinx. He was ready to go to war if the situation called for it.

Chapter 34

The City of Cairo in Darkness

Five thousand years ago electricity didn't exist. The Egyptians used fire and entertained one another with conversations and feasts that lasted hours, even days. Fast-forward to the twenty-first century and electric power has become a necessity. Our entire way of living is based on technology in some way or another, and the ability to communicate instantly with anyone and everyone. To have those ubiquities snuffed out in the blink of an eye brought fear and panic to all in the region.

No light.

No transportation.

No internet.

Chaos flooded Egypt as it fell into darkness. Screams of terror were heard in the streets of Cairo. Any car that was built after the 1980s, which would have been ninety-nine per cent of the vehicles in the Egyptian capital, had been rendered useless by the electromagnetic pulse emitted from the machine beneath the Great Pyramid. All electronically controlled systems, from fuel injection to transmission controls and everything in between, would have been destroyed in that instant, transforming each vehicle into nothing more than an expensive paperweight. God forbid if anyone had been stuck in a dark tunnel doing fifty miles an hour.

Bang! Bang! Bang!

The sound of screeching brakes echoed throughout the city, ending in a gridlock of smashes. That was just the beginning.

Planes fell from the skies as small airliners to jumbo jets exploded all over the place. One Emirates Boeing 777 holding three hundred passengers nose-dived onto the port of the river Nile. A blinding flash came from the point where the plane struck, and a billowing white cloud rose into the air.

One Aegean Airbus crashed into a towering building in haunting imitation of the 9/11 attacks in New York City, and killed hundreds. The enormous explosion was like a fist of orange flame that punched its way out of the structure. Windows shattered and smoke and fire gushed out as the structure collapsed on itself. Thick ash consumed the people caught in its wake as pieces of glass, steel and concrete showered down in a deadly rainfall.

There seemed to be no way of escaping this plague. From afar, it would have looked like a scene depicting the end of the world in a horror movie.

Cairo was turned upside down and the panic sadly and very quickly turned to violence and crime. Bricks were used to smash into stores, and service stations were ransacked and robbed. The alarms did not buzz, there were no police cars, no ambulance sirens. The metropolitan area was etched in charcoal and every man and woman was left to fend for themselves.

One man wrapped his shirt around a stick and lit it on fire like a twenty-first-century caveman. It was official. The beautiful city of Cairo, home to nine million people, had gone back to the brutal stone ages.

Chapter 35

Fearing what he had just triggered, Boyce hurriedly removed the red-spotted dolerite stone from the portal. To his surprise, the blue-white glow that illuminated outward from within the Stargate didn't shut down. It continued to shimmer a translucent wavy cloud that reflected off the inside walls of the pyramid. Boyce took a hesitant step backwards, gazing over to his friends in despair.

'What have I done?' he said, looking down at the stone in the palm of his hand. His heart beat erratically, racing with mixed emotions.

'It's still working without the keystone,' breathed Marie.

'What do we do now?' Joey asked, protecting his eyes from the glare.

'Enter it,' said Youssef quietly with a slow grin.

Terrified eyes turned to the Cambridge archeologist.

'No way!' said Boyce, stumbling backwards. 'I'm not going in that.' He shook his head decisively. 'Who knows what's on the other side, and if we would even survive the journey.'

On cue, Abdul raised his weapon and aimed it at

Boyce, who looked at it tiredly. He tried to assess the situation. He knew there was no democracy here. This was a dictatorship, and the man in charge was destined to get what he pleased. They had uncovered the final secret hidden deep within the Walk of Souls, and the three of them were now in a perilous situation. They were expendable and extremely vulnerable. He'd known it all along.

'Put that gun away,' Marie barked just as Boyce surrendered, his shaky hands held aloft. 'Come on, Youssef, there's no "I" in team.' She said it playfully, trying to calm the situation from escalating into a bloodbath.

Youssef paused in thought for a moment then replied sarcastically, 'There may be no "I" in team, Marie, but there sure is an "I" in win, and that's what I plan to do.' A grin stretched across his face.

'We need to be rational,' Joey reminded him, darting his eyes between the two Arabs about to order the impossible. 'How about we come back with a camera to make sure it's safe? We can use a selfie stick to record what happens as we enter the portal.'

Joey's suggestion was ignored.

'Boyce, you have five seconds to enter the Stargate before Abdul starts shooting,' warned Youssef. 'We all have to make choices in life,' he continued. 'Do you want to live or die? Or do you want your friends to die on your behalf? That's just as easy. It's totally up to you.'

'No! Wait!' pleaded Boyce, unable to form a proper sentence.

'Don't be stupid, man,' said Joey desperately. 'We can work this out.'

Youssef started his life-threatening countdown.

'Five … Four …'

'We can come to an agreement,' interrupted Marie as she eyed Abdul's Glock, which was now pointed in her direction. 'It doesn't have to go down this way.'

'Three …'

Unexpectedly, like a sign from the heavens above, Boyce was thrilled to witness the Stargate's bright glow switch off, leaving them with only the ambient light from the crystal fluttering down from above.

Youssef sighed and glanced over at the now inactive, colorless ring.

Boyce swallowed hard. It was a tense moment for him as he held on to the keystone with a rapidly beating heart. He played scenarios out in his mind and contemplated his chances of survival. It felt like an eternity before someone spoke again and he tried to keep quiet, hoping they would ignore him.

'How long did it stay on without the keystone?' Youssef asked, breaking the uncomfortable silence.

'About a minute or so,' said Marie, once again playing the helpful victim.

Youssef relaxed his shoulders, stretched his neck and flashed a closed smile that made Boyce wonder what he was up to.

'Tonight we have finally discovered the secret Nefertiti promised her husband she would hide,' said Youssef, taking a few steps over to his right. 'The three Pyramids at the Giza plateau were aligned to the star constellation Orion. They were all created for the one single purpose: to produce energy with which to power this Stargate, if that's what this is, found at the belly of the Great Pyramid. We know that now, but there are so many other questions yet to be answered.'

'I agree,' said Marie, nodding her head. 'What I want to know is why was Nefertiti so afraid of Akhenaten's father? What led her to conceal the Stargate in such a hurry?' she continued. 'The stela we found in the empty sarcophagus mentioned that they needed to seal it to save the life of their son and future king, Tutankhamun. Why was he at risk from his grandfather? I don't get it. And the last comment, *he who will open the door will end life as we know it …*' Marie paused to take a quick breath. 'Now that we've discovered the Stargate, have we somehow opened the doors that might lead us to our extinction by a superior race?'

'It sure opens up a can of worms,' said Joey. 'I think it's too risky. We should listen to the queen's warnings and abort before it's too late.'

'Don't you want to know who placed this portal here in the first place?' asked Youssef. 'The mystery of whether we're alone in this universe can be answered.' He licked his lips, obviously enjoying the possibilities. 'And if there are aliens on the other side of this, are they human like us? And the one-hundred-million-dollar question …' he said with a long pause.

'What's that?' asked Boyce, his arm stretched downward, trying to hide the keystone in his fist.

'Was it them who created Homo sapiens on Earth two hundred thousand years ago, or did we evolve from apes like the scientists would have us believe? Or did we flourish from Adam and Eve, as the Bible indicates? The answer to this age-old question is not just a prediction anymore and we don't need to take it on faith. It can be attained right here and right now and I *must* know.'

With that said, he reached for his nine-millimeter and held it sideways like a twenty-year-old thug from the hood. 'Time to find out the truth.'

'Come on, put your gun away,' murmured Marie. 'No one needs to die just to prove who our makers are.'

'Is there any other way?' Youssef retorted, turning to stare into Boyce's brown eyes. 'Switch it back on,' he said through gritted teeth. 'I'll give you three seconds this time. I suggest you don't waste any of them.'

Boyce peered over to his friends with a fearful expression. He thought about making a move, but Youssef and Abdul were both prepared for an oncoming assault. If he attacked, it would only end with a bullet in his chest – or his friends'.

Abdul trained his weapon on Joey and stepped back.

Youssef started counting.

Boyce swallowed hard.

'Three ... Two ...'

Boyce had no time to think, and no options left. He moved over to the portal and inserted the red stone resting in his hand.

'One ...'

The eerie harmonics recommenced. Boyce felt his stomach rise into his throat as the rumbling sound shook the room once more.

Shh-boom!

The Stargate came alive faster than the previous

time, as if it had been pre-charged from the first attempt. Its glow was even more radiant this time, like the sun, causing everyone to look away and cover their eyes.

'How about we test it first?' said Joey in a loud voice. 'Toss something into it and see what happens.'

'Yes,' said Marie quickly, keeping her distance but hoping their captors would agree. 'What can we use?' she said, scanning the inside of the pyramid.

'Abdul, why don't you throw your gun inside,' joked Joey, always one to say the most inappropriate thing at the wrong time.

'Funny man,' mocked Abdul with an irritated expression written on his face. He pointed to the ornate golden chest left on the limestone floor. 'Remove the second bluestone and use the box.'

Boyce nodded in agreement and picked it up, and with an underarm motion, gently tossed the empty container at the light source.

Whoop ... The ring mechanism sucked it in like a fat kid eating chocolate cake and it disappeared, as predicted, into its vortex.

'It's time for a human to enter the portal,' said Abdul, nudging Boyce forward with his Glock.

Marie reacted, placing her petite frame in front of Boyce, obstructing both Abdul and Youssef's line of sight. Joey did the same at the forefront, covering Marie, but it seemed Youssef's patience had run out.

Youssef squeezed the trigger and fired his gun at Joey's thigh – the same leg Abdul had sliced into not so long ago – sending him backwards into Marie's arms as she tried to break his fall. His weight was too great, though, and they both collapsed, toppling over each other.

'Stop this,' cried Marie, struggling back to her feet, while Abdul grinned, seeming to be enjoying the situation way too much. Moaning in pain, Joey lay on his side on the floor, unable to get up.

Youssef stretched out his armed hand and directed his gun at Marie. 'The next bullet has your name on it.'

'Enough already!' shouted Boyce, springing to her defense. 'I'll do it. Just put your guns down.' His words were filled with conviction. If he could save his friends, it was worth the risk.

Marie gave him a hesitant stare as if to say, *What are you doing?*

Boyce rubbed her shoulder affectionately and told her it was okay.

'Boyce, don't do it,' grunted Joey, before Abdul positioned his Glock at the back of the American's head, and he fell silent.

'One more peep out of you and I'll blow your brains out.'

'If I don't see you two again,' said Boyce as a tear ran down his cheek, 'it has been a pleasure to be your friend and I love you both dearly.'

Boyce turned to face the glimmering cloud that he knew would probably be the death of him. He thought about the mid-thirteen-hundreds B.C., possibly the last time the machine had been used by Nefertiti. The small hairs on the back of his neck stood up as he approached the apex of the gel-like structure that looked like water flowing in a ring.

'Please, God don't let this kill me,' he prayed, then stretched out a tentative hand toward it. He was an arm's length away from the turbulent energy field of light. He shut his eyes, took one last deep breath and stepped forward.

Chapter 36

Marie's mouth fell open as her friend vanished into the shimmering light. Her expression was one of utter disbelief as Boyce disappeared into the ring's inner vacuum. He had sacrificed himself to save his friends and now she feared she would never see his beautiful boyish smile again.

Tear marks lined her face. Her blood boiled up inside as she turned around to see the smirking madman, a self-obsessed, murdering lunatic with daddy issues. He needed to be taught a lesson, but the thought of what he would ask for next brought shivers down her spine.

'Are you happy now?' she scowled.

'After so many years, this thing actually works,' Youssef said with reverence.

Abdul nodded his head, dumbfounded.

Joey limped to his feet, avoiding putting pressure on his wounded leg, pain carved all over his face. Dark stains of blood could be seen through the wet jeans that clung to his unsteady body. Marie helped him up by placing her arms under his shoulders, while glaring at Youssef, who still stood in a commanding position with his Glock trained on them.

'Boyce is gone now,' she said, sadness in every word. 'Joey is injured. What now? What is your next move?'

Youssef peered past the couple to the energy field blasting away and took his time to form a reply. From his position, they would have been silhouetted against the blinding light glowing behind them. His eyes glistened, reflecting the continuing wave that was a hundred shades of blue and white.

With an evil smirk that widened when he finally spoke, he commanded, 'Now it's your turn to enter.'

Abdul seemed delighted at the thought that the revenge he had promised Joey was finally coming.

Joey didn't say a word, but his horrified eyes came alive. He sighed, faced the limestone beneath his feet and shook his head disapprovingly.

Marie was livid. She glared at Youssef, her rage building. 'I can't believe your plan is to sacrifice everyone in this room,' said Marie. 'You're a monster.'

'Go find your friend and bring him back,' said Youssef evenly, lowering his armed hand. 'Don't be afraid to step into the light. It seems our ancestors had been doing this for millennia before Nefertiti shut it down. You will be the first woman of the twenty-first century to venture into the unknown and hopefully come back to us with the answers we seek.'

'You realize what we have done,' said Marie with a heavy sigh. 'We have opened the doors to a possible invasion by a galactic army to end all of humankind.'

'That's a risk I'm prepared to take.'

'That's because you're not taking the risk, we are.'

Youssef flashed a sadistic grin.

At this point Abdul tucked his Glock out of sight and stood three feet away. Joey was clearly no threat to him anymore, shaking in his girlfriend's arms as he dealt with the pain of his wounded leg.

Marie paused for a moment to think and looked toward Youssef. He was of average height, wealthy and well educated, a guarded man who most probably had never had a physical fight in his life. He had computer hands, his nails were clean and manicured, and his face was clean-shaven. He was a person who took care of himself with creams and moisturizers.

She darted her eyes over to Abdul. He was the complete opposite. His hands were thick and rough like leather, his face wrinkled and his beard unkempt. Abdul could have been ten years younger than his boss, but his harsh life made him seem ten years older.

Turning back to Youssef, she told herself, *I can take him.*

They had reached the end of the road to the last secret chamber; there were no more rooms to discover. No more death traps or puzzles to solve. This was it. She had known that there would come a time when they would have to fight for their freedom, and now was that time.

She turned to face Joey, letting him stand on his own two feet, her back now toward the enemy. She leaned in and gave her man a loving peck on the lips, then tore off a piece of her dress to wrap around his wounded leg, along with Boyce's sleeve, as the bizarre harmonics continued to issue from the ring.

'Are you okay?' she asked him.

'I'll live,' said Joey, downplaying his pain, trying to be his macho self.

'Before we enter this circle of death, we need to do one more thing,' she said in a whisper against his ear.

'What's that?' asked Joey, gazing into her alluring hazel eyes.

'We need to *dance*.'

Joey's tight-lipped expression and widening eyes indicated that he understood what was required of him. Before they had entered the Sphinx, she had mentioned the term as a code word to revolt and fight back when the time called for it. It was now or never. They needed to turn the tables back in their favor or face an unknowable situation. Joey had to take on the armed, bearded Arab despite his wounded leg, while Marie would try to overpower Youssef.

Marie gave Joey one last kiss and caught her boyfriend's glistening blue eyes. He nodded, game face on. As her lips left his, she slowly built up a frown and clenched her teeth. The anger boiling up deep inside her was ready to explode in the form of a deadly strategically planned attack.

Then without hesitation it happened.

Unexpectedly, she turned at lightning speed as though she was about to take off from the starting blocks.

Joey did the same in the opposite direction, toward Abdul.

Marie pounced on Youssef like a wild cat attacking its prey. Her balled fist collided with his unsuspecting cheekbone, snapping his neck backwards like a willow caught in the wind. He dropped to the ground over the debris of broken bricks as his gun was flung out of his hand and flew through the hole they'd made in the exterior, landing somewhere outside.

Her action had certainly taken him by surprise.

Marie dashed to find the weapon. If she got to it in time she could save her man. She could see him tackling Abdul on the floor, but Abdul was exploiting his weakness and indisputably had the upper hand.

Time was against them.

Exiting the jagged opening with haste, Marie spotted the Heckler & Koch resting by the stone steps where the water began. She reached for it and leaned over to pick it up, just as Youssef came roaring after her.

The businessman's face was consumed with rage. Unthinkingly, Marie aimed and squeezed the trigger, missing him completely. She fired once more and the next bullet seemed to graze his shoulder, but it wasn't enough to stop his charge.

She was too late.

Bang!

Youssef collided with her small frame, causing her to fumble and lose control of the Heckler & Koch.

Plonk ...

The sound of the nine-millimeter breaking the surface of the calm lake made them both turn in panic; their two bodies followed seconds later, splashing into the knee-high water. Struggling for position, Marie found her footing and faced the man who wanted to kill her right here, right now.

Inside the enormous cavern, lit by a crystal

pyramidion on the oldest Wonder of the World, she clenched her hands into fists, the only defense left to her, and prepared to fight for her life. Her fear kept her alert as she lashed out and jabbed her attacker in the nose, causing a stream of blood to cascade onto his white shirt.

Youssef paused to touch and taste his own gore and then, oddly, he smiled, as if impressed with Marie's ferocity.

Marie backpedaled in the water. He wasn't as weak as she had thought and had taken the punch better than she'd anticipated. Then she remembered that he had done time in the French army. This wasn't going to be easy. Her heart pounded almost out of her chest as her arms tensed to strike again. She needed to take him down or she would not live to see another day. She stumbled backwards upon a stone pillar as Youssef moved toward her.

The small monolith was one of the many scattered across the site, its uppermost surface nearly level with the water's edge. It pictured a man's body with a reptilian head, described earlier by Youssef as being the Egyptian god Sobek; the God of the Nile river.

Youssef reached out and grabbed her by the neck. Marie rammed a knee into his groin, and he winced for a second but didn't go down. Releasing one hand from her neck, he directed a stinging backhanded slap across her face. Feeling the burn on her cheek, she threw a hard fist at him that was deflected by his forearm. Still holding her neck, he swung her around and then grabbed her from behind, forcing her arms against her body.

'Don't worry, I will kill you slowly,' his raw voice said, brutal against her ear.

Marie struggled against him, her hands moving from her waist. Youssef seized her elbows, trapping them by her sides. He was too strong. He pushed her roughly, causing Marie to stumble and fall flat on her face into the water.

As she raised herself above the surface, Youssef waded through and forced her back under. It seemed like he had gone mad and was singly focused on ending her life. She tried to loosen his grip on her hair as she entered the water.

'Help!' she screamed, trying to stay afloat as she gulped for air.

Youssef plunged her head under again.

Under the shallow water all she could hear was the sound of her own bubbles and muffled cries. A memory came crashing into her mind. Not so long ago in Paris, the Louvre curator Pierre Savard had forced her head under the cold murk of the Seine River. She had tried to forget the memory of nearly drowning in the city she loved so much. Now, she was reliving it again in an ancient underground chamber in Egypt.

Marie fought and surfaced once more, gagging and spluttering, but she could feel herself weakening.

Under she went again.

Suddenly the sound of gunfire could be heard, coming, Marie thought, from inside the pyramid complex. Fighting to stay alive, she prayed Joey had not been shot again, but she needed to worry about herself now. This time the panic had her heart hammering against her ribs, and every cell in her body was screaming for oxygen.

She swallowed some water. She was near the end, she knew. It was now or never.

Seeing the stone pillar in front of her, she lurched forward and out of the water, coming to rest on top of it.

Youssef's eyes widened as her hand touched the seal over Sobek. 'The God of the Nile river,' he muttered, as he turned toward a roaring sound that was building in intensity. 'What have you done?' he said, bracing himself.

An instant later a burst of rushing water gushed out of the two enormous crocodile mouth holes. The force of the water lifted them both off their feet and swirled them around, like a waterslide ride, while also putting some distance between them. The God of the Nile had unleashed his fury into the super-cavern. To make the situation even more drastically interesting, as the water rose, complete darkness fell upon the outside of the pyramid structure.

Chapter 37

With Marie's plan to strike at the heart of the enemy in motion, Joey used his shoulder to collide with Abdul's chest, winding him and causing them both to stumble near the lip of the Stargate that was still blasting with life. Abdul reacted and reached for his gun. Joey deflected it away from his body and grasped at the man's wrist with his left hand as they rolled on the limestone floor, fighting for balance.

The struggle intensified.

Two shots were fired into the air that ricocheted inside the pyramid's walls, echoing within the super-cavern.

Joey landed two quick blows to Abdul's stomach and managed to knock the Glock over toward the jagged opening that would lead them outside. With momentum on his side, Joey wrapped his legs around Abdul's torso and squeezed as forcefully as he could, even though his thigh ached with the effort. Abdul wasn't having that, though, and reacted with a hard elbow into Joey's rib cage, forcing him to let go.

They both pushed themselves to their feet and began to circle one another, while the blinding Stargate lit up the showdown that had been in the making since the Cairo Museum. Joey felt as if he was back in the boxing ring up against his father, a man he could never beat in the confines of the purposely built arena that was his gymnasium. He thought about all the training that had prepared him to stand toe to toe with a man who was his father's equal, if called for.

Being the son of a notorious gangster who had many enemies, learning to fight had been a must within the family. To be able to defend yourself was to be respected. His father, an old-school fighter, would always tell him, *It's not the size of the dog in the fight, it's the size of the fight in the dog.* It was a quote that had stuck with him. He knew this was a brawl he needed to win. There was no second place if he wanted to live through this evening of hell.

'I have been waiting for this all night,' declared Abdul confidently, with fists raised.

'Well, you better come in hard,' said Joey through clenched teeth. 'Because I'm the wounded dog, and I'm not going down without a fight.'

Abdul shrugged and moved in with his broad upper torso, his biceps thick against his military attire. His rough, dark features displayed his toughness and his darker eyes told a story of a man that would not go down easily.

Joey swallowed as he prepared for the onslaught that was to come.

Abdul threw in a fast jab, and then another.

Joey blocked the first, but the second connected, making his head buzz; a feeling he remembered far too well from the boxing ring. Through the daze of stars, he heard an excruciating ringing noise. His mouth flooded with the taste of blood. He shook it away and raised his hands, this time swaying left to right, as he had been taught by his old man. Defending, but at the same time looking for a clear opening that might show itself.

He wanted to make sure he never felt the sting again.

At that moment Marie called out for help. She was in trouble. Joey's eyes darted outside as he imagined terrible thoughts of what Youssef could be doing to her. Fear rushed through him. He wanting nothing more than to go to her, but he also had a big problem to deal with standing an arm's length away.

Abdul noticed his momentary distraction and smashed him to the ground with another quick punch to his jaw. Joey had been caught off balance and fell hard on his back. First came the blackness, followed by the same ringing noise he had heard moments before, and now he could see blurry colors flying around his head.

Joey had had one simple objective: to take on and defeat the man who was twice his age, but he had failed to do so, utterly. Abdul, with the upper hand, kneeled down and dug his finger inside Joey's bloody bullet wound.

Joey howled in absolute agony. He had never felt so much pain before. He spat blood and saliva out of his mouth, cursing profoundly as blood gushed from his thigh, making him feel woozy and nauseous.

He rose up against the pain and used his free leg to push the leech off, but Abdul just came back for more, attacking at his weakest spot, going for his wound again. He knew if he kept it up, Joey would go into shock from losing too much blood.

In the fetal position, the weight of Abdul on top of him was crushing. From somewhere in the haze of semiconsciousness, Joey noticed that out through the jagged hole in the wall, where he'd heard Marie screaming, was now in complete blackness. It was as though someone had turned off the light switch.

A slither of gushing water found its way inside the pyramid.

Through his agony, Joey's father's voice entered his head as he lay defeated. *Never show fear, that is a sign of weakness. Always remember, you have Peruggia blood flowing through your veins. We are the lions in our jungle, and sometimes we need to unleash our wrath onto our enemies to let them know who they are up against.*

This was all the impetus Joey needed, as he garnered all his remaining strength and rose up like a bull, coming in hard with a push-kick that threw Abdul backwards onto the solid stone floor. He seemed to have hurt his back, as he arched his chest forward and grimaced.

He will not get the better of me, Joey thought with fierce determination, and without hesitation he leaped on Abdul while facing the dark opening. He straddled him like a horse and brought a fist to his face, snapping his nose into a grotesquerie.

The swinging blows continued, one after the other. Joey screamed maniacally, turning into the lion his father had said resided within him, his father's voice still echoing in his mind. He was out of control through the red fog of his rage. Blood poured from Abdul's nose and mouth, covering his entire face. Joey's emotions swirled in his head as he hammered down relentlessly.

Smash ... Smash ... Smash ...

He had had enough of being pushed around and being told what to do. He was going to rise up as the victor in this fight.

Abdul could barely open his eyes now, and he lay limply beneath Joey.

At that moment Joey noticed a figure standing near the jagged opening, bathed in the blue-and-white waterfall of light from the Stargate.

Sadly, it was Youssef.

His face came out of the shadow as he stepped closer. He seemed displeased and completely drenched.

Joey realized what he was up to when a cold smile spread across his devilish face.

Abdul's nine-millimeter lay by Youssef's soaking steel-capped boots. All he had to do was pick it up and shoot, and the Peruggia name would disappear from existence.

Chapter 38

The next couple of seconds happened in slow motion for Joey. A gradually increasing stream of water entered the structure through the jagged hole in the wall and was now pooling around Youssef's shoes. Youssef bent down to pick up Abdul's nine-millimeter. Joey knew he had to think fast. What was he to do? If he did nothing he would die.

The smirk widened on Youssef's face as he brought the gun up and aimed.

Joey reacted, lifting the unmoving Arab to his feet and lugging his dead weight onto his right shoulder, using the man's solid frame as a shield. Abdul didn't react, remaining limp as he was being manhandled, his face in a complete daze, as though he had drunk way too many beers.

Joey was desperate, his choice utter madness, but that was all he had to avoid the impending bullets. Wasting no time, he charged at Youssef, protecting his face as much as he could from the gunman.

Youssef fired his first bullet and missed. The projectile was a little too far to the right, hitting the limestone render wall and creating a loud acoustic sound that reverberated for a few seconds.

Joey was fifteen feet away.

Youssef triggered his next shot. This one was on target; however, it smacked into Abdul's backside. His body arched and he squealed as Joey continued his assault. The protective barrier was working.

Ten feet.

Joey proceeded with a roar. He told himself that even though each stride delivered an excruciating stabbing pain to his wounded leg, he could make his plan work; he needed to.

Youssef fired again. Joey ducked instinctively just as two bullets zinged past his face, one grazing his cheekbone, leaving a sharp sting and a small gash.

Seven feet.

Just as Youssef raised his gun for the final, lethal shot, his eyes blazing with fury, Youssef let out a howling scream of unbearable pain as a weighted EagleTac flashlight struck him in the head. He clenched his eyes and cupped his forehead with his left hand, yelling out an expletive, one that was well known even if you didn't speak Arabic.

The torch plummeted to the ground and splashed up muddy water over his already wet work-wear brown pants.

Joey gained vital seconds.

Four feet.

The time had come for Joey to discard his shield. His breathing became heavy and fast as he tossed Abdul's body at Youssef as though it were a piece of meat. It was met with a violent grunt of fury. Youssef squeezed his trigger-happy finger and unleashed a surge of bullets that tore effortlessly through the soft tissue in Abdul's chest, ending his life.

Unencumbered now, Joey sprang at Youssef with one thing on his mind: to shift the gun away from his hand.

It was going to be close.

Ravaged with bullet holes in his chest, Abdul was shoved out of the way by Youssef, who was searching for a clear shot to strike.

With outstretched arms, Joey grabbed Youssef's armed hand in the nick of time. He bulldozed it to one side as his momentum forced Youssef backwards over the debris of bricks and into the darkness.

Splash!

They entered the churning cold water and the world around them went eerily silent. In a rolling struggle, the two men hit the shallow bottom. Fifteen bullets in the clip plus the one in the chamber were squeezed and emptied into the abyss. Their twisted arms and flailing feet were hidden amid a cloud of breathing bubbles as they locked together, each trying to strangle the other.

In the scuffle underwater, the gun was knocked away and the small backpack carrying the priceless agate cup that could have been the vessel used in the Last Supper, was yanked off Youssef's back and left to drift away.

For once, Joey had the upper hand with Youssef, grabbing his mop-like hair and kneeing him in the face. Breaking the surface, Joey punched Youssef square in the nose as the businessman yelled at the top of his lungs, 'The cup!' He went to retrieve his backpack, but the incoming jets of water separated them and threw them around like rag dolls. The strong jets of water sent the current around the perimeter of the chamber in a clockwise direction, and Youssef disappeared out of sight.

Inside the pyramid, the Stargate portal continued to blast away, its glow reflecting out over the black waters that had once been a calm lake. With his head above water as the current took him round, Joey glimpsed the giant opened-mouthed crocodiles as they effortlessly injected gallons of water into the colossal cavern. The fact that they had been constructed thousands of years ago and were still working so effectively to this day, was a testament to how advanced their engineering must have been – mind-blowing, he mused.

Joey braced his strong leg on one of many underwater stone pillars depicting the God of the Nile, Sobek. Spitting out water, he swallowed and thought about Marie. The flashlight that had struck Youssef in the head and the sudden darkness in the chamber had to have been her doing. He called out to Marie in the hope of finding her unharmed, and not fighting to stay alive with a handful of bullet holes in her chest.

Joey was just catching his breath and gathering his strength when he noticed long, wriggling shadows entering the same pool of water he was trying to get out of. He was definitely not alone now. His heart sank as he realized that he was sharing the same space with agitated reptiles that had more razor-sharp teeth than you could count. These dinosaur-like creatures of the deep had been disturbed and drawn to this very spot. God help the man or woman who crossed their path.

Chapter 39

Four enormous sixteen-foot crocodiles slithered through the water, fighting among themselves, jaws snapping and enraged, having been forced 5.2 miles away from their habitat on the river Nile. The pressure of the incoming water pushed them past Joey, who was still propped up against the stone tablet that bore their image.

Joey turned and eyed the monsters as they cruised with the flow around the perimeter, all-powerful and menacing. In due time, the crocs would reach his position again. Panic gripped him in the cold murky water and he started to swim toward the high point of the chamber, the pyramid, not wanting his last breath to be squeezed from him by the jaws of such brutal killers.

He waded and pushed himself to his left against the force of water, his eyes constantly searching the darkness at his feet just in case another killer loomed ready to take him under. He stumbled, his wounded leg barely responding as he waded in the direction of the steps that were now completely submerged by water.

'Joey!' a voice shouted, and his heart leaped.

It was Marie; she was alive, moving with the current, fighting to stay afloat. 'Help!' Joey saw that she was about to cross the path where the incoming jets of water were pouring into the chamber. There was no escaping the imminent collision that would dump her like a deadly wave on Waimea Bay.

'Ahh, shit!' were her last words as she went under.

Even from where he was, Joey could see her body roll uncontrollably, her hands and feet flailing. To make matters worse, she then hit one of the many stone pillars scattered around the site, and the blow seemed to have winded her. She came up for air, choking and gasping, and Joey knew she was at the point of drowning. Then she disappeared under the roiling water. Her body finally resurfaced, away from the danger zone, but to Joey's dismay, Marie was facing downward and her body was limp.

Without any thought of the risk to his own welfare, Joey dived into the croc-infested water. As he swam he peered anxiously at the moving shadows. His right leg ached abominably and Joey could feel warm blood gushing from his wounds, which would ultimately attract his hunters. But he had to deal with that later. The most important person in his life needed him, so he plowed through the water with an unstoppable resolve.

The first thing Joey did when he reached Marie was to flip her face-up in the water. 'Babe,' he called brokenly, lightly tapping her bluish face. She wasn't breathing and her skin was cold to the touch.

'No, don't die on me now,' he pleaded, holding her head above water as he swam with her toward dry land.

Expecting at any moment to be grabbed by the reptiles who must by now have tasted his blood in the water, Joey was surprised that he managed to drag Marie's dead weight up the stone steps and onto the stone platform surrounding the pyramid, which was now itself an inch deep in water. His top priority was to get Marie inside the pyramid to start the resuscitation process.

That's when a twelve-foot crocodile moved to block his path, emitting a growling *umph* sound as it went. Joey jolted and stared into the beast's yellow-green eyes. Its jaws were shut, but it seemed to be waiting patiently for Joey's next move.

Joey froze and backed away slowly with Marie held flimsily in his arms. He had to rethink his strategy. He would have to walk around the pyramid in an anticlockwise direction to reach the opening. As he reached one corner of the square perimeter, a much larger crocodile, a little over sixteen feet, scurried up onto the platform to block his path, stopping him in his tracks as it roared angrily.

'Holy shit,' mouthed Joey. He was cornered. He thought about trying to climb the pyramid, but it was too steep and too smoothly rendered, and he wouldn't get far carrying Marie's dead weight. Everything was against him right now and every second he waited lessened the chances that he could bring Marie back to life.

The pressure to act built with each moment. Sweat

now ran down his face and he found it difficult to breathe. The anxiety was getting to him. He gently laid Marie's body down on the ground thirty feet away from the two crocs on either side, who watched his every move as they hissed at him.

He began CPR.

With both hands over Marie's heart, he started the compressions as he warily peered at the reptiles in his peripheral vision. 'Come on, breathe,' he muttered.

After fifteen pumps, he blew fresh oxygen into her lungs and repeated the cycle.

'Please, wake up.'

The sound of the growling crocs intensified and their heads lifted in the air, then their jaws snapped open and shut with a loud *pop*.

That's when, astonishingly, Youssef's backpack washed over to the platform near Marie's unconscious body. Joey could hardly believe his eyes, but there was no way he could stop the CPR and reach for it.

'Come on, Marie! Breathe!'

As he forced his palms over her heart the small pack, complete with Youssef's possessions, including his cell phone and what could possibly be the Cup of Christ, brushed up against Marie's body.

'Come on!'

Just when he was starting to feel helpless, Marie suddenly heaved upward, gurgling and coughing water out of her mouth. Taking in gulps of fresh air, Marie flashed a weak smile at her hero as he moved a strand of hair away from her face.

'Welcome back,' he said, lifting her up to her feet.

'Sorry, babe, no time for I-love-you talk. We have two pissed-off crocodiles on either side of us about to pounce.'

Marie's eyes opened wide, clearly analyzing the danger they were now facing. 'Oh my God,' she croaked.

'Tell me about it,' said Joey, frowning. 'I can't believe they haven't attacked us yet.'

Joey kneeled down and grabbed the backpack from the water. That's when he spotted bubbles directly in front of him, three feet away. His eyes boggled. It was another giant crocodile, hiding, lingering, its tail slowly swaying left to right.

'I get it now,' exhaled Joey, dreading what was to come. 'It looks like these crocs are planning a three-way attack and are waiting for their leader to strike first. We're so screwed.'

Chapter 40

Shouldering the backpack, Joey held Marie by the hand and took a step back to where the wall of the pyramid began its upward climb. The enormous crocodile hiding inches beneath the water's surface slowly rose to reveal his beady, peeping eyes.

'Hang on, the cup,' said Joey suddenly.

'This is no time for religion, Joey.'

'No, it's solid.'

'And?'

'And, we can use it as a weapon to pass the smaller of the crocs.'

'You're crazy.'

'Please, if you have any other suggestions, now would be the time.'

Marie hesitantly nodded her head and stood a step away from Joey, who had armed himself with the weighted bag and began to swing it around in a circle, building speed.

'On three we go for it. One ... two ... three ...'

Joey charged first with Marie right behind him. Lucky for them they moved in the nick of time, as the hungry crocodile hiding below the surface sprang to where they'd stood an instant before, snapping his jaws at what he'd probably thought would be an easy meal.

The smaller and much faster killer prepared himself to take a bite with an outstretched neck, exposing his razor-sharp teeth. Joey spun the bag in his hand, building momentum like a cowboy ready to throw a lasso around his bull.

'If there's a God out there ...' Joey prayed, facing the beast in front of him as it moved sporadically, hissing at him.

Joey struck first and swung the backpack smack into the monster's nostrils, knocking a blow to his head that caused the reptile to grunt and retreat backwards into the water. Joey and Marie raced past with thumping strides.

Finally, they reached the jagged entrance to the pyramid.

The blinding light of the Stargate was still as luminous as ever, its harmonic frequency still humming. The water gushed toward it but seemed to bounce off the blue wave of energy that was the portal. It wasn't allowing the mass of liquid to enter, as if recognizing it wasn't a live species.

'The water is rising,' breathed Joey, his eyes scanning the room. 'We've been in situations like this before, but this one takes the cake.'

'What's the plan?' asked Marie, the fear on her face self-explanatory.

'As the water continues to rise we're gonna have to swim back to the vines and climb out of this shithole.'

'What about the crocodiles?'

Joey didn't reply, knowing he didn't have the answer she wanted as he observed an enormous, curious crocodile, perhaps the giant of the bunch at about seventeen feet and possibly weighing over half a ton, stroll toward the source of the light. Its leathery frame crawled through the ring and disappeared.

'You don't see that every day,' joked Marie as the crocodile vanished into thin air.

'At least that's one croc we don't have to deal with.'

'Maybe the others will do the same?'

At that moment about thirteen feet away, the two noticed a pair of crocodiles converging on something on the floor, and within seconds they were shredding into Abdul's dead carcass, like he was dessert, his guts and broken bones torn from his body. The two beasts fought with the parts. Even though Joey hadn't liked Abdul, he felt sick to his stomach watching the man's flesh disintegrate. No man deserved to go that way.

'We're going to be eaten alive in this place.' Marie turned to her side to heave, but no vomit came out of her mouth. She tried to not look at the sight, but kept peeking, her expression of horror evident as she held on to Joey's arm.

The smell of the brutalized corpse suddenly hit their nostrils and Joey gagged. He shook his head and looked despairingly around, glancing at the water outside the pyramid that was consumed in darkness, knowing it was infested with crocodiles. Attempting to swim back the way they'd come now was plain suicide.

'Why is it dark out there?' he asked, frowning. 'It doesn't help.'

'Don't you remember how we rested our flashlights against the pyramid to light up the crystal?' Marie reminded him. 'The water knocked them away. Lucky for you I managed to grab one and heaved it at Youssef's head.'

'Thank God you have an amazing throw,' said Joey. 'You saved my life.'

'Joey, I'm not going out there to be croc bait,' cried Marie. 'I don't want to die.'

Joey embraced her as she drew a deep breath of pure dread. 'If that exit is off the cards, it only leaves us with one other option,' he said slowly.

Marie nodded her head in agreement. 'I'm with you. I'd prefer to take my chances with the Stargate.'

It was then that Joey glimpsed the shadow of a man's frame inside the pyramid. The figure was carefully tiptoeing through the water so as not to attract the attention of the man-eaters that continued to munch away at Abdul's carcass.

Youssef, the slippery bastard, now stood silhouetted against the Stargate. It seemed like he'd been waiting for the large crocodile to enter first before he moved to cross the threshold himself. He would have come to his own realization, like Joey and Marie had, that entering the portal was the only way out of this godforsaken place.

Youssef turned his head, his body facing the light of the gel-like solid structure, and gave them a mocking smile, knowing that to reach him, they would have to pass the two crocodiles that had tasted human flesh.

'Son of a bitch,' breathed Joey. 'He has the blue keystone.'

Youssef had just done the unthinkable.

He approached the structure's mechanism panel and removed the other, smaller red stone that Boyce had inserted to ignite the Stargate. Then with his middle finger he gestured back at Joey dispassionately and took a step forward.

Chapter 41

Youssef vanished, leaving Marie and Joey exposed and vulnerable. Time was against them if they still wanted to exit via the Stargate.

'No!' cried Marie, tugging on Joey's arm. 'He took both stones in with him.'

'Don't panic,' said Joey, trying hard not to panic himself. 'We still have a minute or so before it shuts down.' He clenched his fists, displeased with himself. 'I should've killed him when I had the chance.'

The water was still gushing into the pyramid, forming a vast lake.

'We have to move,' he said, knowing that it wasn't going to be easy with two crocodiles blocking their way. 'Are you ready?'

'As ready as I'll ever will be,' she replied, trembling.

They both moved forward, trying to be as inconspicuous as they could as the devils fought with their prize.

All of a sudden the feasting crocodiles paused, as though they could feel the vibrations of more prey close by. Joey pointed to the bricks by his feet and slowly and quietly leaned down to pick one up. Marie did the same, holding the thirty-pound brick with both her hands. They were now armed and ready to defend themselves if the situation called for it.

'Slow,' said Joey under his breath, tiptoeing over to the right.

The crocodile closest to Joey lifted its head and hissed, even though it was facing in the opposite direction. His twin did the same.

'They know we're here,' said Marie. 'They can sense us.'

'We're running out of time, we have to go for it.'

Marie sighed then raised her head to Joey determinedly. 'I'll go first.'

'Are you sure?'

'I think it's the safer option. They'll catch on by the second time.'

'Let's do this.'

Marie let out two quick breaths and on bouncing feet trudged through the water as it lapped aimlessly around them. Joey followed suit. One of the crocodiles turned to face her and she smashed it over the head with her brick, which gave her a couple of seconds to pass, unharmed. The crocodile's pain was evident as it let out a terrifying roar and shut its jaws.

Joey tossed his limestone block at the other hissing beast but missed the mark. It landed in between the two cranky crocodiles, creating a sizeable splash of water that temporarily blinded them. As he ran, he made a decision.

He knew he would not make it if his injured leg came anywhere near their razor-sharp teeth. So what he did next defied all odds: he jumped onto Marie's injured crocodile's head with his good leg and propelled himself to safety.

'Go! Go! Go!' Joey warned as they approached the dancing light.

'Give me your hand,' she said, reaching out, holding it behind her.

Joey grabbed hold and yelled, 'I love you!'

'I love you too,' Marie replied, turning back to face the shimmering surface.

'Let's do this,' said Joey, building up his courage, now inches away from the overpowering light. 'One giant leap for mankind,' he said, shooting a sideways smile at Marie.

'Here we go,' she whispered, squeezing his hand tight, 'see you on the other side.'

Together they took a breath and entered the sloshing pool. The ring's energy reached out, surrounded them, and swallowed them whole.

Chapter 42

Joey squeezed Marie's hand. He thought if they survived this miraculous journey, they would have an amazing story to share with their children one day. He shut his eyes, but even then, the beaming light overpowered his vision, so he opened them hesitantly. It was like being in a fisheye lens that zoomed forward with an incredible acceleration, a roller-coaster ride that dropped but never seemed to end.

The surrounding walls disappeared as the energy took over. He had lost control, and had no sense of gravity or which way was up or down.

He felt a sharp pain at his fingers. Marie continued to squeeze them, crushing them, but gently. He flashed back to when he had taken her to Orlando's Universal Studios and forced her to go on the Hollywood Rip Ride Rockit that had ended with her in tears. She had vowed to never go on a roller-coaster like that again, so he understood the fear she was reliving this very second, and it was a probably a thousand times worse.

The dazzling, intense light faded to what seemed to be a giant wormhole that sent him into what looked like deep space. The dark skies twinkled with millions of glittering stars, now more visible than anything you would see from Earth on the clearest of nights. Joey wondered if he was hallucinating, or maybe even already dead. But he felt the speed increase and with it the pain in his fingers, which made him sense it was all too real. Marie clearly didn't like this.

They passed an assortment of multicolored gas clouds of blues and reds, reminiscent of a vibrant abstract painting. Enormous star constellations of multiple celestial systems sped past them. The vista was breathtaking and other-worldly.

Suddenly a square filled with piercing light loomed up ahead, increasing in size as they approached it.

Shh-boom!

They hit the light. Joey was spat out onto a luscious green floor surrounded by what looked like standing stones. He fell hard on the soft ground, disorientated and freezing cold. It felt like his body was covered in frost. He surmised that this was most likely a by-product of the teleportation process. He turned to see that Marie was by his side, drowsy as though she had drunk an entire bottle of tequila, but she was safe.

But there was no time to recover from the ordeal of the journey. A familiar growling sound now emerged, too close for comfort.

Joey reluctantly raised his eyes to meet the creature's enormous bloody teeth, which seemed seconds away from ripping his head out of its socket. He had reached the gates of hell, he thought, as he wrenched his girl hastily over to the side to avoid what would have been certain death.

No sooner had they escaped the inner circle of stones than they heard an agonized distress call.

It was a man screaming for help.

Now standing a safe distance away, on the brightest emerald-green grass Joey had ever seen, he realized they weren't in hell. The creature that was out to kill them was not the devil; it was a Nile crocodile from Earth. The same giant seventeen-foot croc that had entered the Stargate due to his own simple curiosity.

And to Joey's morbid pleasure, Youssef was the man at its mercy. He was being crushed and toyed with like a wounded animal, as the croc's jaws took hold of him and it munched away.

'Help me,' Youssef called with a broken voice, reaching out a shaky hand that seemed to have lost all its nerves.

Joey rubbed the sharp pain pulsing through his thigh and leaned his weight on his other leg. He took his time and sucked in a much-needed breath, feeling like he had not inhaled during the entire teleportation process. Still woozy and shivering with cold, he struggled to stay on his feet. As he watched the half-ton reptile crack another bone in Youssef's body, he did what any other person would have done in his position.

He smiled.

'Help me,' Youssef pleaded, as his eyes rolled backwards in his head in excruciating pain beyond words.

'I'm sorry, Youssef,' said Joey quietly, 'but you deserve to die.'

Marie faced the other way and vomited near one of

the many outer stone pillars that encircled the site. She held her right hand up against the solid construction and heaved out what appeared to be the remnants of her last meal since arriving in Egypt.

'I discovered this place,' cried out Youssef, as his leg was crunched and chewed on. 'It was me!' he shouted. 'I did this.'

Joey followed Youssef's bloodshot eyes, which widened as he carefully approached. He stopped seven feet away and carefully leaned down to pick up the two colored keystones Youssef had dropped. He knew if there was any chance of getting back home, they would need to replicate the Stargate's ignition process in this alternate world somehow – in theory. All he could do at this point was hope this would be possible.

Youssef's eyes dulled.

Joey watched him struggle as he drowned in his own blood. His punishment had been meted out. He wanted the last person Youssef would ever see to be him.

Joey knew he had a glint in his eye, a darkness. It was only fair that Joey wreaked his vengeance after Youssef had brutally murdered his uncle and put them through hell.

'Revenge is a bitch,' he uttered, satisfied.

A hint of a smile appeared in his face.

Youssef fell limp and died a most suitable and agonizing death.

Chapter 43

Planet X

With its strong legs, leathery skin and sharp teeth, the disgruntled animal now decided to wander out toward the lush grass fields, perhaps in search of water to wash down its meal. His extreme ferociousness and aggravation was without doubt caused by his entry into the wormhole, a first for his breed.

'Poor croc got the ride of its life,' joked Joey with a shake of his head as the reptile grunted some more and disappeared over a nearby hill.

Gazing out beyond the standing stones, Joey and Marie saw that the sky was consumed in an orange glow comparable to a scene in a Monet oil painting. It was breathtaking to say the least. The air was fresh and pure but there was no sign of life to be seen apart from the crocodile. Two full-shaped moons hovered in the distance and the landscape was an ever-receding hill of grass and trees.

Marie felt like she was in the countryside somewhere in Northern Ireland. Deep in thought, she cleared her mouth and rubbed her hand up against one of the many giant stones that ringed the site. Stonehenge crept into her mind. This stone circle was laid out in the same geometrical pattern as the structure on Earth that was said to have been constructed in 3100 B.C. by the Druids, high priests of the Celts, who potentially used it for sacrificial ceremonies.

How could this be here? And why was it here?

As a child she had always had a fascination with the prehistoric monument in Wiltshire, England. In her last year of college, she had completed an assignment on the subject that had earned her top marks and praise from her history lecturer.

Each standing stone seemed to be an identical match with Stonhenge. For some reason, these details never escaped her mind, even a dozen years later; a testament to her love of ancient history. The boulders were thirteen feet high, six feet wide and weighed roughly twenty-five tons each, and the horizontal lintel stones above them were positioned with precise engineering and placement.

There was one obvious distinction between the two colossal monolithic structures. The stones were clearly a different color, and probably of a completely different type, as though sourced from two separate worlds possibly millions of light years away from each other.

Inside this ring of taller, linteled sarsen stones were shorter brownish-red blocks, nothing like the blue ones that encircled Stonehenge. Marie knew that the bluestone was a type of volcanic rock or spotted dolerite that many ancient civilizations believed held amazing powers.

They had not been wrong.

The fact that this wonder was here on this planet proved that the assembly on Earth was alien in origin; not built by the hands of humans. Its purpose was much more than just a ceremonial place of worship. It served a specific function.

Joey joined Marie soon after he watched the man who had killed his uncle enter into the darkness of death in the most brutal of ways. Even though she felt sick to the stomach from watching the butchery, she gave Joey the time he needed to find closure.

He proceeded toward her with a limp in his stride, gazing upward with a furrowed brow of recognition as he looked upon the structure.

'It's a replica of Stonehenge,' she called out, observing him studying the rocks that dwarfed him.

'Yeah, but this one is intact,' said Joey.

'How's your leg?' Marie asked, as the dark-red stain seeped through the two makeshift bandages she and Boyce had placed on his wounds.

'It's okay,' he said shortly, dismissing his pain. 'Where the hell are we, babe? Where's the Stargate on this end? And Boyce, did he make it here too?' After rattling out this string of questions, he peered out to the horizon, dumbfounded, wanting answers. 'And why is there a Stonehenge on this planet? I feel like we're in a freaking Ridley Scott movie.'

Marie didn't reply. She herself was trying to make sense of it all. They were probably on the other side of the known universe, she thought. 'We're alive, so we must be breathing oxygen, and that would make this planet not dissimilar to Earth.'

Joey paused for a moment to take in the scale and grandness of the finished edifice in front of them.

Marie said, 'On Earth, it has puzzled scientists as to how an ancient primitive society could have moved these stones two hundred and forty miles to where Stonehenge is now located.'

'Why is that?' asked Joey, turning to listen.

''Cause they weigh four tons each and are found only at one remote place on Earth.'

Joey raised an eyebrow in interest.

'The engineers who constructed them had to build them in a specific place to harvest their energy. Like in real estate today, location is the key, it's everything, and they knew this.'

Joey nodded his head in understanding.

'Did you know that the Great Pyramid of Giza is located at the exact intersection of the longest line of latitude and longitude? It's smack on the midline of our planet and this was done deliberately, just like Stonehenge.'

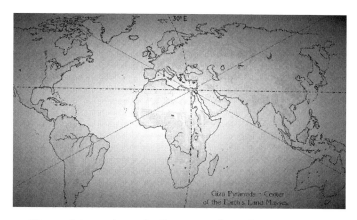

'Everything they built was for the purpose of traveling into deep space,' breathed Joey excitedly. 'And these arrangements were their means of doing so.'

'Hang on,' she said, staring at the items in Joey's hand. 'The trigger stones. I think they're made from the same geological rocks formed here and on Earth. It's all making sense now.'

'What do you mean?' Joey asked. 'They don't look the same color.'

'That's because when you look at these pillars,' Marie gestured over to them, 'you're only seeing the thicker outer layer. Just like the bluestone dolerite of Stonehenge, its core when broken down and shaved appears a brighter and richer shade, like what you're holding.'

Joey raised an eyebrow and held the stones up to look at them more closely.

'The red keystone used to ignite the Stargate on Egypt is linked to *this* Stonehenge, that inner circle of red stones. It's this planet's distinctive key.'

'And why is that important?' asked Joey, always two steps behind.

'It's extremely significant, because the monument in Wiltshire has bluestones.'

Excitement flushed his face as Joey realized the connection.

'Each planet has their own core identification stone,' Joey blurted. 'That means that this bluestone,' he said, looking down at the one in his hand, 'is how we get back home.'

Marie smiled as Joey put it together. 'Some people believed that Stonehenge was actually a giant clock,' she explained, slapping her palm against the perfectly upright and preserved smooth surface of what were known on Earth as the sarsen stones. 'Boy, were they wrong. This turns on its head everything we thought we knew about our past,' said Marie in total awe.

'Okay,' said Joey, trying to put the pieces of this puzzle together. 'So we know that whoever lived or lives on this planet most probably built the Great Pyramid and Stonehenge. We know that the energy created from the Great Pyramid was used to create the wormhole to get us here. And we now know that the ring of standing stones is some sort of advanced docking station that is triggered when you use that planet's identification marker. That might mean that the one on Earth is the mirrored version. The blue keystone should get us home.'

Marie rubbed her naked feet on the soft grass, feeling hopeful.

'Well, we have nothing else to go by,' said Joey, formulating a plan. 'Let's find Boyce and this portal so we can get out of this place.'

Marie nodded her head in agreement and gazed over the landscape. She had been raised a Catholic, and the very fact that this place was real made her rethink everything she had ever come to understand. Her faith was being questioned. The Bible and its scriptures, written a couple of thousand years ago, had been carefully chosen by people who wanted control, power and money. Now she thought them a lot of utter nonsense. Humans were not alone in this universe, and that was now a fact. Not only that, the civilizations that had left behind these amazing structures were incredibly advanced.

She thought that if the people of Earth knew of this civilization's existence, it would cause a considerable deal of chaos and despair. Religion would be annihilated, and people would fear and question who our makers really were, just as she was questioning it right now. Evolution and creationist theories would both be thrown out the window, and scientists would have to re-evaluate our place in this vast universe. The human race was not as unique as it had once thought it was.

Chapter 44

Joey and Marie left Stonehenge and took off across the hills, Youssef's battered backpack strapped to Joey's back and filled with the two triangular-shaped dolerite stones, the Cup of Christ and a cell phone. The thick green grass felt like a comfortable rug beneath Joey's shoes as they hiked north, or in what Marie thought was the northerly direction. She explained that the prehistoric ringed monument back on Earth was aligned northeast to southwest, with the sunrise and sunset at the summer and winter solstices. Joey was lost either way, so he let her make the executive decision.

'I just hope Boyce traveled this way too,' said Joey, leading Marie through the grassy, undulating, picturesque plains.

The countryside may have been in an alien world, but something about it was familiar. It stretched before them and rose and fell like giant waves on a gentle ocean. The air had warmth to it and the sun from above was bathing the landscape in a warm glow that felt pleasant on the skin.

'Is it me, or is it easier to breathe here?' said Marie,

closing her eyes while she tilted her head upward at the blue sky, enjoying the freshness.

'I feel it too,' said Joey, glancing down at the lush grass and resting his hand on his thigh. He winced as the pressure on his leg caused him a great amount of discomfort.

'I can't even comprehend where we are right now.' Marie laughed nervously. 'We're strolling blind on a planet that could be hostile around the next bend.'

Joey half grinned with a closed mouth.

'It's like walking down a dangerous street in the Bronx.'

'We're not in the hood, babe.'

'You get what I'm trying to say, though. It's scary to think what, or whom, we could possibly run into.'

'Don't get ahead of yourself,' said Joey, breathing in the pollution-free air. 'There might be nothing here, no life forms at all. They could've all died out long ago, leaving behind their amazing technology for our species to find one day.'

'I'm sure we'll find out soon enough.'

The walk seemed to be on an incline, and the thick knee-high grass meant that Joey had to push hard on his wounded leg. Thirty minutes in, the agony was written all over his face. His lips were dry and his body was bathed in sweat. With all senses on high alert, he came to an abrupt stop to listen.

'Do you hear that?' he said, his eyes widening. 'Sounds like water.'

Reaching the peak of a hill, a smile grew on his face as he gazed down over a narrow valley that was almost a gorge. Through this gully, a clear stream rushed over a rocky bed that disappeared into the distance.

'If there's water, there's life,' deduced Marie, enjoying the vista.

'Hang on, what's that?' asked Joey, pointing to what looked like a piece of clothing.

The garment was white and it flowed on the riverbed, secured by a rock that was placed on top. A thought came to mind as his eyes darted down to his bloody wound.

'Boyce!' he shouted, and he could hear the excitement in his tone. He knew it was his friend's other shirtsleeve, torn off and left there to inform them that he had come this way. It was only for a brief moment, but Joey forgot the pain he was feeling. It was as if the news had recharged him as he sidestepped down the treacherous slippery hill covered in rock and moss.

Marie followed at her own careful pace.

'He's been here,' Joey said, finding his way to the base. He stepped forward and checked the water to make sure it was safe, then splashed the fresh liquid on his face to refresh himself and took a long drink to quench his thirst. He then balanced himself up against two flat rocks and retrieved the cotton shirtsleeve as the water ran over his hands.

Marie joined him soon after and they both sat by the stream admiring nature at its absolute best. 'Here, let me help you,' she offered, removing the old bloody sleeve and part of her dress tied up against his thigh, and replacing it with the cleaner version. 'We have to make sure the wounds don't get infected.'

Joey thanked Marie and stumbled back to his feet. 'I don't think we have much time before it gets dark.

Let's carry on and find a safer place to spend the night that's not in the open.'

Marie agreed and they continued to follow the stream for nearly an hour with the daylight beginning to slip away to their left. Then they came to a bend in the winding valley and came across something totally unexpected. And it was moving.

But it wasn't Boyce.

Marie sighed out loud.

Joey swallowed hard and the hairs on the back of his neck stood up.

It seemed they had come across life.

The life form in front of them was about three hundred feet away. It appeared to be human, a young male, and maybe eight or ten years old, although there was something odd about him, too. He was playing with the water in the stream, kicking it, and giggling to himself. He wore a brown single garment over his head like a poncho that covered his body down to his knees.

On the side of the hill, a little higher than the stream, small huts with thatched roofs could be identified, built with stone-set walls. This must be his home, and Joey and Marie were the strangers heading his way.

'Be careful, Joey,' Marie warned in a calm, soothing voice. 'We don't know how he'll react to us.'

Joey approached hesitantly, and as he got closer he suddenly realized that the boy had an extremely elongated head.

'Holy shit,' he whispered, his anxiety building. 'Now that's what I call a huge—'

'I see it,' Marie interrupted, talking but keeping her lips closed.

Now only feet away, Joey raised his palm with a friendly smile and said hello. The boy turned and scanned them calmly up and down, as though he was the one confused with their unusual attire. The kid's brown eyes widened when he spotted the top of their circular heads. He reached up and rubbed his own skull curiously, then spoke in an alien dialect that made Joey cringe.

'*Uk buk too*,' he said, his eyes moving between Joey and Marie.

Joey turned to Marie, not knowing what to say or do, and smiled as he asked the boy playfully, 'You wouldn't happen to know English, would you?'

Marie shook her head, displeased with Joey's timing. She loved him for his sense of humor, but there was a time and place to be funny. Joey knew this, but his nerves were obviously getting the better of him.

'*Uk buk too*,' the boy said again. This time he gestured downstream.

'I think he wants us to carry on,' said Marie.

'Yeah, the Starbucks is this way,' Joey joked again, nodding his head, and left the boy, who stood watching and rubbing the back of his head in apparent wonder.

'I can't believe we just spoke to an extraterrestrial,' marveled Joey, stepping away, a little frightened. 'I guess I can cross that off my bucket list.'

Soon after leaving the youngster, they came in contact with a throng of adults this time, who all did a double-take at the sight of them. Joey felt like a tiger at the zoo that had been let out of his cage and everyone was keeping a close eye on it, fearing the unknown. Why was he here, and was he dangerous?

'I'm scared,' Marie said, grabbing Joey by the hand as they entered what seemed to be a large village with now hundreds of aliens going about their own lives, although they felt the creatures' curious stares.

'I think we just walked into the twilight zone,' said Joey. 'Just keep walking and keep your head down and don't look anyone in the eyes.'

They reached an enormous temple structure that was built over the stream and carved into the hill like in Petra, Jordan. A pair of colossal Egyptian-style obelisks flanked the entrance. Each one of them was engraved with two familiar side-profile figures, with the sun symbol atop reflecting its rays downward.

'Akhenaten and Nefertiti,' whispered Marie in a stunned tone.

The square opening was colossal, too high to even distinguish, allowing natural sunlight to flood through. They continued deeper into the building that towered over them. Strategically placed torches were lit, guiding them through the dark sections of the chamber inside the church-like structure.

Everywhere Joey glanced, there were elongated heads of all ages facing in one direction. A gigantic golden medallion was raised high for all to see with the support of thick bulky ropes. Its heavy circular gold construction was positioned precisely over strategically cut-out holes from above that beamed light down upon it, making it the feature of the room, giving the place a euphoric atmosphere.

The majority of people inside were forming a circular symbol with their two index fingers and thumbs raised above their heads while closing their eyes. They appeared to be praying to the golden disc.

'It seems the sun god Ra is still worshiped here,' said Marie, as Joey suddenly felt dizzy and tripped over his own feet, tumbling over and attracting more scrutiny than they were already receiving.

Joey had come to his breaking point. He could not walk any further and was in need of urgent medical attention. It had been far too long and he had lost a copious amount of blood.

Marie scrambled to help him, lifting his head into her lap.

An older woman standing nearby gestured over to them, as she spoke softly to the man standing beside her.

Suddenly, Marie and Joey were surrounded by down-turned eyes.

'Joey?' Marie cringed. 'Oh my God, we're in trouble.'

Joey's head spun, causing him to lose his sight. He could only see blurred glimpses of shadowy men, all with the same overstretched head. He tried to move, but his eyelids felt heavy. He fought with the urge to fall asleep and heard Marie's voice cry out for help, but there was nothing he could do. He was physically defeated. She would have to deal with whatever was coming her way and that frightened him. He blinked continuously in the fight to keep his eyes open, but could no longer resist the urge to close them. He was too weak.

He blacked out.

Chapter 45

Joey blinked rapidly as he opened his heavy-lidded eyes. The last thing he remembered was the strangely deformed heads that had peered down over him. A shadow of a face now loomed from above. In his daze, he thought he had seen an angel sent from heaven to take him to the pearly gates. Was this a dream? Was he dead? Was this the afterlife?

Millions of questions fluttered into his mind as the figure from above passionately rubbed his face, slowly and lovingly. The touch was soft and gentle. He closed his eyes again, and then reopened them. His vision gradually sharpened and the face became clearer.

It was Marie.

'Glad to see those beautiful blue eyes of yours,' she said with a smile. 'You're not going to believe where we are and who I'm with!'

Joey ran his tongue over his lips and slowly leaned upward from the cushioned bed he was lying in. It seemed to be constructed from timber logs and woven bark fibers. It took him a moment to focus. His black jeans had been removed, leaving him only in his red shirt and black underwear. He noticed the bullet wound on his thigh – it seemed to have been cleaned, treated and redressed professionally with a type of gauze material.

'Take it easy, Joey, you need to rest. They gave you a tonic to drink before extracting the shrapnel from your leg,' warned Marie, rubbing her hand up against his back. 'You're probably just feeling the medicine wearing away.'

'Who's they?' mumbled Joey, slouching to the edge of the bed, still feeling woozy. 'I'm so thirsty.'

Moments later, a cup was handed to him, overfilled with water. It was the same agate vessel he had used to deter the crocodiles inside the cavern.

'The Holy Grail,' he said, using it to quench his thirst.

Now refreshed, he paused for a second cup before gazing upward to see who had given him the chalice.

'Time to be resurrected,' said a youthful French-accented voice, stepping into his line of sight with a giant smile over his face.

'Boyce!' said Joey, elated to see that his friend was unharmed. He reached out and pulled him close for a tight hug. 'I thought we'd lost you,' Joey said, moving him away to look into his innocent brown eyes while holding his shoulders. 'Where the hell are we?'

'All you need to know is that we're safe,' Boyce said, grabbing Joey's jeans off the timber floor and passing them over so he could dress himself.

'Are we prisoners?' asked Joey, glancing around the log-built cabin with the darkness of the night visible through a sizeable open window that looked out onto the fields.

'Far from it,' said Marie, opening the door to let two strangers enter.

Joey's eyes widened, unsure of what to expect as he fed his legs into his Levis, moving the material carefully over his bandaged thigh.

An elderly man with a gray beard and bushy eyebrows entered with an amused expression on his face. A young woman, in her early twenties, followed and gave him a warm but fearful smile. The girl's hair was thick and curly and her demeanor was one of innocence and purity. Just by their appearance, they seemed to be related in some way and she seemed to share the man's dimple in his cheek. Joey surmised that the man must be her father.

'He fixed your leg,' said Marie, expressing her appreciation with a grin.

Joey wanted to thank the man, so he turned in his direction and gently patted his wounded thigh then placed both hands together as though he was praying and bowed his head. It was the only way he thought he could express himself without communicating verbally.

The young woman spoke to her father in her dialect, who looked up from his mesmerized stare at Joey's shoes, which seemed to be a novelty for these people who wore straw shoes on their feet. The bearded man smiled and also nodded, mimicking Joey's action as a sign of respect. And that's when Joey noticed his head. It was not huge and elongated. It was normal, which was most probably the reason why he hadn't spotted it initially.

'Can someone please explain to me why these aliens have heads like ours?' he asked, creasing his forehead. 'Where the hell are we?'

'Relax, Joey,' said Boyce, standing by the window. 'I was stunned too when they first brought me here. There are thousands of them living in this one area. I think they might be the slaves or the farmers of this planet. They seem to be happy, simple people and have created a nice community for themselves. They even showed me their ancient book.'

'What book?'

Marie turned with a curious eye too.

'There's an old handwritten codex which I think explains who these people are and where they came from. Maybe even where we came from.'

'And,' said Joey. 'What did you find out?'

'Sorry, I didn't find anything,' said Boyce, walking over to pick up Youssef's backpack. 'The words were scribed in hieroglyphics.'

'The true language of the people,' suggested Marie.

Boyce dug inside and extracted the cell phone. 'What happened to Youssef?' he asked.

Joey shrugged. 'Let's just say he picked a fight with a crocodile and lost.'

'We can use the phone to read the text,' said Boyce. 'We have forty per cent battery.'

'Perhaps it might have information on how we can find the Stargate on this planet to get back home,' said Marie as the young girl watched her with earnest curiosity.

'Now that we still have power left in the cell,

let's not waste any time,' said Joey. 'It might be our only hope.'

Boyce walked over to their hospitable friends and mimed, as if he was turning the pages of a novel. An understanding was met with a smile. The older man stepped to the door with his daughter alongside him, and waved for them to join him.

Chapter 46

Guided by the elderly man and his daughter, they strolled along a line of cabins that seemed to be laid out equidistant from each other. The site appeared to be more like a never-ending caravan park than a planet that was home to an advanced civilization. These people were definitely not superior in any way and they had normal shaped heads. Their clothing was a simple, monotoned brown linen that would have come from a type of flax flower woven into fabric. The construction of the homes was primitive. There were hundreds of them, all identical to one another, with tree logs at their core and a thatched roof made from overlapping bundles of dried plant stalks.

Following the dirt pathway, they passed many log-framed windows, each with their own food aroma perfuming the evening. The inhabitants within peered out of their homes to see what the fuss was all about. Some even stepped outside and expressed themselves by shouting out to their guide, who answered with an authoritative voice that seemed to quieten them down.

Marie noticed that the females were all dressed in the same draped linen clothing and headdress, while the males wore an ankle-length garment with long sleeves, just as the ancient Egyptians would have worn. She wondered what they would have thought of her strange attire as she walked barefoot in her torn formal polyester black gown that would have been quite alien to their eyes.

They found themselves in an open courtyard area that led to a domed church-like structure. The people of the land observed them and parted to either side to clear a passage to what seemed to be a place of worship and importance to their culture.

'Don't be afraid,' said Boyce, holding the phone. 'These people are just curious, just like we are, and they just want to know where we came from.'

The outside of the building was made from stone and smoothly rendered, standing only ten feet high. The crowd followed them with curious eyes as they entered the doorway that was defined by a lancet arch.

'The book is in here,' said Boyce, moving forward to lead with the bearded man and his daughter as he helped carry one of the freshly lit torches.

Into the pitch-black atrium they went, the flickering light just enough to see into the recesses of the building. Cut into the smooth stone walls immediately to one side was an image of what appeared to be Nefertiti worshiping the sun god. The symbol of the gold disc was repeated many times, propelling several downward lines with a tiny hand on the end of each.

'These people must worship the sun here too, like the Egyptians did,' said Joey, looking toward his girlfriend for confirmation. 'What was the god's name again … Ra?'

'You say it as though their god is not important, but what you might not realize is that their sun god and the Cult of Amun-Ra is in fact now the Roman Catholic Church.'

'Get the heck out of here,' said Joey in disbelief.

'It's true,' Marie said. 'The Christian faith is a veiled reincarnation of this sun cult. You understand that the virgin birth of Christ is a retelling of the Egyptian legend of Horus. Two thousand years before Jesus the Egyptians used a symbol they called *ankh*, which means *life*. And later it was adopted and transformed into the Coptic Cross.'

Joey turned to Boyce, who smiled quietly and said, '*Ankh* is depicted as a cross with a loop on top, just in case you were wondering. How about the word used after each prayer?' said Boyce, playing to Marie's passion and seeming to understand significantly more than Joey.

'What, *Amen*?'

'Fantastic point, Boyce, and exceptional timing,' said Marie, giving him a wink. 'Where do you think that comes from?'

Joey shrugged. 'It does sound Egyptian.'

'That's because it is,' said Marie. '*Amen* is another word for *Amun*, as they don't have vowels in their writing. So next time when you pray, remember you're not praying to Jesus, you're paying respect to an all-powerful sun god.'

'You're so hot when you get excited like this.'

'Shut up.'

'Let's carry on. We probably look like we're fighting to our escorts,' said Boyce, who flashed them a smile as if to say everything was okay.

'So they brought you here when you first arrived?' asked Marie as they traipsed down a narrow stone staircase.

'Yeah, after struggling to communicate with them, they led me here.'

Boyce revealed a narrow opening and entered after the bearded man and his daughter. 'Watch your step, it's tight,' he warned, showing the way.

Marie avoided the debris at her feet and was helped by Boyce, who gave her a hand as she stepped into a vast underground hallway with a low ceiling. It seemed to be an ancient cemetery, consisting of arched recesses for tombs that were completely empty.

An eerie feeling washed over her as she bent low to walk through the catacombs. It ended briefly at a small void that was at the end of the row.

'It's just in here,' said Boyce, ducking and entering a decently sized room where they could stand up straight.

Joey entered last. 'Who built this place—midgets?' he said in jest, readjusting his back with a pinched face, his wound still fresh.

'Come on, old man,' joked Marie.

'When we get back home that's it, no more tombs, no more overseas adventures. I hate these tight spaces. I'm so over it.'

The expression on his face was one of utter disdain.

'At least we don't have anyone with a gun bossing us around and threatening our lives.'

'I just want to surf and drink my beer, that's all.'

'I promise, babe, but let's try to find a way home first.'

The feature in the room was a flat, smooth-surfaced stone structure resembling a long six-foot boxed table, on which sat an ancient-looking papyrus. It stretched and spread along the table's length, consuming the area like a tablecloth bearing many different-sized holes. Broken lines and dashes of color were evident in the flickering light of the torch. The writing was in Egyptian hieroglyphics, but the scroll had clearly lain here for a vast amount of time and the humidity and small insects had done their job, making it virtually unreadable.

'It's destroyed,' said Marie, frustrated that this was all they had to go on. 'Even with Youssef's app it's useless. We might be on this planet indefinitely.'

Joey darted over to Boyce, who had a smile on his face. 'What aren't you telling us, Boy?'

The bearded man pushed a lever, disguised as an underground lantern, downward, and a compartment opened up in the wall, just big enough for a person to fit in.

'Trust me, it gets better,' hinted Boyce, disappearing off into one of the empty cavities. 'I'll be with you in a second.'

Marie and Joey entered the tiny void after the girl and her father. The man flashed his torch across the wall, revealing a faded carved drawing. The color had dissipated, but the indented lines were visible.

Marie's eyes opened wide with excitement. 'Two Stargates on two planets,' she said in wonder, tracing her finger over the etching to a mural that told a story.

'That must be Earth,' said Joey, studying it up close.

'If that's Earth, look at the size of this planet. It's enormous, double the size,' Marie said.

Hundreds of small humans with normal, circular heads were depicted with shovels and axes in their hands. They seemed to be working the land near a giant river, with the Great Pyramid lurking in the background. A towering God-like king and queen who bore elongated heads watched and ruled as they sat on their gold thrones.

'That's not why we are here,' said Boyce, interrupting, his flickering torch reflecting over his face as he came into the void behind them. Tucked in his opposite arm he held an A3-sized leather-bound casing. 'This is what we came for.'

Chapter 47

In the shadowy gloom of the old underground crypt, everyone's gaze shifted to Boyce.

'I think the writing in this, when translated, will tell us the story of where these people came from, and hopefully how we can get back home,' he said, holding it up high for all to see.

'Let's hope so,' interjected Joey. 'It's all we have to go on.'

Needing a place to examine the text, Boyce asked everyone to join him in the room with the eight-foot stone table. Joey and Marie didn't waste any time, following him like sheep exiting a paddock. Boyce sat the four-pound book atop the old scroll and carefully turned the first papyrus page as the group encircled the slab.

'Here, hold this,' said Boyce, passing the flaming torch over to Joey, who stood with a perplexed expression, clearly wanting answers.

'Hang on, Boyce where did you get this from?' asked Joey.

'The old man showed it to me,' said Boyce, looking in his direction. The man was almost invisible in the dark, but his friendly smile was apparent. 'He was trying to convey what it was in his own language, but I didn't understand until now.'

'What's that?' asked Marie with a furrowed brow.

'I will explain what I think this is, but first humor me and look at the hieroglyphics on this first page,' he said, pointing out the Egyptian-inspired shapes and lines. 'Now, glance to the far right of the damaged scroll.'

Joey and Marie's eyes zoomed to the edge of the roll.

'It's faint, but it's clearly the same symbol,' said Marie, nodding her head.

Boyce now flipped to the end of the book, which comprised six or so papyrus pages. 'Now, look at this drawing,' he urged, pointing to an image that portrayed an open-winged eagle. 'Then examine the opposite far side of the scroll.'

Marie ran her finger along the old rotten parchment as Joey lowered his fire torch to help with the light. It was extremely faint and torn, but the eagle's right wing was unmistakable.

'As you see, my friends, I think the hieroglyphics on this scroll have been duplicated in this book, probably to maintain the only piece of evidence that these people have about where they came from. It's like their holy bible.'

'Wow, good work,' said Marie, impressed with his findings. 'I'm intrigued. Now let's scan the text before we lose battery.'

Boyce opened the app in question and the bearded man's eyes lit up with astonishment. He followed the device, mesmerized by the illuminating white light of its screen.

Boyce scanned the first couple of pages slowly and steadily and after a minute or so a familiar English-accented female voice began to speak. This made their hospitable hosts glance around the room in search of the lady that was talking, which amused Joey.

'The true gods of this world visited our planet a long time ago, bringing with them their advanced technology. Needing a race to enslave, they found the primitive Homo erectus species and decided to improve on it, helping to evolve us into Homo sapiens, humans. We were engineered to be a primitive society with smaller brains accompanied by many defects, so we could be easily controlled.'

'That sounds about right,' joked Joey, sarcastically teasing his own kind.

'Shhh,' hissed Marie as the voice continued.

'Our population quickly grew and we spread out through the known world, and were told to believe in the sun god, Atum. For the men and women living in the promised land, we were charged with the work of the land, canals and building structures. A portal to travel between worlds was erected deep within the Great Pyramid so they could come and go as they pleased, taking with them hundreds of round-headed ones to help with their own farming needs on their own planet.'

'That explains how these people got here,' quickly interjected Boyce, scanning more pages to be analyzed.

'After thousands of years of coexistence, with the

human race spreading to the vast corners of Earth, new cultures formed, as did their own theories on whom to worship. The king of the time sent his one and only son, Akhenaten, and his queen, Nefertiti, to govern in his name as Pharaoh to the people. During their reign, sadly, they only bore six daughters. Needing a male heir to rule, a round-headed secondary wife by the name of Kiya was chosen, who gave birth to a boy they named Tutankhamun.'

'So Akhenaten and Nefertiti didn't come from Earth after all,' said Marie, watching Boyce scan the next couple of pages. 'It explains why we saw their faces carved into the obelisks on this planet. They were royalty here.'

'In the fifth year of his reign, Akhenaten was instructed by his all and powerful father, Amenhotep, to pass on the one true creator back to the people, the sun god, Atum. The people refused and caused an uprising, not wanting to worship the singular deity anymore. Once word got out to the king, he didn't like how these primitive war-like humans that were evolved by his ancestors were growing in power and disobedience. So an army from his world was to be sent through the wormhole to exterminate them.'

'Now I understand why Nefertiti hid the portal,' said Marie, just before the voice from the phone began to speak again.

'Fearing for her son's life, as he was half-human, she reinstated all gods to gain the trust of the people and blocked the Stargate on Earth so her son could rule over all mankind.'

'Well, that lasted a short nineteen years,' said Boyce, scanning the last page as the shadow of the fire flickered over their faces.

'For this to be successful, the gateway on Nefertiti's home planet posed a risk. The blue trigger keystone, Earth's gateway and identification marker, needed to be removed and destroyed. To save her beloved son, she entered the portal one last time with a task at hand and never came back again.'

'What an amazing woman,' breathed Marie. 'She sacrificed her own life to protect her child, who was not even her own biological offspring. Not to mention that the existence of the human race owes everything to this woman. If it wasn't for her selfless act, humans would not have survived and flourished like we have.'

'Look, it's a nice story and all, but how's that going to get us back home?' Joey muttered, frustration lacing his voice.

'I don't think you understand,' Marie said with a light tone, but her posture said she was ready to argue the point if she had to. 'Our whole existence and where we came from is summed up beautifully in this codex left behind by our ancestors. It means the evolution and creationist theories are all wrong. Our species is in fact alien in origin, mutated by the inhabitants of this very planet. As a Christian this has depleted my faith in a higher power.'

'Yes, but who created the people with the big-ass heads in this galaxy?' said Joey maddeningly.

'Ahh, so you're pitching me the God of the gaps theory,' said Marie. 'Just because something can't be scientifically proven, it doesn't mean you can invoke a higher power.'

'I think some questions we seek will never be able to be explained,' said Boyce, needing to defuse a possible argument. 'At the moment the only thing we should be worrying about is trying to find the Stargate on this planet.'

'And how are we going to do that?' said Joey with a depressed tone, all out of ideas. 'We can't even communicate with these people.'

Silence ensued for a moment.

'The phone,' Boyce blurted.

'What about it?'

'The Stargate would have to be inside a pyramid on this planet,' said Boyce. 'I bet you a million dollars Youssef has a photo of the pyramids on the Giza plateau.'

Marie raised an eyebrow as silence filled the air.

Boyce reacted and swiped through a plethora of personal photos. Some included Joey's uncle, Benjamin, at different times in their lives during the army, graduating from Cambridge, through to their business partnership. And as he had hoped, there was a perfectly cropped vertical image of the tallest Pyramid at Giza. He moved the cell in the direction of the courteous man, while he continued to point at his own eyes, trying to interpret in sign language. 'Have you seen this?' Boyce said.

Joey rolled his eyes in despair.

The man stared at the image up close and the white light bounced back on his aged skin, showing his cracked lines. His brown eyes widened and he moved his head, repeating what Boyce had done and touched his own eye.

'I think he knows,' said Boyce.

Joey did not seem totally convinced.

The bearded man carefully took the cell phone out of his hand and gestured for them to follow him. It appeared that he needed to show them something. His daughter was also telling them to come with a waved hand.

'Let's go,' said Marie as the old man moved quickly with his offspring closely following.

They left the church-like building and headed for the cabins, as the people murmured from outside, most probably due to the white LED light shining from the object in his hand.

'Where is he taking us?' questioned Joey. 'It could be a trap.'

'They mean us no harm,' said Boyce as the elderly man walked among the bungalows.

'You don't think the pyramid is here somewhere?' said Joey, limping on his injured leg.

The old man stopped, faced a cabin and shouted, '*Ku mu tou!*'

'What's going on?' asked Joey.

'There has to be a reason why we're here,' said Boyce.

Seconds later a much younger man exited the hut and stood at the top of the stairs on his wraparound porch looking down on them. He was tall, unshaved and rough looking. He possessed a strong build and a chiseled jawline, like he belonged in a gladiator movie.

He was shirtless, and had an elongated head. But the smile he gave them was not at all friendly.

Chapter 48

Joey's heart raced in his chest. He sensed danger from this man. He wanted to run, but where was he to go? He didn't know his north from his south. He stood there at the mercy of this alien standing only feet away.

Then out from the shadows behind the man stepped an attractive, lean, olive-skinned girl with long, wavy brown hair and a rounded head. She flashed a pleasant smile at all watching as she wrapped her arms around her man and squeezed him tight. By the way she hung on his well-built torso, it was evident that they were a couple and deeply in love.

Knowing that they were an item, Joey felt an instant rush of relief. Perhaps, the extraterrestrial whose race had evolved our species could be trusted after all? If in fact someone from his kind could fall for a primitive human being, it was conceivable that he was of no threat; that's what Joey was hoping, anyway.

A discussion between the old man and the alien began.

'*Shema ab ouk di may,*' said the senior male carrying the bright cell in his hand.

The language was peculiar and seemed to be a mixture of Arabic and Chinese tones. While listening as they went back and forth, Joey thought that anything could have been said between the two. He could have been making a deal with the advanced species to have them captured for a reward for all they knew. Anything was possible at this point. It could go either way and the sad realization was that there was nothing Joey, Marie or Boyce could do about it.

The young masculine gladiator with his perfectly chiseled body gave them a feverish glance and approached the senior with his daughter down the set of stairs as he lifted the phone's bright screen so he could see.

The discussion between the two continued, while Joey stood waiting for a reaction.

The gladiator comfortably retrieved the cell phone and hinted a smile as he examined it. It was obvious from the expression on his face that human technology was still undeveloped and in its infancy. This seemed to amuse him.

He glanced at the Great Pyramid on display, and zoomed in with his fingers, understanding the intellectual design capability.

'Did you see how he scaled the photo?' said Boyce quietly. The fact that he knew showed that they were dealing with an extremely intelligent species.

At this point, the enormous, elongated, giant of a head turned and peered at Joey, which made him swallow hard. The man strolled over to him and handed back the five-inch communication device, and spoke once again in his own language. His voice rose with each syllable and ended with him thumping his fists together violently.

'I'm hoping that doesn't mean what I think it does,' said Joey, taking a hesitant step backwards. 'Does he want a fight?' he breathed.

Joey desperately tried to hide how fearful he was. He controlled the tremor in his voice and consciously willed his body movements to be as relaxed as possible.

'*Na mou!*' the girl shouted from up on the porch. '*Na mou!*'

The gladiator's persona changed to a degree as he seemed to take in a deep breath, readjusting into a less threatening stance. Fear traveled through Joey's veins though, when the alien leaned over and bent down to Joey's level to speak in his face.

'*Akino batook anu!*' he said in a gruff voice, pointing a firm finger into Joey's chest. '*Amanek kil tou,*' he said, before letting out a sigh and turning to leave, returning to his girl for a kiss, and disappearing into his home.

'I think I just wet my pants,' said Joey out loud. 'What in the hell just happened?'

'I think he was threatening you,' said Marie, patting Joey on his shaky arm for support.

'Why would he do that?' asked Joey.

'Maybe he could be risking his own life by taking us to the pyramid,' said Boyce evenly. 'I bet to help or mingle with our kind is banned by his people on this planet.'

'You might have a point,' said Marie as the bearded man's daughter stepped forward, grinning like something positive had been accomplished tonight. She communicated a gesture with both hands resting on her cheek.

'Sleep,' Marie repeated. 'She's telling us to sleep.'

The girl dropped to her knees. Her brown linen fabric touched the dry dirt as she drew a triangular shape with her finger.

'The pyramid,' Marie mouthed.

Her two slender fingers walked toward the triangle.

'They're going to take us,' she said, as the young brunette mimicked the rest gesture one more time, to confirm.

'It looks like we have ourselves a guide after we get some sleep,' said Marie, patting her new friend on the back with a grin and a nod to say she understood.

Now that they had a plan in place, Joey, Boyce and Marie were directed back to the cabin where Joey had woken up from unconsciousness not so long ago.

'I'll go help make the beds,' said Boyce, giving Joey a wink. 'While you two lovebirds have some time to yourselves.'

Joey grabbed hold of Marie's hand and pulled her to the wraparound porch and rubbed his palm against her shoulders even though the night was not cold.

'I've been meaning to get you alone since we landed in Egypt,' Joey quipped as the two moons splashed down a watery silver glow over the landscape, bathing them with light. In the distance, hundreds of trees bearing fruit were lined up and silhouetted against the deep velvety sky as the stars glittered in the heavens above.

'How amazing is it that we can look at the heavens and know that possibly a million light years away is Earth,' said Marie in complete awe. 'How many times have we gazed at the stars and said there has to be life out there?'

'Now we know,' said Joey with a joyous smile. 'That we are definitely not alone. How do you feel about that?'

'I feel small and irrelevant. And we are; we only exist because an intelligent life form decided they needed us for their own propaganda. This news has saddened me to a degree, but that's life, I guess.'

'Well, in my eyes, you're the most important person in this entire universe. To me you're everything.'

'What if we can't get home?'

'Don't be afraid,' assured Joey. 'We'll get through this, we always do.'

Marie leaned her head on Joey's shoulder and shared a quiet moment.

Joey quietly and smoothly reached for his pants pocket. Now was the perfect time to propose. His finger found the ring he had slipped into his pocket before they went on this crazy adventure. He had planned to do it somewhere at the Giza plateau, but he wasn't complaining. He was happy to just be alive at this point.

The art form of popping the question was always a topic among friends around the dinner table. Some had said they proposed on a romantic island getaway, while others had jumped out of a plane. Joey knew he could never reveal the truth. Who would even believe him if he said he had asked Marie to marry him on a planet with an alien species that evolved our kind from the early ape inhabitant back on Earth?

Joey had seen proposals a million times before on TV and the nerves started to get the better of him. Marie was his soulmate and he wanted it to be special. As they both stared up at the flickering stars, he thought about how he would go through with it, which left his heart hammering in his chest.

Joey smiled as he tried to snap out of the state he was in. There was nothing to be nervous about, he kept telling himself. He had been brought up in a criminal family. He had fought against mercenaries in Paris and lived to tell the story. He had got through tonight's many life-threatening situations, and now had entered a wormhole to a habitable planet on the other side of the known galaxy. Now was not the time to chicken out.

He turned to face Marie and stared into her warm hazel eyes. He gave her a passionate kiss, one that was well overdue.

'I have a question I need to ask you,' he said, licking his lips, needing a stiff drink.

Marie stared at him in wonder.

Joey lifted the four-clawed one-carat princess-cut diamond between them.

Marie's eyes widened and her mouth fell open as Joey sputtered, 'I love you, and I want to spend the rest of my life with you. Will you marry me?'

'Of course I will marry you,' said Marie, sliding on her new jewelry, before she jumped into his arms to kiss him.

Chapter 49

Joey woke up to a humming sound that vibrated the bungalow to its core. The early-morning sun had risen and he was the last to get out of bed. He could hear his friends conversing outside and could tell they weren't in any danger by their occasional laughter. He strolled over to the open window, shirtless, and the sound that shook the timbers intensified.

'What in the hell?' he murmured, identifying the cause of the noise. It was a thirty-foot-long dodecahedron-like vehicle that must have weighed a ton. It hovered an inch off the ground in a dusty area that was used as a road.

Taking in the view, he glanced around the alien paddock. The air felt refrigerated against his face. It was that same coolness combined with moisture Joey always loved before he had his morning jog at the beach and his first cup of coffee.

The old man and his daughter sat on the wraparound porch drinking their morning brew, while Marie and Boyce enjoyed the warm sun on a flat piece of grass thirty feet away from the house. She was giggling with Boyce, showing off her new, shiny engagement ring, joking and discussing a possible honeymoon location, and how reluctant Joey would be to take another European trip. The laughter continued as Joey took in their happy faces from afar. What they were saying was true, it seemed every time he left the United States, he ended up in dire circumstances.

Stepping outside on the porch, all eyes turned to him with huge grins.

'Good morning,' said Joey, turning to face his hospitable hosts, who smiled right back with not the faintest idea of what he was saying. The younger female scanned him up and down, clearly appreciating his athletic torso, but he didn't mind. It was her first experience of an earthly human, as everyone she knew would have been born on this planet.

'Joey!' Boyce shouted excitedly as Joey decided to stroll over to them. 'Can you believe this technology?' he said enthusiastically. 'I almost shit myself when I first saw it.'

Marie smiled and approached Joey for a morning smooch. 'Good morning, my fiancé,' she said playfully as the girl on the porch observed intently. She seemed curious to see how this foreign species interacted with each other.

'Congratulations on your engagement,' said Boyce with a friendly nudge on the shoulder. 'It's about time you made an honest woman of her. Now, wake yourself up, you have crusty things in your eyes.'

Joey separated himself from Marie and began to remove the sleep from his eyes with his outer knuckle, while Boyce continued to waffle on.

'The alien driving this thing,' he said, gesturing over to the futuristic vehicle. 'He doesn't seem to be too happy. We don't want to piss him off. Remember, all our eggs are in the one basket now. He's all we have if we want to get home.'

'Can we stop calling him an alien?' Marie said, displeased. 'It's wrong.'

'But he has a massive head,' said Joey in jest.

Boyce breathed in cheerfully, finding his comment funny but true.

'Okay, how about we call him ...' He paused for a couple of seconds. 'Christopher Walken,' sputtered Boyce with a wavering grin. 'He has his same upright sandy-colored hair and pasty complexion.'

An uncontrollable burst of laughter erupted between Marie and Joey.

'You crack me up, Boy,' Joey retorted, trying to keep a straight face.

'Here we go again with the Boy comments,' said Boyce, shaking his head. 'Okay, are we ready to go?'

'Hang on, I'll be right back,' Joey said, quickly darting back inside the cabin. He slid on his red t-shirt and grabbed the mesh backpack that held the two colored keystones, Youssef's cell phone, the battery now dead, and the Holy Grail.

He approached the bearded man and his daughter, who looked up at him and then stood up, realizing this was goodbye. Joey thought about what he could give them to say thank you for their hospitality. Even though their communication was limited to imagery and hand gestures, these people had gone out of their way to help. It showed a spirit of friendship and comradery, despite the difficulty of their circumstances.

Joey leaned over and extracted an item out of his backpack.

'This is for you, my friend,' he said, handing the old man the weighted cup. 'It represents our people back on Earth and the one man who died for our sins. I think it belongs here with you and your people. I'm sure you will keep it safe.'

Even though the older man didn't understand a word or the importance of the vessel, he graciously accepted the gift and nodded his head as though to say thank you.

'*Hur uk poo!*' shouted Christopher Walken, waiting at the back section of the hovering truck. He gestured for them to enter as a staircase appeared from out of nowhere, folding out before them.

'We need to get inside before he changes his mind,' said Boyce, hurrying over. 'I think I know what Christopher Walken does for a job.'

'What's that?' asked Marie, next in line.

'He's a delivery driver. He must take the produce that is farmed here to his people.'

Joey stepped in last to a space that resembled a shipping container with no window. Crates were stacked atop each other all the way to the ceiling, which was webbed with implanted patterns, with the inner dodecahedron marking the core of the vehicle.

Christopher Walken relayed a message at the doorway. It seemed like he was trying to tell them something. He banged on the inside wall then followed with a karate-like chop gesture at knee height. He repeated the movement again as confused eyes observed his every action.

'I think he's telling us to stay low.'

'Either that,' said Joey, 'or he's gonna take us to a place to be chopped up into little pieces to feed to their dog or dragon.'

Boyce tried to hold in the laugh, but failed miserably.

'And this is what I'm marrying,' said Marie, deadpan.

The door was sealed with a clunk as the sound of hydraulic motors vacuumed in the air and the lights were switched on. Concealed in this strangely shaped box, Joey could hear Christopher Walken shouting profusely, as if he was dealing with a stupid species and was clearly upset that he was doing something that was most likely not allowed among his kind.

The humans were evidently a slave race that was kept in check without the need for technological change. Their one key function or purpose was to harvest the crops and they were considered inferior by the supreme rulers of this estranged planet. If caught trafficking, it might lead to a harsh punishment, or even worse, his death. But, the fact that he was on board and executing this feat for his human counterparts was comforting to them.

'At least we have food to eat,' said Boyce, running his fingers over the fruit that was harvested on the site and had been packed for them.

'Let's get to the back,' suggested Joey. A small pass-through hole was present between the crates, enabling them to slide through and hide away from the entrance.

No sooner had they zoomed across the landscape at an incredible speed than the light within dimmed and the metallic surface of the panels started to shimmer.

Joey's eyes widened.

The walls suddenly became transparent, allowing them to glimpse outside.

'That's something you don't see every day,' Boyce mumbled, holding on to the food rack in front of him.

'This sure has been a week of many firsts,' agreed Marie.

Joey stared out at the blurred landscape in wonder. Filled with nothing but nature, green hills and trees as far as the eye could see, he felt like he was on a train looking out the window at an English countryside as the sun spread across the land. All three of them sat down on the hard metallic surface and took in the view, not feeling the need to speak. This moment was special and no words were needed to convey such a memorable and fantastical occasion.

Thirty minutes passed and all of a sudden the vehicle slowed to half-speed.

'We must be near,' voiced Joey, taking it all in. The container tilted to a forty-five-degree angle and dropped into an enormous canyon. It seemed to be guided by a stone pathway that likely had been built for hovercrafts.

During the descent into the unknown, a long silence ensued, only broken by their sounds of excitement and bewilderment.

They stared in amazement, hypnotized by the sheer beauty before them. It was the most gorgeous place

Joey had ever seen. Not even in his wildest dreams could he have conjured up a place so stunning and literally out of this world.

'Where are we?' Joey asked in complete awe.

'I can't believe it's real ...' said Marie, flabbergasted.

'What is?'

'It looks like ... the Lost City of Atlantis,' she breathed.

Chapter 50

Lost City of Atlantis

'Christopher Walken is an Atlantean?' Marie murmured to herself in utter disbelief. She came to a realization that if any species was capable of genetically manipulating the human race it would have been them.

More than 2,500 years ago, a legend originated from an Egyptian priest who spread stories of a past society that enjoyed an abundance of natural resources, military power, splendid architecture, engineering feats, and intellectual achievements, far advanced over those of other lands.

He called it Atlantis.

It was described as an area with rich soil, plentiful pure water, abundant vegetation and animals. Hot springs for health and vigor, and such mineral wealth that gold was inlaid in buildings and was among the precious stones worn as jewelry. Human slaves performed the manual labor and farming, allowing the elite to pursue knowledge and continually improve upon an already thriving society.

'It's exactly how it was drawn on the scroll we found in the library,' said Boyce, turning to face Marie, who looked right back at him, her mind churning, considering human evolution and how it came to be.

'It's no wonder why it has stayed hidden,' said Joey, shaking his head. 'It's been here on this planet all along.'

The vehicle seemed like it had been descending forever. The three bewildered passengers stared out of the transparent window to soak in the view, which consisted of a series of concentric rings alternating between water and land. The water served as canals and helped form natural defenses that would make an invasion extremely difficult. In the innermost circle were palaces and temples that most likely would be to honor the all-important sun god. In addition to magnificent architectural structures, a network of bridges and tunnels linked the rings of land.

It was breathtakingly beautiful.

After a long decline, the container-sized dodecahedron reached ground level and leveled out, and now a swarm of other hovering vehicles swooshed by, all of different sizes and speeds, irrefutably the principal means of transportation in this planet.

The Atlantean race was now in view, going about their normal life. Their enormous elongated heads and poncho-like costumes made the humans feel as if they were at some Star Trek convention where all the freaks had come out to play.

'I hope they can't see us,' Joey muttered, frowning, as they entered the city.

The urbanized metropolis was flooded by a sea of people heading in different directions, a place where buildings grew to the sky with architecture that wowed.

'I don't see any pyramids here,' winced Boyce, sounding nervous.

Marie surveyed, with intrigue, the society that had supposedly evolved the one on Earth, as though humans were their test guinea pigs. This was the same civilization that had been prevented from re-entering Earth, due to a single decision made under Queen Nefertiti's reign, who was clearly also a former Atlantean.

Massive hologram glass panels floated in the air like giant billboards, displaying moving video footage so anyone zooming by could see the latest news. Even in daylight, the visual was unblemished.

'Oh, look!' gasped Marie, pointing. It appeared that the Atlanteans had come across the Nile crocodile. The reptile had been hung vertically on a pulley system in the middle of a plaza, a gaping hole in its skull, between its eyes, oozing with blood. It was clear from the gathered crowd and the reverential way they sliced through its leathery skin that the animal was not from this land.

'I hope this doesn't set alarms bells ringing,' said Joey as they drove onward.

'You worry too much,' said Boyce. 'Must be an American thing.'

'Worrying has kept me alive,' retorted Joey. 'Trust me, when this is all over and done with and I'm back on my beach with a beer in my hand, I'll be another person.'

'It looks like we're not stopping here,' Marie

said with a bittersweet smile, interrupting the men's small talk. To see the Lost City of Atlantis was an unimaginable experience that so many people spoke and dreamed of, but she knew if they roamed these streets it would be the death of them.

Joey shrugged, and that's when the speed of the hovering dodecahedron slowed right down and joined a slower line while crafts on either side whisked by.

'Ha ... traffic,' Boyce teased. 'Who would've thought?'

'This ain't no traffic, there's a blockade up ahead,' warned Joey with a tight-lipped expression consumed by fear. 'It's probably the only way out of this city.'

All three faced the same direction as the panic set in. The slower the vehicle moved the more the transparent see-through walls began to turn opaque, like they were constructed to work only when in motion.

'This is it, boys,' said Marie, exhaling a long breath. 'It's now or never.'

'I just hope Christopher Walken is on our side,' said Joey with a watchful eye. 'For all we know, he could have prearranged our arrest.'

'If he did,' said Boyce, trying to be the voice of reason, 'his human girlfriend, waiting for him, would never let him forget it. We need to trust him.'

'What other choice do we have?' answered Joey, shrugging helplessly.

As the carriage drew near the blockade at a snail's pace, they could hear the Atlanteans talking among themselves. It appeared that they were having an argument, but it also could have been simply the way they communicated, like passionate Europeans who spoke charismatically with their hands. The language definitely didn't have that romantic French lilt that sounded seductive even when cursing.

Fearing the worst, Joey, Marie and Boyce ducked down low behind the crates of apples, hiding as best they could. It was a nervous kind of stress as they wondered how the situation would transpire. Marie asked silently, would they search the contents? Would they come in with laser guns blazing? And if they did, would they become test subjects like the poor crocodile?

The vehicle came to an abrupt stop.

Marie took in a nervous breath as the light flickered on and the walls morphed back to their original solid panels.

Quiet fell inside the vehicle.

Marie pressed her mouth closed and curled herself in the fetal position, while Joey and Boyce laid down low on their backs.

Christopher Walken could be heard speaking. The volume of his voice rose, signifying that something was wrong. Marie closed her eyes and squeezed her thighs closer to her chest.

Christopher Walken had exited the vehicle, his voice now at the side of the carriage. A loud thump was heard against the box; followed by alien words that caused Marie to open her eyes in terror.

Then, just like in a science fiction movie, the top three-quarters of the container's walls came alive with high-tech flashlights that penetrated the surface.

Marie's heart raced as she sucked in a quick breath

and met Joey's gaze, steadily keeping still and dead quiet.

The unseen inspectors weaved their hand-held flashlights left and right, stopping to inspect the cargo inside. Two beams of light scanned the inside of the contents, falling inches above Marie's petrified face, but as quickly as they appeared, they moved away.

Marie quietly sighed, relieved.

At that moment, it became clear to her why Christopher Walken had hit the wall in a karate chop motion when they first entered the container. He was trying to tell them of the safe zone that could not be penetrated from the outside.

It seemed to have worked.

The vehicle slowly moved away from the blockade, and as the speed increased, the lights dimmed and the shimmering walls appeared transparent once more. Their near escape was celebrated with a loud cheer from Christopher Walken, who seemed just as elated as they were that they had survived the ordeal.

'Sounds like someone's happy,' said Marie, as they left the aqua-blue city that would stay immersed in her mind forever.

All that mattered now was finding that damn pyramid that would lead them home. But something in her gut was telling her it wasn't going to be easy.

Chapter 51

After escaping the blockade, one long hour passed uneventfully. The landscape now turned from a lush and healthy green and blue to a dry and desolate orange-brown. In the distance lay a mighty desert of rolling barren hills plagued by dreaded sandstorms. The huge golden sun rose over the parched world where the tops of not one, not three, but eight colossal pyramids emerged.

'We're here!' said Boyce, jumping to his feet, the first to spot the giant triangular structures lining the distance. 'Even from here they seem enormous.'

'There's an entire row of them,' breathed Joey, an elated expression on his face. 'Now, all we have to do is find the one that takes us back to Earth.'

'What if we pick the wrong one?' said Boyce, dreading the thought.

'Then you'll never get to see the last season of *Game of Thrones*,' Joey replied, smiling.

As a French kid who had grown up in a household that didn't have money to travel, the idea of Egypt had felt out of reach for Boyce. The last few days, and being able to stand in front of the Pyramids and the

Sphinx, had been surreal for him. And now, to witness eight magnificent structures on the opposite side of the known universe, he felt giddy with excitement.

At that moment, the vehicle began to slow and their eyes darted to each other.

'What's going on?' Joey asked, as the dodecahedron came to a halt.

The light inside fluttered on and they lost their view of the outside world.

'Why did we stop?' asked Marie, her eyes blinking nervously. 'We're still miles away from the pyramids.'

Joey clenched his fists around the straps of his backpack as the driver's footsteps approached.

Boyce thought about the possibility that their guide could have another agenda. Maybe he was a serial killer who had a thing for primitive humans, and this was just a ploy to feed his addiction?

The entry door opened on a smiling Christopher Walken, who stood waiting.

Boyce blew out a sigh of relief.

The three of them exited to see their alien friend point toward the furthest pyramid on the left, a reasonable hour's hike away. He bowed his head while creating a circular shape with his two index fingers and thumbs.

'What's he doing?' asked Joey, glancing over to his friends, hoping to fill in the blanks.

'He could be describing the Stargate,' said Boyce, noticing Marie shake her head, as if she knew what he was trying to say.

'No, I've seen this before,' said Marie.

'Where?' Joey frowned.

'In the church-like cave we entered before you fainted like a schoolgirl,' said Marie, with Boyce chuckling in the background. 'This symbol must represent the sun god, Amun-Ra. I think he's wishing us good luck.'

'Hang on,' exclaimed Joey. 'He can't just leave us here in the middle of nowhere!'

'It must be the outermost point he could take us to before he puts himself in danger,' said Boyce. 'Look, he did the job he promised his girlfriend he would do. Now, we have to manage on our own.'

Boyce faced Christopher Walken and repeated the sign language back to him, where it was met with a great big grin.

'I think you made a friend,' said Marie as Christopher Walken retrieved a package from his vehicle. He handed them each an apple and gave Marie and Boyce a pair of straw sandals to use while they trekked on the hot sand. He flashed one last smile, entered back into his hovercraft and disappeared into the trackless horizon.

'That Christopher Walken sure was something,' joked Boyce as he slipped on his new shoes and took a bite of his juicy apple. He stepped toward the rolling sandy hills as the sun's rays fell upon him.

Three-quarters of an hour of walking felt like an eternity. It seemed that they had entered a vast desert that would have dwarfed the 3.5-million-square-mile Sahara found on Earth. Their every step sank into the searing sand. The temperature must have been over 100 degrees Fahrenheit and they felt every second of it.

The air was thick and hazy, and each breath was like drowning in lava.

The colossal pyramids grew in size as the dry wind stirred up the wispy sand in their faces, making their hair stiff and frizzy. The sun's never-ending rays beat down upon them mercilessly, as salty sweat dripped off Boyce's nose. He felt completely inappropriately dressed for the climate in his now ragged navy-blue suit pants and cotton sleeveless shirt. The sun burned his exposed skin, but thankfully not his chest and back which were protected by what was left of his shirt. His lips, chapped and dry, longed for icy-cold water.

'Let's stop for a quick break,' whispered Boyce, dropping from where he stood, struggling to get the words out, as he tried to regain some strength. 'I can't go any further.'

'Here, I can't have my best man die out here,' said Joey, cutting open his uneaten apple and offering it to Boyce, who accepted without question. He bit into it like a child stuffing his face into a chocolate cake as Joey shadowed him from the sun with his body.

'Best man?' he repeated as the juices ran down his jawline, soothing his dry throat. 'It would be an honor to stand by your side.'

'Well, it all depends if we make it back to Earth,' said Joey. 'And, if we don't, how good are your farming skills?'

'Don't be stupid,' Marie uttered, not taking the bait. 'We are leaving this place. We're not far now, can we go on?'

Boyce got shakily back up to his feet and shaded

his eyes. He peered across the desert at the God-like structures that rose into the cloudless sky and paused as if he was thinking of something.

'What is it?' asked Joey.

'If these eight pyramids have their own Stargate that take you to eight different planets, I wonder why the aliens decided it was the humans they would bring back here as the slave race?'

'Maybe our evolution was more useful to their faming needs than the other species in the galaxy,' answered Marie. 'I guess we'll never know.'

'Don't forget, we've only seen a small portion of this huge planet,' said Joey. 'There could be other slave groups just as we saw with our kind.'

Fifteen more treacherous minutes and they finally reached ground that was level like an enormous airport runway. The pyramids were perfectly aligned, spaced out from each other at a distance of about half a mile.

Eight lonesome obelisks were also lined up in perfect unison, standing one hundred feet away from their own gigantic pyramids as identification markers.

The sight was breathtaking and frightening at the same time, a mysterious ancient graveyard that was used solely for teleportation purposes.

The eight pyramids were perfectly intact, including the gold capstone pieces that glistened in the sunlight. Erosion had not stripped away their smooth rendered coating, like it had the ones on Earth. It gave the towering structures a completely white ethereal glow.

They stepped up to the obelisk that stood seventy-five feet high, built in a solid yellow granite type of stone. Its markings seemed to be decorated in the Atlantean-hieroglyph language, depicting an image of Akhenaten, the son of the king at the time.

'Tutankhamun's father,' Boyce voiced. 'This must be it.'

Marie rubbed her fingers against the smooth surface until it met a triangular-shaped hole. 'This shape looks familiar. Hand it over.'

Joey dug into the backpack and took out the Earth's blue keystone. He stepped over and carefully slid it into the hole provided. It locked in place and instantly the ground shook and rumbled beneath them.

'Let's hope that whatever you have triggered is friendly,' blurted out Boyce as the sand near their feet began to descend.

'It's an opening,' Marie informed them as it showed itself.

At the lip of the sixteen-foot-wide entrance, a deep tunnel loomed into the darkness as the dust and sand slowly settled. Strolling over to face the drop, lights came alive with each downward step to show the way. It revealed a long descent that would take them to what they hoped was the Stargate.

'Please, God, let there be no booby traps down here,' said Boyce, peering down at the forty-five-degree angle.

All of a sudden, a whistling sound at incredible speed whooshed over their heads, causing them to duck.

'What in the hell was that?' Joey scowled.

Boyce followed the soccer ball–sized, unidentified flying object that wore some kind of helmet shield. It banked back around to face them and stopped to hover with an intent to inspect and record.

'It's a drone,' warned Joey with a rising tone. 'Whatever it's seeing, it's transmitting back to God knows who. We need to move now!'

'Go get the blue keystone, just in case,' Marie suggested, nudging her head over to the obelisk. 'And let's get a move on!'

Joey sprinted back to the pillar and hastily extracted the Earth rock as the glare of the sun reflected off the burning sand.

'Ahh, shit, you're too late!' Boyce yelled, pointing into the distance. 'We have company!'

A spacecraft the size of a fighter jet zoomed by and released a single Atlantean in midair. The soldier landed safely with a jet-propelled backpack that he detached, as he began his full sprint toward his enemy.

'Run! Run! Run!'

Chapter 52

Boyce entered the tunnel in a downward sprint with Marie fast on his heels and Joey at the rear, holding on to the triangular bluestone. The limestone walls encircling them were etched and colored in beautiful shapes and figures. The images seemed to be telling the story of a son who had betrayed his father and his people, but at the speed at which they were descending, all Boyce could see was a blur.

There was no time for observation. The only thing that mattered right now was to trigger the Stargate and get the hell off this planet, before it was too late.

Looking over his shoulder, Boyce saw the Atlantean reach the entrance. He took long, calculated strides like an unstoppable superior force that was determined to achieve his goal, and this petrified Boyce.

'Ahh, God,' breathed Joey, still with the backpack strapped to his back. 'This is going to be tight.'

They entered a super-cavern, the floor of which was covered in knee-high water.

'It's like the one on Earth,' Marie said wonderingly, before slipping face first into the water. For a split second she seemed to enjoy the refreshing liquid that soothed the dryness of her skin, but Boyce wasn't having it.

He immediately helped her to her feet and they bolted for the miniature-sized pyramid, deep within the airport hangar–sized chamber. They ploughed across the watery floor, holding hands as it drenched the lower parts of their bodies. At this point, the straw sandals had been lost in the vast flat lake.

Marie, in her wet black dress, waded across and hit the steps that would take them up to the raised square platform where the hollow pyramid sat.

Boyce couldn't remember the last time he had pushed himself so hard. He was badly out of breath.

Still favoring his good leg, Joey was twenty feet behind them.

'Come on, Marie, keep it up!' Boyce encouraged as they clambered up the stairs and eventually reached the opening, that was never bricked up like the one on earth, to find what they had come here for.

'The Stargate,' Marie breathed, turning to see Joey, who arrived shortly after, constantly darting his head backwards, fear in his eyes.

The Atlantean had reached the water in the super-cavern.

Joey passed Boyce the Earth stone in a hurry. 'Quick, I can hear him!'

Boyce reacted instinctively, inserting the blue keystone with a shaky hand, locking it in place and igniting a spark. The anticipated rumbling sound coming from the ring started up, and the portal blasted to life. Its core shimmered in a cloud of moving energy and matter that reflected the entire inside of the pyramid in a fluorescent blue.

'Let's go!' Marie shrieked.

'Don't forget to extract the bluestone before we enter,' warned Joey. 'Or we'll give them an open invitation to follow us and destroy Earth as they had planned to do four thousand years ago.'

Boyce nodded and extracted the rock from the portal, and just as it had done before on Earth, it continued to light up the room with fifty shades of blue.

That's when the attack came.

Marie screamed to warn Joey, but the Atlantean soldier moved swiftly.

He struck Boyce in the face and then tackled Joey to the ground, forcing his wrist against his chest. An unbearable scream of pain erupted from Joey as he arched his back, hitting up against the red stone in his backpack. He rolled onto his side, defenseless as a wounded animal as the vulture attacked him from behind, getting him in a headlock.

Joey fought to keep himself from choking from the vice that was around his neck and reached back with his elbow, landing a blow on the soldier's enormous head.

'Go, or it's the end of our species,' he yelled, unable to move.

'We only have a minute before the portal closes,' shouted Marie, helping Boyce to his feet as blood poured out of his nose, making him feel dizzy and disorientated.

The Atlantean soldier squeezed his arm tighter around Joey's neck and they rolled to a stop near the entrance of the pyramid, trying to strangle one another. Boyce, seeing his friend in danger, went to help and came in with a football-field goal kick that landed hard under the monster's left armpit, giving Joey a moment's respite, but not enough to get him free of the soldier's grasp.

This aggravated the monster, who went on a rampage of his own, connecting a punch to Joey's jawline that sent him reeling back to the ground.

The alien, who was on his knees now, rubbing his left shoulder with his other hand, turned to face Boyce, clearly wanting to avenge the previous attack.

Marie swallowed hard.

They were next.

He took a step toward them, but Joey was there to hold him back, clinging onto his leg as if he was a child that wasn't going to let his parent leave the house.

'Please listen to me and go!' Joey pleaded, pushing the six-foot-three warrior with bulging biceps in the opposite direction.

'I can't just leave you here!' said Marie, her eyes giant saucers of fear.

'Boyce, take her now!'

'No,' cried Marie, shaking her head, trying to move away from Boyce.

'Do it now!'

The Atlantean powered forward, while Joey moaned in agony as he struggled to stop his attack, hanging on to him and flinging his dead weight on him.

The last thing Marie remembered were her hands being restricted as she was grabbed from behind and manhandled. 'Noooo!' she cried, knowing this was the last time she would see the man she loved, the man she was to marry.

'I'm so sorry,' Boyce said brokenly.

Marie kicked and screamed as her friend made the ultimate decision to pull both their bodies backwards into the dazzlingly bright light of the Stargate.

Chapter 53

Shaking Joey off his leg, the Atlantean turned and positioned himself in front of the portal, creating a silhouette of his broad frame.

He spoke aggressively in his own language.

'*Uk to mentan dai*,' he said in an ice-cold voice, pointing to the ring that continued to blast its energy field.

Joey didn't need to be a genius to work out what he was telling him, which was that he would never let him pass. The Atlantean dwarfed him. He was broader and stronger and most probably smarter, with a brain capacity that likely doubled Joey's.

Joey held his fists up strong, ready to fight, knowing that time was not on his side. Less than a minute was all he had, if that. If the portal switched off, he would be stuck on this planet indefinitely. In his mind he knew he was outmatched, and as the panic and stress hit home, his thoughts wandered back for a moment, to the man he could never beat in the boxing ring. The man who had shown him what a knockout felt like. Joey was thinking about his father, the notorious gangster Alexander Peruggia.

Taking a step closer with fists raised, he faced up

against the Atlantean, but in his mind he imagined he was facing his father. He remembered the teachings he had been given in the ring and played them out in his head in slow motion.

Always watch the shoulders. See the move before it happens.

He had less than twenty seconds or so before it was game over.

It was a standoff in which Joey would either live or die.

He swayed left and right like a true boxer, sizing up his taller opponent, who had a longer reach. This was it, thought Joey, all the fights he had fought in the past didn't matter anymore. They had just prepared him for this moment.

There was no time to make any errors.

A wave of adrenaline surged through him.

The Atlantean jabbed and Joey moved to safety, waiting for the opportune moment, watching his shoulders, studying his fighting stance.

Time was almost up.

Fifteen seconds.

Joey stayed patient, avoiding the incoming jabs that seemed to come in hard with both hands. He realized the alien's left punch was slower and not as outstretched as his right, and he pulled a pained face when he threw it.

It appeared Boyce had injured the beast, thus giving Joey a fighting chance. It was a small possibility, but he was going to take it as it was the only Achilles' heel his opponent appeared to have.

More strong right jabs were thrown. Joey remained composed, waiting for his left shoulder to move.

He could now count the seconds on his own two hands.

A voice flooded his thought process. *Come on, Joey, you can do better than that.*

His father moved in for a deadly right uppercut, Joey stepped back. Then he saw the shoulder in question begin its forward movement.

His eyes lit up.

This was his moment and he jumped at it with ferocity. Joey stopped retreating and came in hard with a right swing that caught the jaw of the elongated head by surprise. To complete the attack, he followed through with a right kick in the alien's genitals that brought him to his knees.

Now with the upper hand, he needed to enter the portal before it shut down. With a bounce in his step, he sidestepped the pained soldier, who tried to reach at him with his free hand, and in a Superman pose he forward-dived into the light in the nick of time, milliseconds before it switched off.

Chapter 54

Earth
Stonehenge, Wiltshire, England

A throng of sightseers from all corners of the world were jostling around the renowned tourist attraction that was the ancient Stonehenge. There were the Westerners. And there were various clusters of Asians and seniors, each group trailing their specific flag as their tour guide babbled excitedly about the sights in different languages.

They all received the fright of their lives when Marie and Boyce appeared out of nowhere from a wormhole that spat them out atop one another.

Like a flock of doves disturbed by the scream of

a hawk, the crowd parted, leaving the unexplained phenomenon that had just occurred centerstage among the bluestones.

'We made it!' cheered Boyce with the triangular bluestone raised victoriously as he held his rib cage with his other hand. The sigh that escaped his dry lips was slow, as if his brain needed that time to process what had happened.

The startled tourists trying to comprehend what was going on turned their cell phones toward them and began to snap away, as Boyce muttered obscenities under his breath.

It was a bittersweet moment for Marie. She was unhappy in a way he hadn't seen before, her grief evident. On the one hand they had made it back home, but on the other, she feared she would never see Joey again.

Boyce helped Marie to her feet and gave her a warm embrace that was cut short by prying eyes.

'Where did they come from?' a bald man in his sixties asked, scratching his forehead.

Marie and Boyce chose not to say a word.

More muddled questions followed.

Boyce grabbed Marie's hand and they walked over to a group of tourists boarding a tour bus. They were chattering with excitement, some in English and some in foreign languages.

With the all-important red trigger stone in his hand, Boyce managed to borrow a cell phone from the driver, telling him it was an emergency.

Marie stood by as Boyce dialed the DGSE

switchboard and was immediately patched through to Julien, who was on ground zero on a military phone.

'Hello?'

'It's me,' said Boyce with a finger in his ear. 'I'm safe.'

'Where are you? asked Julien, the strain clear in his voice. 'I found your tracking device and have been searching for you this whole time.'

'I can barely hear you,' said Boyce, stepping over to the side of the bus, so as not to be overheard. 'You wouldn't believe the adventure we've had if I told you,' Boyce said, Marie by his side watching sadly.

'Where did you say you are?'

'I'm at Stonehenge, sir.'

'Stonehenge?' His voice increased in volume. 'How the hell did you get there?'

'Deep inside the pyramid we found a Stargate and triggered it.'

'You did what?'

'It took us to another planet in the galaxy.'

'Is this a joke?'

'No, sir,' said Boyce, sounding very solemn. 'I wouldn't lie to you.'

There was a long pause. 'It looks like we have a lot to talk about.'

'We sure do, sir,' said Boyce, envisioning his boss's confused demeanor. Julien could be heard on the other end issuing instructions to his soldiers.

'Okay. I'm glad you're safe, Boy. Stay put and I'll organize a chopper to pick you up.'

'Roger that,' said Boyce, now tearing up as he hung up the phone. The fact that Julien had called him Boy caused sadness to run right through him. He tried to contain his feelings, not wanting to affect Marie, who had kept quiet this whole time. His friend had not made it out in time, and was stuck in a place where he would be subjected to scrutiny and God knew what else if he survived.

Boyce handed the phone back to the driver and thanked the man. Suddenly, there came a crackling sound from the ring of stones behind them.

All heads turned to face the electric pulse that was forming.

'The Stargate,' mouthed Marie with excitement.

'It's happening again,' said a woman in her late fifties, who took out her iPhone and hit the 'record' button from inside the bus. A brilliant flash of white was soon followed by the constant click of cameras as everyone within the site with a mobile device took pictures.

'Joey!' Marie breathed with widening eyes, jogging back to the prehistoric monument. 'Please be you,' she prayed, as her heartbeat pounded out from her chest.

Bursts of blue-and-white light briefly opened what looked like a shimmering donut.

Shh-boom!

Joey was spat out from a wormhole that disappeared faster than it had reappeared. His hands broke his fall as he rolled over to his side with the backpack still strapped to his back.

'Joey!' Marie screamed with uncontained happiness.

Joey had a great big grin on his face as he turned to look at her.

Seconds later Marie was all over him. She threw herself onto him, kissing him, touching him, just wanting to feel his heartbeat against hers. One of his hands clasped around her lower back, the other stroked her hair. With each soft touch more tears of happiness fell, tears neither of them wiped away.

'I can't wait for you to be my wife,' said Joey as they embraced in a passionate kiss.

The confused sightseers watched their heartfelt reunion and did what tourists do: they took a picture.

* * *

Ten minutes later, a black Apache chopper emblazoned with a British flag arrived to collect them. In the cockpit was a pilot and single commando dressed in his complete military attire and weaponry.

'We've been instructed to pick you up,' said the soldier in accented English as he helped them on board.

Boyce thanked the man and grabbed him by the arm, needing to share something.

'In the interests of national security, we need to confiscate the phones and cameras of everyone here at Stonehenge, including everyone on all the buses,' instructed Boyce, thinking about the consequences of the events leaking out. 'People have been recording footage that needs to remain classified.'

The soldier nodded his head, understanding what needed to be carried out, and stepped outside to talk to the pilot. He gave him the winding signal so he could go and the blades came alive and lifted them into the fresh morning sky.

Joey slid the backpack onto the empty seat in front

of him and they all smiled at each other as if to say, *We did it, we made it home!* It was a quiet moment of contentment.

'What took you so long to get out?' Marie asked him. 'I thought I would never see you again.'

'I almost didn't make it,' Joey answered. 'But I'm glad I did, thanks to something my father said that stuck in my head.'

'Can you imagine the discussions the Atlanteans are having on their planet right now?' said Boyce, fearing a possible attack. 'What if they use the Stargate?'

'They can't,' Marie told him. 'We have the only keystone that could lead them to Earth. The portal is useless without it.'

'What if they have an extra one hidden away somewhere?' Joey said, causing Boyce a degree of discomfort.

'Don't you think if they had a spare,' said Marie, moving forward in her seat, 'they would have used it already, in all this time since Tutankhamun's reign? Trust me, they have nothing. Nefertiti made sure of it.'

'Yes, but we have their keystone,' said Boyce, eyeing the backpack to his right. 'What's stopping us now from visiting them again? It's in our DNA. We want to investigate the unknown. We *need* to investigate the unknown. In time, someone stupid will open the portal and this time the Atlanteans will be ready.'

Boyce stared into his friend's eyes. 'That's why you know what needs to happen right now,' he said, tapping the bag. 'Let's eliminate the possibility of a future threat.'

Joey and Marie agreed with a solemn nod.

Boyce dug his hand inside the backpack and removed the red stone, the single piece of stone that could easily open the door to the Lost City of Atlantis and send the Atlantean army to Earth to exterminate the race they had fashioned.

The chopper reached the Mediterranean Sea, then passed the volcanic island of Santorini. A carpet of blue water stretched out before them. It was now or never.

'This is for our survival,' Boyce said, about to heave it out of the window.

'For our species,' repeated Marie with a smile.

'Do it,' said Joey.

Boyce flung the triangular-cut rock outside the helicopter and they watched as it fell fast and vanished into the dark blue abyss.

Chapter 55

Egypt, Cairo
Giza Plateau

After a long chopper flight back to Cairo that seemed to last forever, they arrived at a city engulfed in flames. Burning in a sea of red, yellow and orange, from the air they could see a plethora of airliners that had crashed, leaving nothing but devastation and destruction in their wake.

'Oh my God, it looks like a war zone down there,' said Marie, who peered out of her window as the helicopter banked left to avoid the smoke that came from a commercial Aegean Airbus that had plummeted into a towering building.

'What the hell happened here?' Joey blanched.

Nothing but gray dust and ash blanketed the city.

Boyce shook his head. The scene was quite unbelievable, shocking really. His mind was sent reeling, unable to comprehend or process the images below him.

Marie questioned the pilot as to why there was so much devastation.

'I've been told it was an electromagnetic pulse that caused Cairo to completely lose all power,' he said out loud over the sound of the churning rotor blades from above. 'All planes with a direct flight path over Egypt were affected and fell from the sky.'

'What about us now?' Joey interrupted. 'Are we in any danger?'

'No, sir, not to worry, all electricity has been restored.'

'Do they know the cause of the blackout?' asked Boyce, curious to find out if it had been due to a possible terrorist attack.

'No official report has been shared as yet, but many fellow operatives have said they saw a beam of light coming from the Great Pyramid.'

Marie's shoulders hunched together like she was trying to disappear inside herself. 'Holy crap,' she breathed, her face ashen. 'We did this,' she said, digging her face into her palms. 'We caused all this heartbreak and death when we triggered the Stargate.'

Joey realized the cause and effect of their actions.

His downcast face showed an expression of utter disbelief and regret.

'Don't feel too disheartened,' Boyce said, reaching out to lovingly touch his friend's shoulder. 'It's tragic, yes, but on the other hand we saved humankind. Don't you ever forget that small fact.'

In the distance, the river Nile could be seen snaking like a giant python as it disappeared into the horizon, but today a strange phenomenon was happening. Raised beds of bubbling waterfalls flowed endlessly.

Marie and Joey had no words.

The Apache chopper hovered near the Pyramids and landed on a flat piece of land not far from the Sphinx. As it hit the limestone bedrock, it blew away the loose sand and attracted the attention of an armed military team.

In the center of what appeared to be a group of elderly men was Julien Bonnet. He was dressed in his soldier's uniform and was chatting away to men in dark suits. Men that looked like they were important and possessed a certain amount of authority and power, like men in government that ran the country and its secrets.

Avoiding the rotor blades that eventually came to a halt, Marie, Joey and Boyce walked over to join Julien, who gave them a strong and proud welcome handshake.

'You three never seem to do anything small, do you?' he said with a charismatic smile, pleased that they were all unharmed. 'Last time you were all together you uncovered Alexander the Great's final resting place and now you have discovered the treasures of the Hall of Records, and if what you're saying to be true, a Stargate.'

'Have you seen it, sir?'

'I've seen photos on my phone,' said Julien, raising his cell for all to see. 'My men penetrated all the way to the Stargate you found, retracing your steps using thermal imaging goggles.'

'It's not flooded anymore,' Marie said to Joey, commenting on the last secret chamber room.

'Word of warning, sir, make sure your men don't touch any stones around the lake of water, unless they want to go for a swim with killer crocodiles.'

'Noted,' replied Julien.

'We sure do work well as a team,' said Boyce, turning toward Marie, who flashed him a friendly wink.

'So the secret about Alexander the Great's resting place is true,' wisecracked Joey.

'Sorry, boss, you let that one slip,' said Boyce, glancing upward at the towering general. 'I never said a word.'

A serious expression now showed on Julien's face and all smiles disappeared.

'You realize all this mess you see around this city was created when you ignited that thing,' said Julien, turning to face the Sphinx. 'I was almost a victim myself,' he said. 'That's my chopper over there.'

Julien gestured to a large burnt-out piece of black metal that had crash-landed in the distance. He paused for a moment in mid-thought. 'Ahh, by the way, something you might be pleased with, we found a survivor.'

'Who?' asked Joey, frowning.

'Your friend Hazim. The poor man would have died if we hadn't arrived in time. We tracked your footprints down a flight of steps.'

'You found the wooden lever to open the secret doorway,' said Joey. 'The Walk of Souls.'

'It led us straight to him,' said Julien with a half-smile. 'Once we pumped him with the right drugs, he explained all about your hostage situation with Youssef. He's getting the medical attention he deserves right now. We flew him to Al Maadi Cairo Military Hospital.'

'I'm so happy to hear that,' Marie sighed.

'It has been prearranged. When he recovers from his injuries, he will be promoted to the Cairo Museum Director of Antiquities and is going to be rewarded for finding the Hall of Records.'

'What about us?' joked Joey. 'Don't we get a finder's fee?'

'No!' said Julien bluntly. 'You three can't be seen to be involved in any way, for the greater good of Egypt. It has been decided that most of the treasures inside the Hall of Records will be sold to help repair the city, and the rest of the contents will be placed in the new Giza Museum.'

'So, the cover-up begins,' said Boyce.

'It needs to be that way,' said Julien, with a hard finger up and at his three explorers, like a teacher warning his students to behave.

'Yes, of course,' they all replied, not wanting to upset the general.

Then he lowered his voice significantly. 'So tell me, are we alone in this universe?'

'No, sir, we are not,' answered Boyce evenly.

Julien nodded his head, as if taking in the information he knew to be true anyway.

'Are we at any risk?'

'Not anymore,' said Joey. 'We made sure of that.'

'The Atlanteans don't have our Earth keystone,' said Boyce. 'So they can't activate the Stargate on their end to bring them to our planet. They pose us no threat.'

'Atlanteans?' Julien repeated, blinking with disbelief. 'As in the Lost City of Atlantis?'

'That's exactly what we are saying, sir.'

'This is Earth's identification marker,' said Joey, extracting the triangular-shaped spotted dolerite stone and handed it over so Julien could inspect it. 'It's useless unless you were on their planet and wanted to come back to Earth.'

'It's the same rock type found in Stonehenge,' said Marie.

'And that's where it brought you back.'

All three nodded in confirmation.

'All these ancient sites on Earth are linked, sir, for the one purpose of traveling between worlds. That's why the Great Pyramid's axis is aligned to true north and has been built on the midline of our planet.'

'So how does Stonehenge fit in all this? Why would they have their entry point there and not in Egypt?' asked Julien, trying to understand it all.

'I wondered about this on the flight over here,' said Marie. 'Then I remembered a small mathematical detail from back in college delineating the distance between the two great monuments. Amazingly they are three hundred and sixty kilometers away from each other on a metric scale, which is important as it's a direct reference to a three-hundred-and-sixty-degree circle. For the portal to work with the universe, there could only be one exit spot on our planet, one precise location, so they built Stonehenge there.'

'It doesn't explain how they traveled back to Egypt, though,' voiced Joey.

'They must have brought with them those long dodecahedron vehicles, like the one Christopher Walken drove,' said Boyce. 'This would explain the metals that were scattered across the cave floor we swam over before we faced the quicksand.'

'Who's Christopher Walken?' Julien looked profoundly confused.

Marie chuckled for a brief moment, but no one gave Julien an answer.

'How about the key that activates our portal and takes us to their planet?' asked Julien. 'Where is it?'

'I'm sorry. We lost it in the Stargate,' said Boyce, looking out blankly at the dry barren surface that was the desert.

Julien studied the boy carefully. He was avoiding eye contact. Boyce knew his boss could tell he was lying, but he let it go. 'That's a shame,' he replied after a long pause. 'You three look like you could use a shower.' He turned to Boyce with a proud smile. 'I think after what you've been through you deserve some holiday leave.'

'That would be much appreciated.'

'But not before you write me up a detailed debrief on what you saw on Atlantis, and I mean everything.'

'Of course.'

'Where will you go?' he asked.

'America, sir,' said Boyce with a smile toward his friends. 'I have a wedding to attend.'

Chapter 56

Atlantis, Farmland,
Holy Church of the People

The old man was ushered into the scroll room by his daughter. It seemed by the tone in her voice that she had uncovered something. The parchment stretched over the table had deteriorated to the point where you could see through it.

The young girl pointed to a symbol carved into the stone table beneath the parchment. The wise man moved in closer to examine it. He had never seen this before in all his years. An Egyptian cartouche was engraved in its core.

He ran his eyes downward, moving away the ancient papyrus to discover that this was no table; this was someone's tomb. With the help of his daughter, they slid the lid over to one side to discover a body.

It appeared to be a female with an elongated head.

He would not know it, but he was staring at the dead remains of Queen Nefertiti herself. The woman who had sacrificed her own life to protect her child,

Tutankhamun, and single-handedly saved the human race from being wiped out.

His eyes widened and his jaw dropped when he spotted the item in her hands.

She held a triangular-shaped bluestone.

Earth's stone.

ACKNOWLEDGMENTS

I want to thank my beautiful wife Marie, and my two boys Alexander and Leonardo who supported me and put up with me, throughout this amazing journey.

A special thank you goes out to Tania Kondoulis for being my beta reader, who read the novel in its infant stages.

A huge thank you once again goes out to my genius editors Brianne Collins and Alexandra Nahlous for giving this book life and making it the best it could possibly be.

Last of all to you, my dear reader, for picking up my book. I truly hope you have as much fun reading it as I did writing it. I would love to hear from you. I can be contacted via social media, or on my website **www.philphilips.com**

ONE MORE THING …

If you loved the book and have a moment to spare, I would really appreciate a short review where you bought the book. Your help in spreading the word is gratefully appreciated, as it helps other readers discover the story.

Mona Lisa's Secret

A Joey Peruggia Adventure Series Book 1

Joey is the great-grandson of Vincenzo Peruggia, the man who stole the original Mona Lisa in 1911. Along with his girlfriend, Marie, an art connoisseur, he stumbles across his father's secret room, and finds himself staring at what he thinks is a replica of da Vinci's most famous masterpiece.

BUT IT IS NO FAKE ...

The Louvre has kept this secret for over one hundred years, waiting for the original to come to light, and now they want it back at any cost.

With Marie held hostage and the Louvre curator and his men hot on his trail, Joey is left to run for his life in an unfamiliar city, with the priceless Mona Lisa his only bargaining chip. While formulating a plan to get Marie back with the help from an unexpected quarter, Joey discovers hidden secrets within the painting, secrets which, if made public, could change the world forever.

In this elaborately plotted, fast-paced thriller, Phil Philips takes you on a roller-coaster ride through the streets of Paris and to the Jura mountains of Switzerland, to uncover a secret hidden for thousands of years ...

MORE FICTION FROM PHIL PHILIPS

Last Secret Keystone

A Joey Peruggia Adventure Series Book 3

When a cargo plane carrying an ancient vase crashes into the Atlantic, the DGSE – otherwise known as the French CIA – immediately suspect it's deliberate. The vase is believed to hold a key that gives entrance to a hidden cave on Easter Island: a site connected with ancient Egypt and an otherworldly portal discovered deep beneath the Great Pyramid of Giza.

Joey, Marie, and Boyce are once again caught up in a dangerous adventure, forced on them by a trained assassin who is on his own spiritual quest for answers … A ruthless man who will stop at nothing to get what he wants.

His objective: to find the last secret keystone, and with it activate the portal once again. Joey and his friends must stop him – at any cost.

In this fast-paced thriller, Book 3 in the Joey Peruggia Adventure Series, Phil Philips takes you on a roller-coaster ride from the giant Moai statues of Easter Island to the Greek island of Santorini and back to Egypt, where the fate of humankind once again rests with the most unlikely of heroes.

Fortune in Blood

A NOVEL OF MURDER, THEFT, BETRAYAL AND MONEY ... LOTS OF IT ...

Joey used to be a carefree surfer kid on Venice Beach. But as the youngest son of a notorious gangster, it seems he can't escape the life. Soon he's forced to prove himself by leading a team in the heist of the century. Will he be able to pull it off?

Vince was always worried about getting to lectures on time ... and spending time with his hot girlfriend. But everything changes when he's embroiled in his detective father's world. Now he's on the run for his life from the mob.

FBI Agent Monica is smart, beautiful, tough and unyielding. Caught in the middle of the mob and the police, her loyalty is being questioned by both sides. But Monica seems to have her own agenda ... In a world where corruption is rife, she will be tested to the limit.

Who can be trusted and who will be left standing? And who will ultimately escape with all the money? A showdown is set in motion and no one will be left unscathed.

In this elaborately plotted, fast-paced thriller, Phil Philips takes you on a roller coaster ride that will keep you guessing until the very last page.

Guardians of Egypt

*Short Story - Prequel to the
Joey Peruggia Adventure Series*

When Julien Bonnet finds the remains of an ancient city under the Red Sea, he unleashes the might of the Guardians of Egypt. They carry the burden of destroying ancient sites – and anyone who discovers them – to keep their secret safe.

Only this time, they messed with the wrong guy. Killing him will not be as simple as it seems

Get a FREE copy when you sign up to my mailing list. You also will be notified on giveaways and upcoming new releases. www.philphilips.com

Printed in Great Britain
by Amazon